GUILD OF DRAGON
WARRIORS

JAXON'S SANCTUARY
BOOK I

I0679161

NEW YORK TIMES BESTSELLING AUTHOR

A K MICHAELS

Edited by Missy Borucki

Cover Design by Sassy Queens of Design

Formatted by FancyPants Formatting

Proofread by Tammy Payne and the girls from A K Michaels' Minxes

ISBN13: 978-0-9935223-2-1

DEDICATION

I would like to dedicate this book to a very special person. One who has the sweetest soul and a heart of gold.

She and I "talk" every day, and if I need to, she is always there for me to bounce ideas off. She is truly one of the nicest people I've come across and I'm blessed to have her in my life.

So, this is for you, Stracey, my little ray of sunshine. Thank you for everything, honey, I really appreciate it beyond words.

CHAPTER ONE

Jaxon's flight was far slower than his normal speed, exhaustion overtaking him as his beast fought to heal itself. He was under no illusions of how seriously injured he was and knew he'd need to recover in Dragon form within the healing caves of the mountain range surrounding his home.

He wasn't far, but the short distance he still had to cover seemed like miles away. His massive wings beat against the cold night sky, his breathing labored as he swooped over the top of the mountain. A rumbled notification slid from his throat to alert any guards he was there. The last thing he needed was for one of them to attack if he surprised them.

His mind wandered . . . a flash of a woman running desperately in a forest tugged at his consciousness, causing his heart to flutter. *"What the hell was that?"* he thought, shaking his head clear as an answering soft bellow came from his right and he wasn't too surprised when Sapphire flew down to join him. Her Dragon's

1

eyes filled with concern at the state he was in. Jaxon tried to reassure her, using their blood bond link, but he was near collapse and he was certain he'd not allayed her fears.

She flew directly in front of him, leading him towards the very back of the valley where their camp was and the large outcrop of rock that led to the healing caves. Sapphire hovered above the opening as Jaxon made a harsh landing before falling forward onto his scaly chest. Sapphire's huff of concern reached his hearing but he didn't have the strength to reply.

His beast was literally on its last legs and it took every ounce of his energy to shuffle forward, out of sight, and disappear inside the darkness. As soon as he was ensconced within the cave he relaxed his mind, allowing his beast to take over and look after them both.

He was vaguely aware of his Dragon dragging itself further inside the mountain range, heading toward the warm flowing spring that would heal him. Pain lancing through the great body as its wounds rubbed on the harsh granite, opening wounds that had barely started to heal. Soft grumbling sounds erupting from its throat as he felt as if his injuries were being dragged over broken glass.

Jaxon had never felt so relieved when he smelled the unique scent of the healing spring.

That was until his beast hauled itself into its miraculous warmth, then that was the most relieved he'd ever felt. Absolute peace, warmth, and tranquility swept over him as the water engulfed his Dragon.

His beast allowed itself to drop down through the water to rest on the very bottom of the deep pool. Its wings still unfurled and drinking in the healing qualities of the magical liquid. Jaxon wasn't sure how long they'd need to languish in the mountain, but he was certain it would be at least a full day, maybe more.

Even then, once they'd leave the spring, it would be days before he was fully fit again. Wounds inflicted by Demons always affected Dragons adversely, and he'd had a damn lot of them today. Although he was badly wounded, his thoughts were on his Second in Command, Terigan, and his Ice Dragon, Allyssa.

Both of whom were so grievously injured that their Goddess, Zeeandra, had to take them to her home to attempt to restore them back to full health. His worry for both of them hung heavy around his heart and he'd contact Zeeandra as soon as he was well enough to find out how they were progressing.

He also knew Sapphire and the rest of his Warriors would be anxious to know where their comrades were and why they hadn't returned with him. Although, he thought Sapphire was savvy enough to realize that if he was so badly injured, then Terigan and Allyssa probably wouldn't have fared much better.

His mind was drawn back to the bloody carnage as he languished in the water, going over the battle and wondering if he could've done something different that would have saved the other two. His heart ached as he replayed the moment Terigan fell from the sky after being hit by a blast from the King of Hell, Basilius.

Jaxon had dropped like a stone, hoping to catch Terigan before he smashed into the ground, but he'd been too far away. Then, through their mind-link, Zeeandra had ordered him away, worried that Basilius would mortally wound him. He'd shot back up into the air although every fiber of his being protested against leaving Terigan lying prone on the ground.

Even though Zeeandra had tried to calm him, his anger grew at the same rate as his exhaustion. But knowing Zeeandra's commands were prudent, he'd watched from a safe distance, hoping he'd be able to get to his friend. But then a damn Angel had appeared and engaged Basilius in an unholy battle. Jaxon had no chance to get to Terigan until the Angel had defeated the Demon King.

He knew, through their blood bond, that Terigan lived, but he was so badly injured that Zeeandra worried he may not survive, even with her help. She'd whisked Terigan away, ordering Allyssa to go with her too. The Ice Dragon was also wounded seriously, and their Goddess wished to heal them both. Jaxon refused to take up her offer, deciding instead to return home to his "sanctuary" and ensure all was safe there.

He couldn't stop his beast from turning and heading away from his Goddess and back to the valley where he'd spent years building a small village for those they rescued. He knew the time was coming when their exploits would be exposed, and the reason for the camp would soon be known to all.

They weren't stupid, they knew the day would arrive, but it seemed to now be looming in front of them and Jaxon feared for all of them. He would always do what the Guild had been created to do: offer safe harbor for those in dire need.

As his beast relaxed at the bottom of the pool he floated off to sleep, a dream taking over.

He flew high in the sky, his stomach clenching as he watched a woman speeding through a forest clutching a bundle to her chest. Although the figure wore a cloak which billowed out behind it, he knew that a woman hid beneath. How he knew that he wasn't sure, only that he did. Every instinct inside urging him to save her. He had to save her. His heart stuttered wildly as Demons appeared, chasing the mysterious woman who now attempted to avoid detection, hunkering down with whatever she was carrying clutched tightly to her chest. He could feel her terror as the Demons drew ever closer to her as she tried in vain to conceal herself and the precious bundle in her arms. He couldn't make out her face, even though he tried, but her soul called to his as he sped up, trying to reach her.

She meant something to him. What? He had no idea, only that she was important. No, more than important; she was vital to his future.

His Dragon rolled over, the dream disappearing like a wisp of smoke from his mind. His beast sighed as its strength grew, wounds healing, and finally rose to the surface. Jaxon felt the partial strength within his beast, knew it would still be days until he was battle ready again, but he was fit enough to return to camp and check on things.

Shaking its body as it clawed itself out and up onto the rock, his beast let out a bellow of relief. *That was a close call,* Jaxon thought as his Dragon claws scraped over the rocks on its way back to the entrance. As he drew nearer he saw dawn just breaking over the opposite mountain range, its beauty making him pause and take it in.

As soon as his head exited the cavern, Sapphire swooped down, Jaxon used their bonded link. *"How long have I been in the spring?"*

"Two days," she answered, her magnificent beast hovering in the sky, cocking its head to the side as it sized him up. *"You all right? You still look as if you could sleep for a week."*

"Yeah." His Dragon shook itself off before flapping its wings and taking to the sky. *"I think I could but too much work to do. How's things been?"*

Sapphire's Dragon kept pace with his, her worry for him very obvious. *"Quiet. Nothing happening really, so you can rest and heal. I'll look after things with Skar and Katarina's help."*

"Nothing needing my attention right now?" Jaxon felt his strength waning on the short flight down to the camp.

"No." Sapphire's long neck twisted to stare at him. *"You sure you should've gotten out of the healing well? You don't look so good, Jaxon."*

"I'm fine." Jaxon fought to hide his exhaustion. *"Nothing a few hours in bed won't heal."*

"I think you need a couple of days in bed." Sapphire's Dragon huffed out a puff of smoke. *"You're no use to anyone like this. You're way past*

tired and I don't want to see you out and about until at least tomorrow. All right?"

Jaxon's beast swiveled to glare at her. *"Since when did you start to play nurse?"*

"Since you came back almost done in and still look like death warmed up," she retorted cheekily.

"Well, it just so happens I am tired, so I'll let you off with all the fussing, this time."

Sapphire glided beside him as they slowed for landing. *"Zeeandra has been in touch. I thought you'd want to know that Allyssa is doing much better and should be home in a day or two."*

Relief flooded Jaxon as they landed in the backfield, before asking worriedly, *"Terigan?"*

"She says he's alive but he is still badly wounded." Sapphire transformed in a flash, standing in her usual black jeans and tee, hands in her pockets. "She isn't giving us any guarantees for his survival but she says he's a fighter and not to give up on him."

"Fucking Demons." Jaxon now stood dressed casually in jeans and not his usual leather, battle uniform. "I kinda wish Basilius was still alive so I could kill the fucker for all the damage he and his Demons have done."

Sapphire reached over, her hand gently placed on his shoulder. "We've heard some stories filtering through already. Sounds as if it was bad."

"That's one word for it," Jaxon ground out. "They lost so many people, Sapphire, so many dead and the blood lay in large pools in some areas. The scent was so strong it almost made me gag."

"We heard a rumor about a white Wolf." Sapphire cocked her head to the side as they started walking back to camp. "Is what they're saying true? Or is it one of those battle stories that grows more outlandish with each telling?"

Jaxon shrugged. "Depends what you heard. But, I'm telling, you I've never seen such a large beast and, boy, could it fight. It tore through Demons as if they were children and left a trail of devastation in its wake. I'm glad it was on our side, that's for sure."

"Sounds like it was an amazing sight." Sapphire's eyes shone as she carried on. "Is it true that this Wolf was the Witch from the prophecies? This girl called Rose, that's her name, isn't it?"

"Yes and yes." Jaxon shook his head in wonder. "She's got some heart in her. I'd go so far as to say she has a Dragon Heart and a warrior one at that."

"Really? Now that does surprise me. You don't usually have anything good to say about Wolves."

"There were quite a few Wolves there, some were killed, but they fought well and showed a hell of a lot of bravery faced with the hordes of Demons that they were up against." Jaxon sighed heavily. "But Rose was like a beast possessed, her size and strength certainly helped everyone, and with Allarde right there by her side, jeez, it was something to see, Sapphire."

"Is he as good looking as everyone says?" Sapphire grinned up at him cheekily.

"What kind of question is that to ask?" Jaxon scowled at her. "He's a man and I don't generally notice what they look like. I'm only interested in whether they're a threat or not."

Sapphire punched his arm lightly. "But is he? Come on, Jax, you must've noticed."

"No, I did not," Jaxon said firmly. "I only saw how well he fought by his mate's side. That was all I was bothered about."

"We also heard there was a Demon fighting alongside the white Wolf. Is that true?"

Jaxon gave a small nod. "Yes, she was tiny with blazing red hair and she fought like a fiend. I can only assume she's a Fire Demon 'cause she was certainly lobbing fireballs around all over the place."

"I can't quite believe a Demon fought against the King of Hell." Sapphire looked off into the distance. "Kinda makes me think that if there's one there may be others that aren't so bad."

"I believe that may be the case, but," Jaxon's tone hardened, "I'll continue to treat any Demon we come across as an enemy. They've worked with the Witch-Hunters from the beginning and have killed many humans, Supernaturals, and a few of our brothers and sisters of the Guild. I won't be letting down my guard anytime soon, Sapphire."

"I know," Sapphire agreed. "I'll be the same but it'll be interesting to see where things go from here."

"Yes," Jaxon conceded, "it will."

Sapphire stared hard at Jaxon, curiosity in her eyes. "What were the casualty numbers?"

Jaxon shook his head sadly. "Always the battle analyzer, Sapphire."

"I like to have details, you know that." She shrugged. "I write every detail down, you're aware of that, it helps me predict for future conflicts."

"I know." Jaxon sighed. "So many dead, and so many brave warriors cut down, I'm afraid I don't have exact numbers but I'd say more Demons died than us. With our Dragons attacking from overhead and the ground forces fighting, including a powerful Witch I saw throwing Demons all over the place, I'd say our side came out on top. However, if the Angel hadn't arrived I doubt any of us would be here."

Sapphire patted his shoulder. "I'm grateful he decided to show up and help. Angels can be fickle creatures, we both know that. But regarding the losses, that is the way it has always been, Jax. Good against evil and there are always casualties. No point brooding about it."

"I know." Jaxon stopped outside his cabin. "It was a fight I'd rather not relive but my brain won't shut down."

"Maybe once you've slept and healed properly you'll feel better. Away you go and I'll let everyone know not to interrupt you."

"Thanks." Jaxon pushed his door open, glad to be home, and alive. He'd thought on more than one occasion he wouldn't make it out of the fight still breathing, so he was thankful as he wandered along the corridor towards his bedroom. Kicking off his boots, his bare feet padded across the plush rug at the side of his bed and tumbled down onto it. The soft feathers molded around him, a soft groan escaping as his eyes slid shut, sleep pulling him under. A sliver of a memory of a woman running in the forest briefly surfaced, only to disappear as exhaustion took over.

CHAPTER TWO

Sapphire shook her head as she walked away from Jaxon's cabin, her worry for their leader rumbling around inside her. *"At least he's here and on his feet,"* she thought as Terigan's plight washed over her. If their Goddess couldn't tell them he'd definitely survive, then Terigan was definitely in a far worse state than Jaxon.

"Are you okay?" The soft, gentle voice of Bliss interrupted Sapphire's musings.

Turning around she tried to smile at the young woman. "Just a little concerned for Terigan, that's all."

"Oh." Bliss frowned. "I'm sorry."

"For what?" Sapphire asked, confused, though she should be used to it. Bliss was a Dragon, but different than most. She was a very sensitive soul who always worried for others far more so than for herself.

"Because you feel bad." Bliss shrugged. "I hope you feel better soon."

"Thank you." Sapphire felt touched by the younger woman's thoughtfulness, and smiled.

"Did I see Jaxon? Is he feeling better?" Bliss asked quietly.

"He's not fully healed, but Jaxon is being his usual self and has left the healing waters early." Sapphire sighed in exasperation. "I wish he'd stayed within the mountain for at least another day, but you know what he's like."

Bliss smiled, her eyes twinkling. "Yes, he's always thinking of others first and he's a little obstinate when it comes to taking care of himself. Isn't he?"

"That he is." Sapphire chuckled. "Obstinate is exactly what he is."

"Is there anything I can do to help?" Bliss cocked her head to the side looking thoughtful for a moment. "I could make him some of my healing tea, if you think it would help?"

Sapphire smirked at Bliss. "I think that would be a very good idea. At least then he'll sleep for a while and, hopefully, heal faster."

"Okay," Bliss said and turned away. "I'll go and get some ready for him."

"Wait." Sapphire stopped the young woman. "Once you've concocted it can you bring it to me? I'll take it to Jaxon, I need to speak to him anyway."

"Sure." Bliss shrugged. "I'll drop it off in the morning, if that's okay? I'll have to go and find some of the herbs I use as I'm running low. I should've thought on that earlier, I'm sorry."

"No apologies necessary." Sapphire tried to hide the smirk that was tugging on her lips. "Tomorrow will be perfect as I've sent him to bed for the rest of the day."

"Oh, okay, I'll bring it to you just after dawn." Bliss wandered off, muttering to herself as she went.

Sapphire chuckled as she carried on her way, knowing that Jaxon would be forced to rest the next day too after having some of Bliss' secret concoction. All she needed to do was make sure he ingested it. He most certainly wouldn't drink the healing tea, knowing it would knock him out for at least twelve hours. However, if Sapphire managed to add it to some food then he'd be none the wiser.

Well, that's what she hoped, because he'd be royally pissed at her deception if he realized what she'd done. *"Shit, he'll know as soon as he wakes up,"* she thought, shrugging as she sauntered through the camp. *"I'll deal with the fallout afterward, once he's had more time to heal."*

"You look deep in thought. What's up?" Skar's hoarse voice stopped her.

He was leaning against the side of his cabin, weapons and cleaning materials at his feet. Sapphire went over to join him, the

15

disfigurement that he got his name from didn't mar his roguish good looks, his dark ebony skin masking the extent of the scar. "Jaxon left the healing pool far too early so I'm trying to figure out how to get him to take Bliss' healing brew, and still keep my hide intact."

Skar laughed heartily as he shook his head. "You're taking your life in your hands playing that game, Sapphire."

"I know, but he needs to rest." Sapphire scowled up at the huge hulk of a man next to her. "He looked like shit and he hardly put up any fight when I told him to go and sleep. That alone tells me how badly hurt he still is."

"I see your point." Skar picked up one of his battle swords and started to clean it lovingly with cloth and oil. "However, you know he'll be aware what you did when he wakes, if not before, so you better make yourself scarce or he'll have your guts for garters."

"I'm already planning ahead." Sapphire grinned. "I'll take him a nice hot breakfast tomorrow and in the afternoon I'll head out and see how Zane's getting on with his mission. That'll take me far enough away that Jax should've calmed down by the time I get back."

"Has Zane checked in?" Skar stopped cleaning his weapon, looking down at Sapphire. "I've not heard anything through our link, but then I suppose he could've done a private one on one without the rest of us knowing."

Sapphire shook her head. "No, that's another reason I'm going to go and check on him. I asked him earlier, privately, if things were okay and he gave me a rather curt 'I'm busy' which isn't like him. If I leave tomorrow afternoon, I should reach him before nightfall. I know the area he's travelling in has a lot of Vampires but that shouldn't cause him too many problems."

"Has he found the one he was sent to look for?" Skar resumed his weapon cleaning.

"I'm not sure." Sapphire nibbled her bottom lip. "Again, that's not like him either, not keeping us in the loop. I hope he's all right."

"What information do we have on his target?"

"Only that a woman was in need of our aid and shelter." Sapphire tapped her chin with a finger. "It came from a reliable source, one of our contacts, but the message was sketchy at best. I've tried phoning but there's no answer. That's not to say our contact is in an area that has a good reception, it happens, a lot, so I'm not overly worried. Zane is more than capable of looking after himself, but I'll go and see if I can lend a hand."

"Okay, and if I see Jaxon on the warpath, I'll try and distract him." Skar chuckled. "I've got a good bottle of Scots Whisky that I'll share with him while I get him to tell me about the battle, especially the part about this supposedly huge white Wolf."

"I asked him about it." Sapphire raised an eyebrow. "Apparently what we've heard is true and he sounded quite in awe of the beast."

"Really?" Skar asked, surprised.

"Yes, really." Sapphire nodded. "Oh, and just for the record, the Wolf *is* a woman. See, we're not just pretty faces, we can kick ass too."

"Oh, my dear Sapphire," Skar's voice grew serious. "I know that. You and Allyssa, as well as all the female Dragons are more than capable of handing we men our asses."

"Maybe not all of us." Sapphire nodded toward Bliss' cabin. "I don't think Bliss could hurt a fly, it's just not in her."

Skar disagreed. "I think if the situation arose and an innocent was in need of protecting, she'd come through. I know she's not exactly the norm when it comes to our race, but I honestly have no doubt that if any of the children, or their parents, came under attack, she'd protect them."

"You think?" Sapphire queried, not sure at all if that were true.

"Yes," Skar said firmly. "She's pure of heart and violence isn't something that comes easily to her, unlike the rest of us, but I truly believe she has it in her if the situation called for it."

"I'll take your word on that, although I'm not entirely convinced."

"It's a gut feeling," Skar reiterated. "Now, is there anything you need me to do today? I'd thought I'd get some of the older kids together and practice some self-defense, but if you need me for something else I'm free."

"No." Sapphire nodded to the mountain range surrounding them. "Katarina is on guard duty and Brydon will relieve her later. I've put Katarina in charge of organizing the guard Rota so she'll let you know if you're needed."

"Okay, that's fine with me." Skar looked up into the sky. "I wish some of our guys would get back though. We're stretched a little thin at the moment."

"Amber and Opal are due back later today." Sapphire squinted up at the bright sky. "Their recon didn't have any results though. They couldn't find anyone in the area that appeared to need our help so they're on their way home."

"Good." Skar grunted. "I'd like a few more back here too."

"What's on your mind?" Sapphire queried.

"I'm not sure, just a feeling, and I've learned to trust my 'feelings' over the centuries, Sapphire." Skar's eyes roamed around the perimeter of mountains. "I hope I'm wrong but I feel something is coming our way and I don't mean anything good."

"I've always trusted your instincts, Skar." Sapphire's guts twisted with anxiety. "Maybe I shouldn't leave tomorrow."

"No, you definitely should go." Skar turned to smirk at her. "Unless you want Jaxon skinning you alive."

"I'd rather forego that pleasure," Sapphire replied sarcastically.

"When are Aric and Amos due back?" Skar asked of the twin Dragons who went everywhere together.

"Tomorrow at some time." Sapphire felt a shiver run through her, although she had no idea why. "They're bringing back a couple of teenage kids whose parents were killed, both Witches that were in hiding."

"Damn it!" Skar kicked out, sending a cloud of dust into the air. "Those poor children, I hope they're all right."

"They're not injured but I doubt they're okay," Sapphire enlightened him. "Their parents managed to hide them using magic but Aric informed me that they saw their parents being killed."

A growl rumbled up from Skar's chest, his anger clear. "Fucking assholes, those poor kids, what will you do with them?"

"I'll ask Bliss to look after them to begin with when the twins arrive with them." Sapphire gave him a sad smile. "If anyone can help them, it's her."

"Good idea." Skar agreed. "I'm more than willing to help too, but this," he motioned to his ravaged face, "might scare them more."

"Thanks for the offer." Sapphire paused for a moment. "One of them is a boy and I know that one of the emotions he'll have is the feeling of helplessness at being unable to help his mom and dad. So, you might be able to help after all. You could offer to teach him how to look after himself, and others. You could tutor him in the art of self-defense and maybe help him to feel a little more in control. What do you think?"

"That might work." Skar nodded. "I'll let Bliss have them for a day first so she can work her magic and then I'll see what I can do for the boy."

"His sister is only a year younger so you could include her too. After all, she'll feel the same way as her brother but if she's not interested then leave her with Bliss."

"Okay." Skar focused back on his weapons. "I'll do my best for them."

"I know you will." Sapphire patted his shoulder. "I'm going to check in with Katarina and make sure everything's been taken care of before I leave tomorrow. How's the food stocks? Do we need anything that I could try and get when I'm away?"

Skar shook his head. "Food is fine, I caught some deer yesterday so we've got plenty of meat. I think that we'll need to do a supply run for some other things soon though. Bliss has a list of what's running low, like clothes and maybe some toys for the younger kids. Who woulda thought little 'uns could destroy toys so fast?"

Sapphire laughed. "Yeah, I know. All right, I'll check with Bliss and get her to organize a run for when we're back to full complement. I don't want to leave the camp vulnerable, especially now."

"Okay." Skar stopped cleaning the large sword in his hand, giving her a hard look. "Our purpose here is going to come out soon, you know that, don't you?"

"Yes," Sapphire admitted. "I suspect there'll be some fallout about that too. There are people out there who think their loved ones were abducted, or killed. They have no idea that there's so many Witches safe and sound here."

"It may be that when it comes out that there'll be some people whose hopes are raised, thinking someone is here, safe, and that's not the case. So many *were* seized and killed."

"That's true too." Sapphire sighed heavily. "It's going to be a bit of a mess for a while."

"I'm not entirely comfortable that we've 'come out' but that was Jaxon's call and I support him one hundred percent." Skar frowned. "I just hope the innocents we've been protecting aren't put in harm's way."

"I would've done what he did too." Sapphire shrugged. "The truth is he couldn't have done anything *but* help. The alternative would be to turn our back on everything the Guild stands for and we can't do that. I just hope Allyssa and Terigan are healed soon and can come home, I miss them, even Terigan's bad jokes."

"You're right, of course, but you can't be serious about Terigan's jokes." Skar chuckled. "Nobody can miss those awful excuses for hilarity. Not even you."

"What?" Sapphire screwed her eyes, glaring at him.

"You don't have a sense of humor and his jokes are abysmal, no denying that, Sapphire."

"Pfft," Sapphire turned on her heel, scowling at Skar over her shoulder. "I do so have a sense of humor so go boil your head, big guy."

Skar guffawed as she strode away, outraged he thought she didn't have a sense of humor. Of course she did, she thought Terigan's jokes were funny. Well, maybe not funny but mildly amusing. In any case, she missed the big guy, Allyssa too, and wished they'd return soon.

CHAPTER  THREE

Jaxon was still wiping the sleep from his eyes as he answered the knocking at his door to find Sapphire waiting with a covered plate in her hand. "What's up? Is something wrong?" he asked as she swept inside.

"No." Sapphire made her way to his kitchen, placing the plate on the table before rummaging around for silverware. "I thought you could do with some good wholesome food so I brought you breakfast."

"Breakfast?" Jaxon asked perplexed. "It's barely past dawn and you just woke me up. Correct me if I'm wrong, but weren't you the one who told me I had to rest?"

"I know, but you need sustenance too, so here's some food and then you can go back to bed." Sapphire went to work brewing coffee as he sat down.

"I'm up now, I'll not be going back to bed." Jaxon removed the cover, inhaling the aroma of fried bacon, eggs, hash browns and even some sausage. "Who made this?"

Sapphire turned round, her eyes wide. "What?"

"We both know you don't cook." Jaxon smirked as he inhaled again, but deeper, savoring the aroma of the perfectly cooked food. "And this is far too good to have come out of your kitchen, so spill. Where did you steal this from?"

"Hmmf." Sapphire huffed as she turned her back on him to prepare coffee. "I asked Bliss if she'd cook you breakfast and, for the record, I'm a little put out about your aspersion on my cooking abilities. I'm not that bad."

Jaxon started to eat, the taste exquisite on his tongue as he ate the delicious offering. "Not that bad? Jeez, Sapphy, when you offer to cook for people they run screaming to the hills."

"That's it." Sapphire spun around. "I'm out of here, no thanks necessary for me bringing you food *and* making you coffee!"

Jaxon grinned as she stomped away in a huff, enjoying the food too much to bother if he'd put her in a bad mood. "Best I've had in a while." He continued to eat slowly so he could savor the food.

When he was finished Jaxon yawned, his eyes drooping, and his body feeling as if he'd flown half way around the world. "What the hell?" he said aloud, his legs growing heavy as exhaustion overtook him. He made his way back to his bedroom, sinking down onto his bed.

As his head hit the pillow, realization dawned, anger flaring as he cursed, "Damn it. I'll pay you back, Sapphire." That was all he managed before sleep engulfed him entirely.

Sapphire grinned as she slammed Jaxon's door, her mission accomplished and feeling happy with herself it had gone so well. He needed more rest than she knew he'd take, so a little helping hand on her part was worth the fallout she'd suffer when she returned to camp.

That wouldn't be for a few days yet and she hoped he'd calmed down by then. If not she'd stand tall and take her punishment, it was a small price to pay to aid their leader's recovery. For now she'd check everything in the camp was all right before leaving in search of Zane.

She'd played things down the day before while talking with Skar, but the truth was that she was concerned at Zane's silence. Normally he'd update them morning and night while on a mission, so his lack of communication was out of character and something she was troubled about.

So troubled that she was going to leave early. The sooner she found Zane, the quicker she'd find out what was going on. With her mind made up Sapphire hurried through the camp, ensuring everything was in order, before making her way to an area of large open grassland. She transformed quickly, her large but sleek Dragon taking to the air with ease.

Sapphire used the Dragon blood-bond mind-link. *"Kat, I'm leaving early to go find Zane. I'll keep you informed of what's going on."*

Kat replied immediately, *"Okay, Sapphy, take care and stay safe."*

"I will," Sapphire responded as her beast soared over the top of the mountains, engaging her Dragon magic to disappear from view of everything but other Dragons.

Even with her giant wingspan, it would take a few hours flying before she reached the area where Zane had been sent. She relaxed into the flight, allowing her mind to wander as her beast's wings beat a steady rhythm as she flew over the ravaged land below. The devastation of the town she now looked down upon causing her great sadness, with a good dose of anger. The thought of other supernatural beings trying to overrun weaker beings always brought out her warrior side.

Sapphire took her vows as a member of the Guild very seriously. Taking care of people in need, no matter who, or what, they were was ingrained deep inside her soul. She didn't care if it was a Witch, human, or anything else. If they were pure of heart and needed their help then they got it.

The fact that the Guild's missions over the last couple of decades mainly involved rescuing Witches didn't bother her in the least. That it was because they were being hunted by Demon Witch Hunters bothered her greatly. Most people weren't aware of who'd been behind the great massacre of Witches, but the Guild knew, without a doubt, that it was Demons.

She *hated* Demons, but if what Jaxon had said was true, that there were *good* Demons, then she may have to amend her thinking. Until she came across one that wasn't out to kill her, or anyone else, then she'd continue with her hatred boiling beneath the surface.

On and on she flew, her Dragon eating up the miles and she tried again to contact Zane. *"Zane, I'm headed your way. Are you all right?"*

There was silence for a few minutes, her worry increasing by the second, before he answered,

"*All right isn't exactly what I'd say, but I'm now on the trail of the woman we were alerted to.*"

"*You haven't found her yet?*" Sapphire queried, wondering what was taking him so long.

"*No,*" Zane sounded exasperated. "*She's as slippery as an eel. I've lost her more than once and I'm not the only one looking for her.*"

"*Demons?*" Sapphire asked, disgust dripping from that one word.

"*Yes, there's a band of Hunters here but I'm not sure this woman is a Witch so I've no idea why they're trying to capture her.*"

Sapphire's beast bellowed in anger, its wings beating furiously to close the distance between her and Zane. "*Why didn't you summon assistance?*" she asked, annoyed.

"*I'm handling it.*" Zane sounded just as displeased.

"*Why are you so obstinate?*" Sapphire ground out, infuriated that he'd not asked for help.

"*Sapphire, I've gotta go, I'm a little busy here,*" Zane said quickly.

"*What's going on?*" Sapphire asked worriedly. Waiting on a response that didn't come causing her to increase speed again. Her Dragon flew across the skyline like a bullet, trained on the spot in the distance where she knew she'd find Zane.

She didn't bother to contact him as she flew, too intent on closing the gap between them. Her sleek, black beast raced onwards and only when she sensed Zane's closeness did she contact him again.

"Zane, I'm nearby, where are you?"

Silence for a moment before he huffed out, *"I'm to the west of you, I can see you, look over, can you see the stream between the trees?"*

"Yes."

"I'm there."

Sapphire turned mid-air, her massive body rushing toward the ground with breakneck speed, her wings furling in, then fanning out to slow her descent. She now saw Zane, in human form, kneeling beside the stream. There was just enough room for her to land and she did so with ease, transforming quickly to rush over to Zane.

He was hunched over the water, splashing water on his white, pinched face. "You okay?" she asked, standing at his side and looking down at him.

"I'll be fine." Zane rose, groaning as he did so, a hand moving to cover his side. "Just a few broken ribs that are healing fine. I'll be good to go in a few minutes."

Sapphire looked around, on guard. "Is it safe here? What happened, Zane?"

"I had to deal with a Demon who was getting too close to the woman." He scowled as he rubbed his side. "It's safe. I flew away so I could rest for a bit to heal."

"What is wrong with you?" Sapphire's voice rose angrily. "Why do you always feel the need to do everything by yourself? You should've asked for help before this, Zane, and you know it."

Zane nodded, his face tight with anger. "I know, I'm sorry. I thought I could handle things on my own."

"You *always* think you can do that." Sapphire huffed out. "But we are a *Guild*, Zane, we work together and you need to stop trying to be a lone wolf. It puts you, and others, in danger."

"All right!" Zane snapped. "I said I'm sorry so can we just move on?"

Sapphire gave him a hard stare before inclining her head. "Tell me what you know of this woman. Do you have a name, or any other information?"

"No." Zane looked chagrined. "I've been following her for days but she keeps getting away. How she does it I have no freaking idea. She's using magic of some sort but it's not like Witches' magic, it's different, and I have no clue as to what it is."

"Intriguing." Sapphire thought for a moment. "Maybe she's using a spell to hide the fact she's a Witch?"

Zane shook his head emphatically. "Nope. I can sense that, and she is not a Witch. There's something else too."

"What?" Sapphire asked as she pondered on what magic the woman was using.

"I think she has a baby with her." Zane frowned. "I can't be certain of that though . . ."

Sapphire interrupted him. "What do you mean you can't be certain? She either has a child with her or she doesn't. Surely you've seen this child if she has one."

"When I've spotted her she's usually cradling something in her arms, but it's wrapped up, so I can't say for sure what it is." Zane shrugged. "But the way she holds it shows me she thinks it's something very precious and she carries it like a child. Maybe I'm wrong, it could be something else entirely, but I sense it's a baby."

"Shit," Sapphire cursed, running a hand through her ebony hair. "I guess we need to be careful then. We can't run the risk of injuring a little one."

"My thoughts exactly," Zane agreed. "That's why I've not 'caught' her yet. I've been playing safe, but those damn Demons are on her tail constantly. I've had a couple of run-ins with them just to give her a chance to escape."

"Has she seen your Dragon?" Sapphire queried.

"I would assume so." Zane cocked his head to the side looking thoughtful. "I thought if she saw I was trying to help then she'd reveal herself to me."

"How's that working out for you?" Sapphire said "I mean, of course she's going to come out of hiding and show herself to a blinking huge fire-breathing Dragon. Yeah, I can just see that happening."

"I thought it would help her understand I was there to help," Zane said curtly.

"Okay, we need to try and find her, and this possible child, as soon as possible." Sapphire nodded toward his body. "How're you feeling? All right to go and see if we can find her?"

"I'm fine," Zane barked. "I'll go first and then you can follow me."

"Let's go." Sapphire walked away, giving him plenty of room to transform. Her Dragon was large, but Zane's was far bigger. Almost same size as Jaxon's, which was saying something.

Zane changed quickly, his red-toned beast standing magnificently before her. Sapphire waited, watching as the Dragon took flight, shooting straight up into the sky, then hovering above. She saw him stretching his neck, checking all around before giving her a nod and a rumble to let her know all was clear.

Sapphire moved from the trees she was backed up against, striding to the middle of the clearing to morph and join Zane in the air. Her jet black beast would be invisible shortly, once it grew dark, without the aid of their magic. Zane's brighter color would always require the assistance of their Dragon abilities to be avoid detection, unless he wished otherwise.

She flew to Zane's side, using their link to communicate. *"Which way?"*

"Last I saw her she was a few miles to the south, but she'll have moved on by now to get away from the Demons I was fighting."

"Okay, lead the way."

Zane's Dragon veered off, flying low over the trees. He sped along for a bit before slowing down, hovering over a clearing. Sapphire looked down, seeing signs of Zane's encounter with the Demons. The earth messed up, blood spots covering a large area, and a tree or two ripped from the ground to lie broken on the ground.

"How many Demons?" Sapphire asked as she looked at the devastation below.

Zane was slow to answer. *"Three."*

Sapphire rumbled in annoyance. *"Three? For goodness sake, Zane, you shouldn't have taken on three Demons. How the hell did you survive?"*

"I'm not sure, but I did, so all's good."

"All is most definitely not good." Sapphire grew angry at his foolhardiness. *"Once we rescue this woman and get home, you're grounded. Do you hear me? You'll not be going on any further missions for the foreseeable future. I'll let Jaxon deal with your stupidity."*

She could feel his anger through their link. Zane remained silent and she gave him points for that. Usually he'd argue until he was blue in the face. If he'd said anything, anything at all, she would've ordered him home and took on the mission herself, after she'd called for reinforcements.

"What's that?" She nodded toward a greenish wisp of smoke that meandered off to the right.

"That's her," Zane replied. *"It must be some kind of trail she leaves due to her magic but I've never come across anything like it before."*

Sapphire flew lower, scrutinizing the trail, something flickering in the back of her mind. She'd seen something similar, a long time ago. *"Impossible."*

"What is?" Zane asked.

"You'd know an Angel if you saw one, wouldn't you?" she questioned.

"*Of course I would, she's not an Angel, Sapphy. If she were, she could easily take care of a Demon or two.*"

Sapphire stared intently at the green tinge lingering in the area. "*Of course she could. I must be wrong.*"

"*Definitely,*" Zane reiterated. "*If she were an Angel she could easily escape this realm and not be in danger from anything, far less Demons.*"

"*I know that,*" Sapphire grunted back. "*All right, let's follow and see where it leads and pray we don't meet those damn Demons again.*"

CHAPTER FOUR

Sapphire grew tired as they tried to pick up the woman's trail. Over and over they circled around, spiraling ever outwards, with no sign of the woman to be found. Darkness fell, the moon became bright in the sky when she finally gave up. *"We'll find somewhere to rest up and start again in the morning."*

"I've got a camp set up in the mountains to the west," Zane advised. *"There's food and blankets and I'll get the fire going, it's snug once it heats up."*

"Good," Sapphire replied tartly. *"I do hate being cold."*

She followed Zane's Dragon as it veered off, flying higher in the dark night sky toward the far off mountain range. Their speed picked up now, no longer trying to track someone on the ground. Zane sped up and she matched him, weary to land and rest. After flying for hours to reach Zane, she was now exhausted and needed sleep.

Relief flowed over her when she spied where Zane was leading her: A large outcropping in the middle of the range in front of them with a huge dark circle behind, which obviously led to a cavern of some sort. Sapphire hoped Zane was right regarding it being warm, she *hated* to be cold.

Zane flew faster on the approach, only slowing at the last possible moment, and landing gracefully on the outcrop. As soon as he was down, he transformed and went inside the cave. When he'd left the opening clear, Sapphire touched down, morphing quickly, ensuring she clad herself in warm clothes, and turned to look out over the forest one last time before heading after Zane.

She found him inside the cave that was much smaller than she'd thought, a fire already flaring and heat beginning to warm up the area. When she joined him, Zane walked back to the entrance, picking up a makeshift windbreaker made from branches entwined together.

"This keeps the worst of the cold out," he explained as he set it upright.

"Good." Sapphire looked around, spying a mound of blankets near the fire.

Zane returned to shuffle through a large backpack, pulling out some meat, veg, and a small camping stove. "I'll make us something to eat." He pointed to his pack. "There's bottled water in there if you want a drink."

"Thanks." Sapphire grabbed one and sat down, cross-legged on the floor. "Cold," she complained before snatching a blanket to sit on.

"You'll be warm soon," Zane reiterated as he went to work.

Sapphire watched as he made quick work of getting food on to heat. His strong, large frame casting flickering shadows on the cave's walls. She sighed at the thought of her comfortable bed as she waited for the area to become warm. "So, Zane, when we get back, I think you need to have a meeting with Jaxon. You should've called for help when you realized Demons were on this woman's trail."

"Whatever," he mumbled as he stirred the food.

"Don't 'whatever' me." Sapphire's anger grew at his nonchalance. "We can't afford to lose any more Dragons. There's few enough of us as it is."

"I know that," Zane conceded quietly.

"Well then, you should know better." Sapphire shook her head sadly. "We can't lose any more, Zane, you included."

He looked over at her, his eyes full of mischief. "My apologies for being an idiot. Again."

Sapphire groaned at the insincerity in his voice. "You better try harder than that with Jax, or he'll murder you."

"I thought I could handle it, okay?" Zane said curtly.

"Yeah, right, and how's that working out for ya?" Sapphire snorted. "You got the woman? Did you have to fight off Demons?"

Zane focused on the food, refusing to look at her. She waited him out until finally he looked up. "Okay, I get it, Sapphy. No need to rub it in."

"Zane," Sapphire exhaled, trying to rein in her annoyance. "I know you think you're invincible, but against Demons any one of us could be mortally wounded. You know the rules. If there's more than one, then you contact base and ask for reinforcements."

"I'm sorry." Zane's tone of voice seemed far more apologetic this time. "I didn't want to waste time waiting for reinforcements. I thought I could get the job done alone. I admit, I was wrong."

"Yeah," Sapphire agreed. "I know that's what you were thinking and you have *got* to get rid of this lone wolf persona. We are a team, Zane, a team who counts on each other to do things properly so none of us gets hurt. Or worse."

"I guess it won't come as a surprise when I say I prefer working alone." Zane's lip tugged up at one side.

"No, really?" Sapphire feigned surprise.

"Sarcasm doesn't suit you," he ground out.

"I know you're relatively new to the Guild, but you've gone through the rigorous years of testing we all had to go through. So, Zane, you are well aware of how we work and if you can't do that then you shouldn't have joined in the first place. Simple."

"Don't say that." Zane's head snapped up. "I'm proud to be a member of the Guild, I just find it hard to ask for help."

"Trust issues much?" Sapphire's tone dripped with sarcasm, and she saw him visibly wince.

"You could say that," he admitted softly.

"The only thing I have to say about that is, get over it," Sapphire said firmly. "We don't have room for a rogue in our ranks."

Sapphire stopped, noting the slump of Zane's shoulders, her annoyance dissipating as she watched the young Dragon. "I'm sorry if I seem harsh, Zane. Look, all you need to do is remember the rules and don't break them. They're there for *all* of us to follow and I'm telling you now, if there are still three Demons on that woman's trail tomorrow then I won't hesitate to call for back-up."

"I'll do better in the future," Zane spoke quietly before nodding toward his pack again. "There's a couple of tin plates in there, could you grab them, please?"

"Sure." Sapphire did as he asked, holding them out as he dished up.

"It's not gourmet food but it's warm and nourishing." He placed the empty cooking tin down before taking a couple of forks out of his pack. "Here." He put one onto each plate before taking one and sitting down.

Sapphire sat back down, noticing the area had heated up nicely. Starting to eat, she was a little surprised at how good the food tasted. "Nice, thanks," she mumbled through a full mouthful, tucking in and finishing every last morsel.

Zane remained silent, cleaning up when they were done, walking away into the dark at the back of the cave. Sapphire called after him. "Where you going?"

His voice echoed as he answered, "There's a small stream back here, I'm going to wash up this stuff."

"Okay." She looked around for a place to settle down, moving small stones out of the way so it would be as comfortable as sleeping in a cave could be. It wasn't the first time she'd done it, and it certainly wouldn't be the last, but she didn't have to enjoy it. She much preferred her soft bed with its thick comforter so she hoped they could get this assignment done and dusted and get back to camp.

Zane reappeared, replaced the now clean plates and tin in his pack, then found a spot near the fire and lay down, tugging another blanket over himself. "We'll get an early start and see if we can find her tomorrow."

"All right, goodnight." Sapphire yawned, exhaustion taking her over into a deep, dreamless sleep.

Jaxon woke refreshed, if not totally healed, and headed into his attached bathroom to have a quick shower before dressing and stomping outside, slamming his door behind him. His eyes scoured the area in search of Sapphire, but he couldn't see her anywhere. His face set in a stony glower, he strode through the camp, his anger flaring brighter with every step.

Skar was walking toward him, but when he saw Jaxon, Skar veered off to the right. Jaxon snarled. "No you don't. Skar, get your ass over here. Now."

Jaxon changed direction to intercept Skar, who'd stopped, his eyes down and shoulders slumped. Jaxon closed the distance quickly, standing toe to toe with Skar's hulk. Jaxon's jaw clenched as he ground out, "Where is she?"

Skar's eyes didn't meet his, looking somewhere over Jaxon's left shoulder as he feigned innocence. "Where's who? Is there something wrong?"

Jaxon's blood pressure rose as he fought to control himself. "Don't. I'm warning you, I'm not in the mood for deceit, Skar. So, tell me, where is that slippery, devious, and scheming Sapphire?"

Skar shrugged. "I'm not entirely sure."

"Did you not hear me?" Jaxon poked Skar's broad chest. "I'm not in the mood. Where the hell is she?"

"I'm telling the truth." Skar finally met his eyes. "She went out yesterday to try and track down Zane, but I've not heard anything from her and I have no idea where, exactly, they are."

"Zane is out on a mission?" Jaxon asked. "Where and what's the task?"

"I'm not certain where he is right now." Skar shrugged. "Kat will know the general area. He was sent out after a tip was received from a contact about a woman needing our help. That's all I know, Master, honestly."

Jaxon eased off Skar when he used his official title, knowing the man spoke the truth. "All right, I'll speak to Katarina and find out where she's sneaked off to."

"If you don't mind me saying, you still don't look a hundred percent, boss. You sure you're okay?"

"Excuse me?" Jaxon bristled, raising an eyebrow.

"I'm just saying," Skar mumbled, taking a small step back.

"Well, don't," Jaxon snarled. "I'm fine, and definitely fit enough to tan Sapphire's hide for slipping me some of Bliss' knockout concoction."

"How badly hurt were you in the battle against those Demons?" Skar asked, his tone sincere. "I hear Allyssa is doing much better but Terigan is still not out of the woods yet."

"I'll admit I was wounded pretty badly." Jaxon shook his head. "And it was a hell of a fight, Skar. I'm amazed any of us made it out alive."

"The white—" Skar started but Jaxon interrupted him.

"Wolf, yeah, all true what you've heard."

Skar whistled, shaking his head. "I'd like to meet her one day. This Rose person sounds intriguing and quite the warrior."

"She is," Jaxon agreed. "I've a feeling we'll hear from her when she finds out what we've been doing here."

"Why?" Skar looked confused.

"Her mother was a Witch and was taken when she was a child," Jaxon informed him. "Or so I've heard. I imagine she'll want to know if we have any information on a woman named Marie O'Connell."

"And do we?" Skar asked.

"I've a pretty good memory and the name doesn't ring any bells with me, but I'll get Bliss to check our records, just in case."

"If she were here, surely she would've let herself be known when all the rumors about this Rose person filtered through." Skar scratched his head, looking thoughtful.

"You would think, yes." Jaxon nodded. "So I guess I was right and she's never been here."

"That's a pity." Skar looked over towards Bliss' cabin. "I've got to go, I'm planning on introducing myself to a couple of teenagers the twins brought back yesterday. They're with Bliss right now but Sapphy thought it might be a good idea if I tried to teach them some self-defense."

"All right." Jaxon turned away. "I'll speak to Katarina and then I'll be contacting that little weasel to give her a rollicking."

"Don't be too hard on her." Skar tried to soften the blow he knew would soon be landing on Sapphire. "She was just trying to help."

"I don't give two figs if she was trying to help," Jaxon spat out. "She drugged me and I will *not* allow that to go unpunished."

"Okay, okay." Skar held his hands up, palm out. "Sorry I said anything."

"Just remember, Sapphire deliberately drugged me unconscious, so in an emergency situation I would not have been available. That is not acceptable and she *will* be punished."

"Yes, sir." Skar bowed his head before stepping away. "Now, if you'll excuse me, I'm going to set up some weapons and an area to take the kids to."

"Fine." Jaxon waved him away. "I'll go and find Katarina."

"She's in the communal hall having breakfast," Skar told him. "She was on duty last night so she'll be going to bed soon."

"Then I'll go and find her now." Jaxon about turned and headed toward the large building set in the middle of the camp.

The building housed a huge commercial kitchen that could feed large numbers of people at a time. Most of the camp's community ate there on a daily basis and it was run with an iron fist by an old Witch, Emmalina, who'd been there for almost twenty-five years. Although she rarely answered to her given name, much preferring Em, saying it made her feel young to be called by her childhood nickname.

Jaxon pushed open the door, the noise assaulting his ears. Most of the spaces were taken, the smell of breakfast heavy in the air as he looked around for Katarina. Failing to spot her, he used their link. *"Katarina, where are you?"*

"Having a well-deserved meal after a long night. Why, do you need me?"

Jaxon scanned the throng of people again looking for Kat's brown hair. *"I'm at the door, where are you?"*

"Oh, I see ya." Kat's hand shot up, waving him over.

Jaxon weaved around tables and young children who played, while their parents tried to get them to eat. Reaching Kat, he nodded at the man sitting next to her who shifted over to make room. Jaxon sat down and before he could open his mouth to speak, a plate of food materialized before him. Em gave him a cheeky wink. "You're looking a little peaky, Jaxon, eat and get your strength back."

"Thank you." Jaxon smiled up at the old woman.

"Pfft, it's what I do, no need to thank me." She shuffled away, picking up empty plates as she went.

"She never stops, does she?" he mumbled as he started to eat.

Katarina sipped on some OJ before replying. "Nope. She's got more energy than I'll ever have, that's for sure. I've no idea how she does it."

"Me neither," Jaxon admitted.

Katarina returned her glass to the table. "So, boss, why were you looking for me?"

Jaxon finished his mouthful of food before talking. "What's going on with Zane, and also, has that conniving snake in the grass, Sapphire, been in touch?"

Katarina's face sobered quickly. "Zane's doing his 'one man army' thing again and no, Sapphy's not been in touch. I assume you're angry with her?"

"Damn right I am." Jaxon shook his head. "She was wrong, Katarina, no matter that she thought she was doing the right thing. I'm the Master of the Guild and it's my decision whether to take any kind of medication, especially something that'll knock me out for almost a day."

"I told her it was a bad idea." Katarina's tone was deadly serious. "She didn't listen."

"She'll have to be punished when she gets back." Jaxon speared a piece of bacon. "I've not decided what yet. I may ground her for a month. That'll get her panties in a twist."

"Damn, Jaxon." Katarina's eyes widened in shock. "That's a hell of a long time to ground any Dragon, far less Sapphire. You know she flies every single day, she was born to be in the sky."

"Well, maybe it'll make her stop and think on her actions in the future." Jaxon frowned. "What she did crossed the line, and I won't put up with that kind of insubordination. Not even from her."

"Maybe a week?" Katarina countered. "A day is torture for her, a week will be hell, but a month, jeez, I think it'd kill her."

"I'll think about it," Jaxon conceded. "But she's not getting off lightly. She has to learn that I won't tolerate behavior like that."

"I understand." Katarina yawned. "Is there anything else I can help with?"

"No." Jaxon focused on his food. "You can go get some rest. If I need you, I'll let you know."

"Thanks." She rose, picking up her plate, glass, and silverware to stack it on one of the trolleys dotted around the cavernous room. "I'll be in my cabin if you need me."

"All right." Jaxon inhaled deeply, smiling. Em's scrambled eggs were the best he'd ever tasted and he was going to enjoy every bite.

Only then would he contact Sapphire and Zane to find out what was going on, and he'd give her a headache she wouldn't forget. He'd make damn sure she didn't repeat her act of insubordination.

CHAPTER

FIVE

Zane woke Sapphire before dawn. Stretching her arms before rubbing the sleep from her eyes, she was pleasantly surprised that she'd slept so soundly. Zane looked as if he'd been up for a while and she noticed two cups steaming beside the dimming fire.

"That's one of Bliss' morning tea blends. It's hot and helps get me going when I wake up."

Sapphire snatched one of the steaming mugs. "Thanks, I love her blends of tea. She has one for just about every occasion."

Zane smirked. "I know. I think I've got all of them."

"You have a plan for this morning?" she asked as she sipped the warm brew.

"I think we should look for the woman's trail again near where we left off last night. See if we can pick her up again."

Sapphire agreed. "Okay, let's hope we have better luck today."

Zane frowned, his face showing his concern. "I'm getting more worried with each day, especially if that bundle she's carrying is a child. The thought of Demons getting their hands on a baby turns my blood to ice."

"Me too." Sapphire rose, looking around. "Hmm, where have you been, you know, *relieving* yourself? I need to go before we set off."

Zane pointed to the back of the cave. "Down by the stream, it's the only place that's available."

"No problem, that'll do fine." Sapphire started to fold her blanket but Zane stopped her.

"That's all right, I'll do that."

Minutes later, Sapphire returned to find everything cleared away and the fire doused.

"Ready?" Zane asked as he removed the windbreaker.

"Sure. Let's go find this woman and get her to safety." Sapphire hoped they didn't encounter any Demons. She *hated* damn Demons.

Zane transformed, his beast taking flight immediately to hover outside over the ledge, waiting on her. Sapphire was aware that he was also checking for danger, feeling relieved when he obviously found none. She stood in the middle of the outcrop and morphed quickly, her massive wings lifting her easily into the dawning sky.

"I hope we find her today," Zane mind-linked.

"Me too," Sapphire agreed as she swooped after him.

Their journey took them back over the area they'd been searching the previous day, there was still no sign of the woman. Several hours later Sapphire was getting exasperated. *"Any ideas?"* she asked Zane curtly.

"Stay patient and widen the search on each pass," Zane replied.

"Duh, like I hadn't already thought of that," Sapphire snapped back.

"Wait, what's that over there?" Zane's great head swiveled around to their left where a faint green hue swirled around the tree line.

"That's same type of smoke that we saw yesterday." Sapphire's excitement grew as they sped toward the trail.

"Yeah, it's what I've always seen just before I catch sight of the woman, and then she goes and disappears before I get the chance to let her know I'm here to help."

"Here's hoping we manage to snag her this time."

As they drew nearer, she almost shrieked when Jaxon's angry voice bored into her head. *"Sapphire! If you weren't out helping Zane, you'd be grounded for what you did. Do you hear me?"*

Zane's head spun toward her and she knew Jaxon was talking to them both. She took a moment to answer, trying to sound apologetic.

"I'm sorry, Master, but you were almost dead on your feet and I thought you needed the rest."

"That was not your decision to make, Warrior." Jaxon's tone was icy cold. *"I am Master of the Guild and you showed gross insubordination, deviousness, and deceit. I'm extremely unhappy, Sapphire, and you'll be suitably punished on your return."*

Sapphire winced, regretting her decision to slip him Bliss' healing potion. *"I'm truly sorry."* She tried to lessen the blow she knew would fall on her return.

"Too late for an apology. You should've thought before you acted. Now, give me a report on your situation, and Zane, it has not gone unnoticed that you haven't been checking in."

"Sorry," Zane replied softly.

Sapphire sighed, the action causing smoke to leave her beast's mouth, before she answered. *"We're on the trail of a woman, who may, or may not, have a small child with her. She appears to have some kind of magic that she uses to evade detection but we're on her trail right now."*

"Any other problems I should know about?" Jaxon asked brusquely.

Sapphire looked over at Zane pointedly. *"Apparently, there are some Demons also looking for her."*

Zane huffed as they waited on the explosion both knew would come, and they didn't have long until Jaxon shouted in their heads. *"What? Demons as in plural? How many?"*

"Several." Zane tried to avoid the question.

"Several intimates more than one, Zane, you know protocol regarding that. Why didn't you request assistance?"

Sapphire held her breath, knowing Jaxon would be angry at the lapse of their rules. Zane's tone was very subdued as he replied. *"I thought I could handle it."*

"You know what thought can do? Get your ass killed! You'll be reprimanded when you return. For fuck's sake! What is wrong with you two?"

Sapphire groaned at Jaxon's cursing, it wasn't something he usually did when speaking in an "official" capacity. She knew they were in deep shit for him to have lost his temper like that. She remained silent, not having an answer that would help and knowing if she tried to pacify Jaxon that he'd only grow angrier.

Zane wasn't as savvy as he hurried to fill the silence. *"I apologize, again, Master. I didn't think."*

Sapphire rapidly shook her head at the young Dragon, knowing his words would add fuel to the fire. She was right.

Jaxon swore again. *"Fuck! You didn't think! All those years of training to drill into you how we do things, and why we do things, and all of a sudden you 'didn't think'! I may have to reassess your ability to attend to an assignment alone, Zane."*

Zane's eyes locked on Sapphire's, his anxiety showing clearly. *"Anything you think is appropriate, Master."* Was all he managed.

"So, are you two safe at the moment? Or do you require any further help?"

"We're fine . . . shit, wait a moment." Sapphire's enhanced sight caught a glimpse of several bodies among the trees. *"Houston, we have a problem."*

"Shit." Zane swore as he saw what she motioned toward.

"What? What is it?" Jaxon asked urgently.

"Demons," Sapphire replied tersely. *"Quite a few, at least four or five that I can see. There may be more."*

"Do not engage," Jaxon ordered. *"I'm on my way and I'll bring the twins and Skar with me."*

"What do we do if they find her? We can't let them capture, or kill her, Jax," Sapphire ground out, her concern for the unknown woman growing. *"She must be pretty damn special if they're going to this length to get her."*

"Stay hidden and keep your eyes on the situation. We'll get there as soon as we can," Jaxon said calmly.

"*All right,*" Sapphire conceded, knowing deep inside she'd never be able to stand by and watch if the Demons cornered the woman.

"*I'll cross that bridge when I come to it,*" she whispered.

Zane's Dragon head nodded, understanding what she meant. He too would be compelled to engage the enemy if the woman was in danger. That much was clear to Sapphire and she'd be right by his side if it came to that.

"*I'll follow the Demons.*" Sapphire's beast turned to fly toward them. "*You keep trying to find the woman. Hopefully, the others will get here in time.*"

"*I hope so too, because I'm not leaving her to whatever fate those bastards have in store for her. Not happening, Sapphire.*"

"*I'm aware of that,*" Sapphire snapped. "*I wouldn't expect you to, but let's hope we don't have to intercede until Jaxon and the rest arrive. Now go, see if you can find this elusive creature that has a horde of Demons after her.*"

"*I'll do my best,*" Zane replied before swooping away, his speed picking up to zoom across the treetops.

"*Good luck,*" Sapphire muttered as he grew smaller with every flap of his wings.

She looked back down, spying the Demons, and following them from above. She *hated* Demons and hoped she'd have the chance to take several of them out before the day was past.

Jaxon sped toward Skar who was walking toward him. "Get ready to leave on a mission. Sapphire and Zane need our help."

Skar frowned. "I'm not being rude, boss, but are you fit enough to go on an assignment?"

A growl rumbled up from Jaxon's chest as he glared at Skar. "I'm fine."

Skar didn't look convinced but he nodded. "Whatever you say, Master. What's going on with Sapphire and Zane?"

"Demons are after the woman they're trying to find." Jaxon was just about to mind-link with the twins when he saw them leaving the meal hall. "Aric, Amos, over here."

The striking men jogged over, Amos grinning as he arrived. Aric was his usual, quiet self, almost surly as he joined them. Amos nodded to Skar before focusing on Jaxon. "What's up?"

"Zane and Sapphire need our help. We leave in ten minutes so hurry." Skar hurried away as Aric frowned.

"What's the mission?" Aric asked.

"Excuse me?" Jaxon raised an eyebrow.

Amos punched Aric playfully. "Doesn't make any difference what it is, *does* it, brother?"

Aric shook his head. "That came out wrong, Master. I just meant do we take weapons to use in human form? Knowing what the mission brief is would let me know that."

"I doubt we'll be in human form." Jaxon scowled. "It's Demons we'll be up against."

"Alrighty then." Amos grinned, nodding. "I'll grab my mission pack and we'll meet you in the field."

"Ten minutes," Jaxon reiterated.

"Nine now," Aric said as he turned and trotted away, his jet black hair flowing behind him.

"Tick tock." Amos laughed as he ran after his brother.

Jaxon shook his head at their backs. The twins were so different it amazed him they were even related. They were identical apart from coloring, and of course, nature. He was well aware at how well they performed together, but sometimes Aric's demeanor grated on Jaxon's nerves.

Shaking off his annoyance, Jaxon headed to his cabin to pick up his own mission pack. They all had them, large enough for some food, water, blankets and camp-fire cooking utensils. It was easily carried in their Dragon's claws and a must-have if planning to be away from camp for more than a day or so.

Having no idea what they were flying into, he would ensure they all took theirs along. Jaxon only hoped they'd arrive before Sapphire and Zane's hands were forced. Despite his orders, he knew, without a doubt that they'd intervene if the Demons managed to find the woman. Truth be told, he couldn't blame them, he'd do the same, no question about it.

Pushing open his cabin door and snatching his pack from just inside, Jaxon closed the door behind him, before linking to Kat. *"Katarina, Zane and Sapphire require assistance. I'm taking Skar and the twins with me and we're leaving right away. Can you take over and keep an eye on things while we're gone?"*

"Are they all right?" Kat replied, sounding worried.

"At the moment, yes."

"Okay, I'll look after things here, but I'm a little worried we're going to be shorthanded if we have any problems."

Jaxon sighed, his mind running over where everyone was. *"Brydon and Amber are due back this morning."*

"Good." Katarina sounded relieved. *"I'm glad, I don't want us vulnerable while you're gone."*

"You won't be. Send them a message and tell them to hurry back."

"I'll do that now. Take care and keep me informed of what's going on."

Jaxon smirked at the obvious concern in her voice. *"I will."*

He carried on out of the camp, Skar catching up to him as he strode toward the large field they used for taking off. "All set?" he asked the huge man beside him.

Skar inclined his head. "Sure. How far away are they?"

Jaxon exhaled, thinking for a moment. "At least a few hours and that's us going full out."

"So, basically, we're between the Devil and the deep blue sea?" Skar commented. "We fly all out and arrive to a fight tired. Or we conserve our energy by going slower and run the risk of Zane and Sapphire being in trouble."

"That's it exactly," Jaxon agreed. "I'm going to keep in contact with Sapphire and if it seems as if we have more time, then we'll slow down, but to begin with I'd rather we used our speed to get us there as soon as possible."

"No problem." Skar stopped, plopping his pack down.

Jaxon turned around at the sound of feet rushing toward them. Amos and Aric were apparently having a race, with Amos in the lead and whooping with glee.

"Tick tock! We made it with three minutes to spare, boss." Amos slid to a stop, a wide grin on his face.

"Yes, you did." Jaxon couldn't help his lips tugging up at the younger Dragon's enthusiasm.

Aric arrived a second or two after his twin, his face somber, as usual. Jaxon gave him a nod and filled them in. "Zane and Sapphire are tracking a woman in need of our assistance and there are Demons on her trail. Yes, Demons, as in plural, so we need to get to them promptly. We'll fly high and use the thermals to aid our speed. Everyone okay with that?"

Amos saluted with two fingers to his temple. "Sure thing, boss."

Aric barely inclined his head and Skar walked farther away before replying. "Let's get going. We don't have time to spare on chatting."

With that Skar transformed, his magical beast looming over the rest of them. His gigantic claws snapped up his pack that now appeared tiny against his immense form. The beast's wings flowed out to the side, flapping once to lift it effortlessly into the air.

Jaxon strode over and mirrored Skar's movements as the twins flanked him. All three transformed, grasping their mission packs and gliding up into the air. Skar waited for them above and as soon as they joined him, Jaxon nodded toward the west. *"This way."*

They fell in beside him as he soared higher and higher until he felt the welcome uplift of thermals, using them to increase their speed. On and on they flew and after an hour or so he connected to Sapphire.

"How's it going at your end?"

"We've split up. I'm keeping an eye on the pesky Demons and Zane is trying to locate the woman."

"Okay, keep me updated." Jaxon closed the link, focusing on getting there as quickly as possible.

CHAPTER SIX

Sapphire glided above the treetops, her eyes glued to the Demons progress below. She winced several times when they stopped to turn their heads skyward, even though she knew her Dragon's magic hid her from their sight. They might have "sensed" something but unless she engaged in battle, they would not be able to see her—something she was extremely relieved about.

The morning had started with three Demons. Now there were five. Two more had joined the original group and they seemed intensely focused on their prey. Once again she wondered what was so special about the woman they so diligently hunted.

Zane's excited voice brought her out of her musings. *"Sapphy, I've found her trail."*

"Thank goodness. We've been up here for hours."

"I know," Zane replied, obviously relieved. *"I think she's just up ahead, I'll let you know in a few moments if I see her."*

Sapphire looked down and noticed the Demons appeared to be moving faster. *"Shit,*

Zane, I think the Demons have her trail too. They're on the move and they're speeding through the forest."

"Fuck! Sapphire, I can see you, you're not far behind me."

"Which means they're not far behind her." Sapphire kept pace easily with the Demons, her eyes locating each one as they ran through the forest below.

"I see her and she's definitely carrying something."

"Is it a child? Is that maybe what those fuckers are after?"

"The way she's holding the bundle, I'd say it's a baby."

"Damn it. Hold on, I'm going to see how far out Jaxon and the rest of the cavalry are."

Sapphire opened a link to include Jaxon in a three-way conversation. *"Jaxon, we're in a bit of a bind here. How far away are you?"*

Jaxon replied instantly, *"Not far, why? What's going on?"*

Zane cursed, *"Damn it to hell! I can see them. They're right on her tail. Sapphy, we need to do something or they're gonna get her."*

Jaxon's calm tone surprised even Sapphire. *"Zane, hold off. Wait for us for as long as you can. We'll be there soon so hang off until they're almost upon her."*

"What if they hurt her or the baby?" Zane's strangled cry caused Sapphire to speed up to join him.

"Are we certain there's a baby?" Jaxon's voice was now filled with concern.

"It sure looks like that's what she's holding," Zane said quickly.

At that moment, Sapphire caught sight of him and sped through the air towards his location. *"I'm almost with you, Zane, just keep your eyes on her and I'll keep mine on those Demons. Oh, Jaxon, by the way, their numbers have increased. The original group were joined by others a little while ago."*

"How many?" Jaxon ground out.

"Five," Sapphire revealed.

She could feel Jaxon's anger through their link, his voice tight and controlled. *"Five? Dang, it looks like we're in for a bit of a firefight. I've opened the link to include everyone. Skar, Amos, Aric, there's five Demons on the hunt for this woman and it looks like she's got a baby with her. Be ready to engage as soon as we arrive. We're about ten minutes out."*

"Fucking Demons," Skar growled.

"Sounds like fun," Amos chuckled.

"Brother, we work together as usual, you distract them and I'll go in for the kill." Aric's voice sounded cold and detached.

"Fine by me," Amos replied.

Sapphire drove her Dragon down as low as possible to keep a close eye on the Demons progress. *"Just get here ASAP, guys."*

"We will," Jaxon answered quietly. *"Just make sure you and the boy are still alive when we do."*

"I'll do my best, boss." Sapphire watched as Zane lowered his own beast, his legs tucked tight against his body.

"Zane, where is she?"

Zane's voice seemed to boom in her head. *"She's trying to hide. She's in a hollow tree just below me, on the west side of that clearing. Wait, shit, yes, it's definitely a baby. I can hear it crying and if I can, then so can those Demons."*

"We're only a few minutes out. Stay calm, Zane, we'll get her."

"Hurry," Zane's strangled cry tore at Sapphire's heartstrings.

"I'm here," she told him and he glanced around toward her.

"We'll stand guard and if they get too close we'll engage and keep them at bay until the others arrive."

"I can't allow those slimy bastards to get their hands on that baby, or her," Zane spat out, his voice full of hatred.

"I understand that, but we need to hold off for as long as possible to let the guys reach us. We stand a

better chance of saving them both if we have them here to help us."

"*Sorry.*" Zane's beast turned its eyes to her. "*I just can't lose track of her again. I've worked my ass off trying to help her and she keeps slipping through my fingers.*"

"*We'll get her,*" Sapphire reiterated strongly.

They kept themselves hidden and their eyes peeled, watching the Demons below. They slowed their progress, taking more care as they drew ever closer to the hiding woman. Sapphire's superior sight meant she could see the female trying to shush the babe in her arms, but to no avail. The small bundle wailed and drew the Demons ever closer to the woman's hiding place.

"*We can't wait much longer,*" Zane mumbled.

"*Just a few more moments.*" Sapphire saw the Demons slowly reaching the other side of the clearing from where the woman was concealed. "*Hold it, hold it, Zane, wait until we have a clear shot at them. Wait, a few seconds more.*" Sapphire readied her beast for battle, drawing nature's magic inside her massive form. "*Hold it.*" Two Demons cleared the trees, unhurriedly making their way forward.

"*Sapphire,*" Zane urged, worry in every syllable.

"One, two, three." Sapphire pointed her Dragon's head down. *"Now!"*

Her beast plummeted toward the Demons, staying hidden until she was ready to blast them with her scorching flames. The fiends must have heard something or felt the air displacement, whatever it was, they looked above and at that moment she spat forth a flume of flaming fire to engulf the one nearest to her.

The Demon's screams as it burned brightly below were ear-shattering and eerie in the still forest. A moment later, Zane's Dragon let loose a huge fireball that impacted the ground in front of the remaining Demons. Sapphire veered left, hoping to catch another one by surprise, but that ship had sailed and they were now returning fire.

As the Demons regrouped, Zane and Sapphire dodged around the sky as lightning bolts flew up at them with increasing speed. A large shot of God knew what was fired by a large, ugly son-of-a-bitch toward them, and she felt herself being blown backwards. Sapphire used her colossal wings to stabilize herself as she fought to regain control.

Zane didn't fare any better, in fact, he was blown much farther than her. She saw him spin head over heels twice before he regained control.

"No!" he screamed as her eyes were drawn back down to the ground.

The Demons now closed in on the woman who still cradled the baby, her eyes flitting between the Demons and the Dragons in the air. Sapphire caught sight of Zane's red beast; it tucked its wings in and fired downwards with a speed she knew he wouldn't be able to stop.

"Zane, no, don't!" Sapphire yelled through their link, knowing he was going to sacrifice himself to aid the woman's escape.

A mere second later, Amos' electric blue beast swooped down and across Zane's path of descent. Sapphire gasped with relief when she saw their Warrior support had arrived. Zane changed his trajectory, letting out a blast of fire before soaring high once more.

"Thank goodness you lot arrived," Sapphire gasped.

Jaxon's Dragon plunged down, his beast focused on the two Demons closest to the woman. An ear-shattering roar erupted from him a moment before his fire rained down to obliterate their enemy. His triumphant bellow was music to Sapphire's ears.

"Zane, keep your eyes on the woman and child, we'll do the rest," Jaxon ordered. *"Sapphire, you watch my back, I'm going in again."*

"Sure." Sapphire flew above Jaxon to ensure he wasn't attacked while his attention was elsewhere.

She could hear the sounds of battle from Skar and the twins, and the relief that encompassed her was all-consuming. She'd believed that she'd lose not only the woman and the baby, but Zane too, and now they were easily dealing with the Demons below.

It was mere moments before there was no trace of any Demons, however, the woman still huddled in the clearing with the child in her arms. Zane flew down, landing in the scorched earth of the clearing and transformed. Sapphire noted he clothed himself in casual clothes and not his usual battle attire.

He held his hands up as he approached the woman. "We're here to help."

Jaxon landed too, transforming quickly and striding forward, almost pushing Zane out of the way in his haste to get to the woman.

Sapphire wasn't sure what was going on but she dropped down to join the men. Once she'd morphed she jogged over, hoping a woman's face might ease the other's fear. She definitely didn't expect the Master of the Guild to be acting as he was.

Jaxon hurried to see the woman and child, confused about what was happening inside him as fleeting thoughts of a dream slipped to the surface. He felt as if he'd seen this entire scene play out before—a bit of déjà vu—but that was impossible. A feeling overtaking his body the moment he'd arrived, one that screamed to him that he had to ensure their safety. Their? Or one of them? He had no idea as he strode over with a scowl on his face.

Zane was holding his hands up and trying to talk to the woman, but Jaxon just brushed him away before stopping and staring at the disheveled woman and child. Jaxon saw fear in her eyes and he tried to calm her. "We won't harm you."

Her pure white blonde hair flew out behind her as the downdrafts of beating wings hit. The cloak she'd been wearing billowing out behind her. Pale grey eyes flickering up and then focusing on Jaxon. "Really? How do I know that?"

Zane stepped beside Jaxon. "I've been trying to find you for days. Surely you must know I wasn't trying to hurt you."

She looked scathingly at Zane. "What? Am I supposed to just stand around and wait for a Dragon to eat us or burn us to death? I only ever saw a Dragon. How was I supposed to know you were also a man?"

"What?" Zane asked confused.

"You're a *Dragon*! I didn't even know they were real so when I see a huge beast that's shooting flames at the ground, guess what, buddy, I'm making a run for it."

Jaxon smirked at her sassiness and Zane's open-mouthed shock. Sapphire joined them and tried to talk to the woman. "I'm Sapphire, and this lummox here is Zane. This," she pointed to Jaxon, "is our leader, Jaxon, Master of the Guild of Dragon Warriors, and we help people that are in need. I'm sorry if Zane scared you but he was only trying to protect you from the Demons hunting you."

The woman only glared at Sapphire before turning her emerald green eyes back to Jaxon. "At least that's something. I thought I had Demons *and* Dragons on my tail."

Jaxon stepped forward, cocking his head to the side as he tried to figure out what the woman was and at the same time understand what was going on inside him. Strange emotions ran through him causing him to be abrupt as he spoke. "I assure you we won't let any Demons get their hands on you, but, tell me, what are you?"

Her eyes skittered away as she refused to answer. "None of your business, Dragon."

"It doesn't make any difference to our purpose." Jaxon spoke with authority, his eyes glued to hers, unable to force his away. "We'll take you and the child to safety."

"Where?" she asked, her eyes sweeping around, and above. "There's nowhere that those *things* can't find me."

"Yes," Jaxon said firmly, "there is. Our home is protected and you and the child will be safe there."

The woman looked at the bundle in her arms, then back at Jaxon. "She's cold, tired, and hungry. I ran out of milk for her and I've not been able to stop running long enough to get her more. I'm afraid I've not been doing a good job of taking care of her but I couldn't leave her to the Demons."

Sapphire stepped closer. "Aren't you feeding her yourself?"

The woman frowned for a moment before realization dawned on her face. "Oh, she's not mine. I heard her cries and came across her in the forest. Nearby was a woman's corpse; the infant's mother, presumably . . . anyhow, I picked her up and took her with me. I'm not sure it was a good idea, what with those horrible things chasing me."

"I see," Jaxon said, although he didn't really, he was impressed with her bravery. "Well, we have people at home that can look after her, and you."

The woman snuggled the child even closer as she squinted at Jaxon. "How do I know this isn't some kind of trap? I mean, you *are* Dragons, after all."

Jaxon scowled. "What's that supposed to mean?"

"Don't Dragons eat babies for breakfast? I've read tales of that and since I didn't even know you existed, how am I supposed to trust you?"

"I can assure you we will not harm you, or the child." Jaxon smirked. "I much prefer bacon and eggs for breakfast."

Amos' voice broke in through their link. *"Boss, I've tried reading her and I can't. That's never happened before."*

Jaxon knew what Amos meant, he also could not figure out what she was. Although, Amos had greater psychic abilities than any of them apart from Bliss, so Jaxon's interest was piqued even further. He tried to explain who, and what, they were. "We are members of the Guild of Dragon Warriors, and we are tasked with helping people in need. Since the beginning of the inter-species war, we've been focused on helping Witches escape those that hunted them and we've been kept busy with that. We offer sanctuary to any that are in need of it. Our camp has humans as well as Shifters and Witches, in fact there are more species than that there, but I don't think we have the time to go into everything in detail. So, first of all, do you have a name?"

"Of course I do." She raised an eyebrow. "But I'm not sure I want to give it to you."

Sapphire exhaled loudly. "For goodness sakes, we just saved your ass, lady. We're here to help."

The woman's eyes spun to Sapphire. "Excuse me if I'm not exactly in a trusting mood. I've been running for years and so far I've done okay."

"Didn't look like that from where I was," Sapphire grumbled.

"I'm tired and the little one is needing attention." The woman stared hard at Jaxon. "If you try to hurt her, or me, trust me, you'll live to regret it."

Jaxon held his hands up before him. "I promise we'll take good care of you both."

"You better," She muttered.

"I assume that means you'll come with us?" Jaxon said with a smile, feeling far happier than he should at that thought.

"I don't have many other options right now." She looked down at the child who'd fallen asleep. "She really needs food and I think she's caught a chill."

"We have people who can check her out for you." Zane joined the conversation. "She'll be well looked after."

"All right." The woman huffed. "How do we do this?"

Jaxon stepped back. "You can either ride on my back, or I can carry you both. It's up to you."

"Either of those will be too cold for the child." She bit her bottom lip and Jaxon's stomach clenched.

With what, he had no idea. This stranger was affecting him in ways he couldn't understand and that piqued his interest at the same time as annoying the hell out of him.

Zane held up a hand. "I've got blankets in my camp in the mountains."

"No need." Jaxon looked around, spying the mission packs they'd brought, and dropped when they joined the fight. "We've got some here. Sapphire, Zane, can you grab a couple so we can wrap them up?"

Jaxon waited until they'd gone to do his bidding before edging closer to the woman. Her eyes locked with his as he stopped in front of her. "What's your name?"

She looked up into his face, confusion and fear on hers. "I'm Sidra Aurora."

"And will you tell me *what* you are?" Jaxon pressed.

"No, not at this time." She reached with a hand to touch his face.

When her skin touched his, a calmness he'd never before felt overtook him. Her eyes bored into his and he felt her mind glance against his. Jaxon jerked, breaking contact, not entirely sure why his heart rate picked up speed, and glared down at her. "What was that?"

"Nothing." She shrugged. "Just trying to see if you are who you say you are. I won't entrust you with this little one until I know for sure you won't harm her."

Jaxon was about to question her further when Zane and Sapphire rejoined them, both holding warm blankets. Sapphire's eyes darted from Jaxon to the woman and back as she said, "Here's something to keep you and the baby warm."

Sidra took the offered blankets and wrapped one around her body like a sling. She struggled to tie it around her while still holding the child.

Sapphire held her arms out. "I'll hold her while you sort that out."

Sidra paused, obviously reluctant to hand the baby over. Sapphire sighed. "I won't hurt her."

"Okay." Sidra passed the child to Sapphire and then deftly folded the blanket into a baby sling. Once she'd got it done to her satisfaction, she held out her arms and Sapphire gave her the child back. Sidra placed the sleeping babe in the sling and tucked the warm blanket around it before taking the second one from Zane and wrapping it around herself.

"All set?" Jaxon asked, still confused at how his body was reacting to this stranger.

"I suppose," Sidra said reluctantly.

Sapphire retreated first, morphing quickly and taking flight, followed by the twins and Skar. Zane then moved the fallen mission packs out into the open, and stepped back. One by one, the Dragons swooped down to retrieve a pack before soaring back into the sky. Zane turned to Jaxon. "Should I go get mine? It's in a cave over there, in the mountains."

"Leave it," Jaxon ordered curtly. "And don't think you won't be reprimanded for doing your own thing on this mission, again."

Zane nodded, looking chagrined, then transformed, his massive beast pausing before he joined his fellow Warriors in the sky. Jaxon glanced at Sidra. "I'll transform and I'll get as low to the ground as possible. If you grab onto my leg, I'll hoist you as high as I can. I'm afraid after that you'll have to pull yourself up onto my back. If you sit as close to my front shoulders as possible, there are some small indentations there that you can use to settle yourself into. It won't be the most comfortable journey, but it's the best we can do this far from home."

"Okay." Sidra looked uneasy as she nodded. "You won't let us fall?"

"No, I will fly low to the ground as it's too cold higher up." Jaxon gave her a reassuring smile. "I promise to try not to jostle you too much and you can lean forward and lie between my shoulder blades. As I said, there are indentations there that make it pretty safe for a rider."

"So you usually have people riding on your back?"

"Not usually." Jaxon shook his head. "But there are occasions where it's unavoidable. Like today."

"All right." Sidra tucked the blanket tighter around her. "I guess we should get going. I'm worried about the baby."

"Okay." Jaxon strode to the middle of the clearing, transformed, and watched Sidra closely as she slowly walked toward him. He could sense her apprehension as she grew nearer, his size and appearance causing her to breathe faster.

He held out his front leg, offering it to her, and she slowly climbed on, hanging on for dear life as he lifted her as high as possible. After that, she hauled herself the last few feet up onto his scaly back. Sidra shuffled around until she found the depressions in his huge back, settling herself there and holding onto him for dear life.

He wished he could tell her that she was safe, that he wouldn't let anything happen to her, but he couldn't. Dragons were magical beings, but even they couldn't talk while in their beast form. He gently rose into the air, his ascent far slower than normal, as he joined the others waiting for them.

"*All right, let's get going.*" He mind-linked to the rest. "*I want to get home before dark.*"

With that, they swooped back toward their haven, Skar and the twins taking up positions to guard Jaxon. "*Sapphire, you go ahead and have Bliss and Em ready to check these two over. We'll need milk for the baby and clean clothes. Heck, we'll need everything that a baby needs, including a warm bath. She's rather pungent at the moment.*"

Sapphire's Dragon picked up speed, breaking away from them. *"Will do, and I'll make sure there's a hot meal ready and waiting for you boys."*

"Thanks," Jaxon replied as he focused on staying on an even keel so as not to upset his precious cargo.

The journey was long, and mostly silent, with Amos cracking a joke or two during the hours of flight. Around the halfway mark, Jaxon felt Sidra change her position, lying down against his scales. Soon afterwards he heard her breathing change and he felt certain she'd fallen asleep.

He flew even more carefully, not wanting to wake her, and tried again and again to figure out exactly what she was and why he was reacting to her. She was not a Witch, although he sensed magic inside her. She was not a Fairy, although he sensed an affinity with nature inside her. She definitely was not a Shifter, well, not any he'd come in contact with, and he was pretty sure he'd met them all.

Not a Goblin either, nor any other Supernatural species. What the hell was she?

Hopefully, once they were safely back at base, he'd get it out of her. If not then he'd ask Bliss to see if she could decipher exactly what Sidra was.

He'd felt "strange" from the moment she'd made contact with his face. Something inside him felt "off" and he wasn't sure what was going on with that either. He tried to focus on what was happening inside him, and failed. All he knew was that something happened when her skin touched his, and he wasn't entirely happy with any of it. He was Master of the Guild and always knew what was going on, especially inside himself. Not having a clue about this strange woman was beginning to annoy the hell out of him and his mood worsened as they drew nearer to his home, his sanctuary.

A fleeting memory of a dream flickered in his brain of a woman running through the forest. However, when he tried to grasp more details he failed. Was it Sidra in the dream? If so, why and how did he see her before they'd ever met?

Sidra was an intriguing puzzle, and one he planned on solving. As soon as possible.

CHAPTER SEVEN

Jaxon felt relief course through him as they drew nearer the mountain range that guarded their village, his home, his sanctuary. He always felt the same when he returned, no matter if it were only an hour or days. Today, however, he felt even more relief as they returned home, knowing that Sidra and the child would be safe here. That fact eased the tension that had been running through him since he'd first caught sight of her.

He'd picked this spot himself, many years ago, when he'd been awarded the honor of becoming Master of the Guild. He and his Dragons needed a home, one that was easily defended, and the valley had been perfect. The first few cabins being built by him and his Warriors alone. Now there were dozens of homes scattered around the area and there were hundreds of people living there. Most of whom the Guild had rescued and brought here for their own safety.

There was a mix of beings, from Witches to Shifters, but all had one thing in common: they'd needed the Guild's help.

Jaxon let out a rumble of greeting to any guards keeping watch for danger. Katarina's great beast swooping up from a hidden spot amongst a mound of rocks. *"I'm glad you got back in one piece."* She hovered in front of Jaxon, waiting for them to reach her.

"I am too," Jaxon replied. *"I'm looking forward to some hot food and a long, hot shower."*

"Food's waiting on you as is Em with a room full of baby stuff." Katarina chuckled. *"She said she's keeping the baby for a day or two to make sure it's all right. Then she'll vet some couples before handing it over."*

"That's just what I expected." Jaxon caught sight of Brydon's Dragon in the distance. *"What's Brydon up to?"*

"He's making sure everything's all right," Katarina said. *"Bliss has been feeling weirder than normal and is a bit jumpy. Brydon took it upon himself to try and ease her concern, so he's been flying extra guard duties and going out farther to ensure nothing is heading our way."*

"I see." Jaxon spun his head around, trying to locate anything "off" in the area. *"We both know Bliss can get over excited but her warnings are usually spot on. I think we should double the guards too, just in case."*

Katarina's beast snorted, a puff of smoke escaping as she shook her head. *"Oh ye of little faith,"* she said sadly. *"Already done."*

"Thank you." Jaxon bowed his head toward Katarina as they dived down into the valley. *"I'm sorry, Kat, I'm tired and more than a little unsettled with our new arrivals."*

"How so?"

"I have no idea what the woman is," Jaxon admitted. *"I can't read her and all I know for sure is that she is not human."*

"Really?" Kat asked, surprised. *"Now that intrigues me a hell of a lot."*

"Me too," Jaxon said and touched down gently as the rest of the team landed around him. Katarina stayed airborne and bid them goodbye.

"I'm staying on duty for another couple of hours. I'll see you later." With that her Dragon pointed itself upwards and sped off into the night.

Jaxon stood still as Sidra and the child still slept on his back. Sapphire jogged over to join them in the field. "Welcome home, guys, there's food in the mess hall and Em is waiting there to take care of the baby."

Jaxon gave his body a shake, not enough to unseat Sidra, but to wake her. He felt her shuffle about, yawn, then gasp aloud. "Where are we?"

Sapphire stepped closer as Jaxon lowered his beast down onto the ground. Sapphire stepped up onto his foreleg, reaching out to help Sidra. "This is our home and a sanctuary for all that need it. Here, hand me the child and we can get the two of you some food and warm you both up."

Sidra stayed where she was and he could feel her nervousness as she answered. "I think I'll keep hold of her for now."

Sapphire shrugged. "Sure, if that's what you want."

Jaxon waited as Sapphire helped the woman from his back then transformed, clothing himself in casual jeans and tee instead of his usual battle leathers. Sidra was obviously spooked, and he didn't want to unsettle her any further than necessary. She scrutinized him closely before turning to follow Sapphire back to the camp.

The intense look in her eyes caused Jaxon's stomach to clench and he took a moment before trailing behind. This woman was throwing him off balance and he wasn't sure why. All he knew was that it had him in a thunderously bad mood. Stomping along, he saw her glancing behind, whether to make sure he was following, or possibly because she feared him. Whatever the reason, every time her eyes flitted toward him, the strange feelings inside him grew which caused his bad mood to worsen.

"Sapphire, is Bliss in the hall? I want to speak with her," he growled out as Sidra once more looked behind her.

"Yes." Sapphire slowed, raising an eyebrow at his tone. "She's waiting for you. She's got her panties in a twist about something, but then, when doesn't she?"

"Her *feelings* have proved accurate in the past." He frowned at Sapphire. "Only a fool would disregard her warnings."

Sapphire stopped, facing him fully and glaring back at him. "I'm not a fool. I just don't understand half of what she says."

"Hence the need to talk." Jaxon passed her and Sidra, continuing to stride purposefully toward their main dining hall.

"Grumpy much?" Sapphire spat out to his back, which caused him to spin around, eyes locking with hers.

"Don't think I've forgotten your shenanigans, Sapphire. You're grounded unless you ask permission to fly or I give you a direct command. Understand?"

"What?" Sapphire gasped.

"I said, you're grounded." Jaxon sneered "That little trick of slipping me some of Bliss' knockout brew has earned you a punishment. Suck it up, Sapphy."

"Damn it." Sapphire shook her head. "I hate being grounded."

"Exactly," Jaxon snarled as he strode away.

"What's wrong with him?" she asked quietly.

"No idea," Amos quipped. "He's been quiet all the way home and he didn't laugh at any of my jokes. Not a one."

"I don't blame him for that." Sapphire chuckled. "Your jokes are lame, Amos, everyone knows that."

"They are not," Amos replied, shocked.

"Hmm, yup, they are," Sapphire said.

Jaxon picked up speed, leaving them behind as he headed towards the hall, pushed the door open, and walked into the welcome warmth. Em was sitting at a table, Bliss opposite, but when he entered, the old woman jumped up with a speed and agility that belied her age.

"Jaxon, I'm glad you're home." Em looked behind him expectantly. "Where's the child?"

"They're coming." Jaxon ignored Em, making a beeline for Bliss. "I need a few words with Bliss before they arrive."

Bliss cocked her head to the side, returning the cup she'd been sipping from onto the table. "Yes, Master? What can I help you with?"

"Firstly, the woman that we rescued," Jaxon turned to make sure they hadn't arrived yet, "I need you to try and read her. I can't figure out what she is, only that she's not human, and I don't like having a being here when I have no clue what they are. Or what they're capable of."

"Certainly," Bliss agreed. "I'll do my best but I usually have to touch someone to get anything worthwhile."

"Just do your best and if you get the chance try and shake hands with her." Jaxon heard the stampede of boots a moment before the twins ran inside, noisily shouting. Well, Amos shouted as Aric looked around hungrily.

"Food, food. The returning heroes need food." Amos laughed as he picked Em up and spun her around, kissing her cheek before replacing her onto the floor.

"Let me go, you young ruffian," Em scolded, hitting Amos' chest. "There's plenty of food on the table there."

"Yummy!" Amos sped over to the laden table, grabbing a plate and heaping food onto it. "My favorites, Em, you are a culinary queen, thank you."

"Pfft—" Em waved an arm at him. "You say that all the time, Amos. I could feed you gruel and you'd still say that."

"That's because you can make anything taste delicious, mighty queen." Amos bowed low before sitting at a nearby table and tucking in.

"Silly boy," Em said, although her eyes twinkled wickedly.

The rest of the team joined them, the men heading straight for the food, and then Sapphire and Sidra walked in. Em went straight over, holding her arms out. "I'll take the little one. I have milk warmed and ready and then I'll give her a nice warm bath and get her into some nice clean clothes."

Sidra looked down at Em, indecision on her face. Em huffed, her eyes locked on Sidra's. "I promise the child will be safe with me. I won't let any harm come to her. Now, woman, hand her over and get yourself some food. Oh, by the way, I'm Em, nice to meet you."

Jaxon watched as Sidra seemed to make a decision, nodding as she untangled the babe from the confines of the makeshift sling. She kissed the child's head before handing her over. "I'm afraid I don't know her name. I've been calling her Lucky because if I hadn't heard her cries then she would've died next to her mother in the forest. I know it's not exactly a girly name but it's what I've been using."

Em took the swaddled bundle from Sidra, looking down at the awakening child. "I think Lucky is a fine name and we'll use that for now."

"Okay." Sidra's hand swept across the baby's face before finally relinquishing her to Em's care.

"I'll take good care of her," Em emphasized before nodding toward the table behind them. "There's plenty of food there, and after you've eaten, we'll see about getting you cleaned up and a place to sleep."

Sidra nodded, her eyes staying fixed on Em and the child as the old woman walked away toward the kitchen. Sapphire took Sidra's elbow, leading her to the food, her voice friendly as she motioned to the plethora of items available.

"I'm sure there's something you'll like here. Grab a plate and come join us."

Sapphire picked up a delectable pastry, then left Sidra to join Bliss at the table. Jaxon watched closely as Sidra placed several items onto a plate then poured herself a glass of juice. His heart speed up as she shook her head, her long blonde hair flowing across her back. He felt a tug in his pants, scowling as his obvious attraction for the mysterious woman reared itself. Jaxon forced his arousal away, gritting his teeth in anger at his body's reaction. Sidra's eyes briefly met his as she looked around as if trying to decide where to sit, Sapphire's arm waving her over.

"Come and sit down." Sapphire gave the woman a warm smile.

Sidra joined, albeit reluctantly, and sat opposite Bliss who cocked her head to the side, her emerald eyes scrutinizing Sidra. Bliss waited until Sidra was comfortable then held her hand out over the table. "Hello and welcome to our home. My name's Bliss."

Sidra looked at the hand and hesitated before shaking it quickly and tugging her hand free of Bliss' hold. Jaxon saw Sidra frown, her head spinning to spear him with an accusatory glare. "Well played, *Master*," Sidra spat out as Bliss' face whitened in shock.

"Bliss, what's wrong?" Sapphire asked as Bliss started to shake her head.

"Nothing, I'm all right," Bliss whispered, her eyes seeking Jaxon's.

"Bliss, are you sure? You look a little peaky," Jaxon prodded, wondering what had caused her pallor to change. Was this woman, Sidra, some kind of threat? A threat that he'd brought into their camp?

"I'm confused." Bliss turned back to Sidra. "You can't be."

Sidra shrugged. "I've no idea what you're talking about."

Jaxon looked between the two women, addressing first Bliss then the stranger in their midst. "Bliss, is the camp in danger?" His eyes locked with Sidra's. "What are you?"

Sidra remained silent as Bliss exhaled. "I don't think we're in danger from her. But, I think others will come looking for her. That's if anyone knows of her existence. She's unique, Jaxon, and I am sure there will be ones who would wish to capture her for that."

"Is that so?" Jaxon kept his eyes on Sidra, his tone cold as ice even as his heart stuttered in his chest at the thought of her being in danger once more. "I'll ask again, what are you?"

"I'm sure your little spy here can tell you." She nodded toward Bliss who blushed in embarrassment.

"I'm not a spy. I just have certain gifts that we need to use from time to time."

"You're two faced, that's what you are," Sidra ground out, her hands flat on the table, as if she were trying to hold herself back from doing something stupid.

Bliss shrank back as Sapphire leaned forward, her eyes blazing. "Don't you dare talk to her like that. Who the hell do you think you are? Coming in here when we've saved your ass and calling people names."

Sapphire wrapped an arm around Bliss' shoulder, tugging her into her side. "It's okay, honey, just ignore that bi—"

Jaxon cut her off, well aware of Sapphire's fiery temper. "Enough, Sapphy."

Sapphire grunted as Skar sat down on Bliss' other side. His hand grasped Bliss' shaking ones and whispered down to her, "It's all right, sweet-cheeks, I think our *guest* is a little upset at the moment. She doesn't seem to trust any of us, yet."

Sidra shook her head. "I'm sorry. I'm tired, grumpy, and I don't know any of you so pardon me if I offended you. But you did use the ruse of shaking my hand to try and find out what I am."

"I didn't try," Bliss mumbled. "I know what you are."

"No, you don't," Sidra said forcefully through clenched teeth.

"Yes." Bliss nodded, her eyes searching for Jaxon's. "She's a hybrid, one I never thought still existed."

Sidra slapped a hand on the table. "Don't, don't you dare say it."

Jaxon reached over, snatching Sidra's hand and holding it firmly against the wood of the table. He tried to ignore the tingling sensation that ran up his arm from the contact. "Don't you threaten one of my Dragons."

Bliss looked distraught as Sidra glowered at her. "I'm sorry, but you may not be safe here, and if you're not safe then that means none of the others are safe. I have to tell him."

Jaxon snarled, releasing Sidra's hand as if it had burnt his skin. "Tell me, Bliss. What the fuck is she?"

Bliss gasped at Jaxon's curse, her hand flying to cover her mouth. Jaxon sighed. "I'm sorry. I didn't mean to swear at you, but please tell me what the heck is going on."

"She's . . . she's . . ." Bliss' eyes flickered between Sidra and Jaxon. She jumped when Sidra pushed her plate of food away violently.

"For goodness sake." Sidra leaned forward, banging her head on the table a couple of times before sitting back up. "I'll tell you or we're going to be here all night."

Bliss relaxed immediately and every pair of eyes in the room locked on the stranger. Jaxon nodded. "Go on."

"My mother was Fae." Sidra shrugged. "Nothing special about her apart from the fact she was expelled from her tribe for her friendship with someone the elders thought was 'out of bounds.' She left, or rather, was thrown out with a bag of possessions and nothing else. She'd refused to stop seeing this person and she ended up living in a small cabin he built her in the forest, away from prying eyes. They grew closer and if what she told me was true, she was head over heels in love with him, and he her."

Sidra stopped, a painful expression crossing her face. Jaxon reached out to comfort her, jerking his hand back when he realized what he'd been about to do. "And?" he said gruffly to cover up his action.

"She fell pregnant, nearly died having me, and kept me hidden from everyone and everything, for most of my life." She stopped again as her eyes filled with unshed tears. Jaxon saw her swallow before continuing. "However, I am apparently like a bright flame that attracts dirty moths to it, and we had some close calls until my father was eventually killed and my mother not long after. I've been on the run ever since. Oh," She tapped her chin as if deep in thought, "I think that's about the past five years or so."

Jaxon felt her pain but frowned at her obvious omission. "You still haven't told us what you are? Who, and more importantly, what was your father?"

Sidra stared into Jaxon's eyes defiantly. "My father was an Angel."

Jaxon recoiled as if she'd hit him. "Impossible. Don't you mean a Fallen Angel?"

"No." Sidra shook her head. "I meant what I said. He was an Angel, although he'd started to lose some of his powers because he was spending so much time here with my mother and me. That's how those damnable Demons managed to kill him. If he'd been at full strength, they wouldn't have stood a chance."

Jaxon heard the intakes of breath all around him, Amos' shocked tone whispering, "Shit, doesn't that make her a you-know-what? Aren't they a myth? I'm sure they're a myth. She must be lying."

Aric shushed his twin. "Be quiet. I want to hear what she has to say."

Bliss pulled away from Sapphire, her eyes wide and excited. "So, you are a you-know-what?"

"Yeah." Sidra gave a half smile. "I guess I am."

Jaxon couldn't believe his ears, his insides churning with excitement, and trepidation. "If this is true then you're probably the first for many centuries. I can only vaguely remember a time when there was any here on earth, and I've lived a very long time. No wonder those Demons were hunting you. It was you they were after, not the child."

"Duh." Sidra pulled her plate of food back toward her, picking up a piece of fried chicken and sniffing it. "Those damn things have been on my tail on and off for years. Every time I think I've finally lost them and settle down, up they pop, and I'm off and running again. I'm usually good at escaping, but once I found the baby, I was pretty damned screwed."

Skar cocked his head to the side. "You could've left the child to escape."

Sidra glared at him, her eyes flashing with anger. "Don't be such an idiot. Nobody would leave a baby in the path of Demons."

"Just checking." Skar smirked.

"Well check this." Sidra blew a kiss toward Skar and the next moment he flew backward, head over ass, to land on the floor in a heap.

CHAPTER EIGHT

Bliss let out a strangled cry as Jaxon grabbed Sidra's hands, holding them tightly in his. "Stop that!"

Sapphire pulled Bliss to her side, shushing her and pointedly asking. "It's okay, sweetie, she won't do that again. Will you?"

Sidra shook her head as Amos chuckled, walking over to hold a hand out to Skar. "Need a hand, big guy?"

Skar knocked Amos' hand out of the way. "I'm fine, I think." Skar rose and shook his head at Sidra. "That's some punch you've got, even if you didn't actually touch me. How the hell did you do that?"

Sidra shrugged nonchalantly. "Just a little magic power courtesy of my father."

"I'm impressed." Skar righted his chair and sat back down.

Sapphire leaned forward. "So are you saying you're one of those extinct creatures? Is that what you're telling us?"

Amos joined them at the table, sitting on the corner and frowning. "I've heard you say stuff about a 'you-know-what' and now you're mentioning something that's extinct. I know I'm a lot younger than you guys, but just what the hell is she? Come on, enlighten me."

Sidra picked up some more food, popping it in her mouth as she raised an eyebrow toward Jaxon. He sat back, crossing his arms, and finally said aloud what had been running through their minds. "It's extremely rare for an Angel, not a Fallen Angel, but a fully-fledged Angel to have offspring with *any* species. I'm by no means an expert but from what I've learned over the centuries any couplings with humans led to the women dying in pregnancy. Any other species didn't fare much better although there have been instances of live births. Those special children were, and I can't believe I'm saying this out loud, but they were Shifters, with magical powers, and well, they . . ."

Jaxon shook his head and Amos urged him on. "Out with it, boss, what kind of Shifters were they?"

Jaxon turned to look at Sidra as he answered. "Unicorns."

Sidra held up her hand. "Ah, but not the normal, run of the mill Unicorns that you read about in folklore. We actually have wings and can fly too, sort of like Pegasus."

Amos snorted, his face a mask of disbelief. "Yeah, right, pull the other leg why don't you. I know I'm young, which you lot are always reminding me of, but I'm not an idiot. Unicorns aren't real, they're only in fairytales."

Skar grinned up at the younger man's face. "They are real, I saw one when I was a boy, and a most magnificent sight it was to behold. I hold that memory dear because they were rare, even then."

Jaxon nodded. "I too have seen one, in fact I met the creature, back when I was a lad living in the Highlands of Scotland. Scotland has many heraldic symbols with a Unicorn on it and although rare, there were a few that lived there in my youth. This is no tale, Amos, I assure you of that. If Sidra is indeed the progeny of an Angel, then she is, in fact, a Unicorn Shifter."

Bliss mumbled as Amos' jaw dropped open, "They'll come for her."

"Yes." Sidra sighed. "I'm afraid that Bliss is right. I've never been able to stay long in one place before they found me. Someone is investing a heck of a lot into capturing me."

"This is a well-protected area, we'll keep you safe." Sapphire breathed out, her eyes twinkling with excitement. "When can we meet your 'other half' so to speak?"

"Maybe tomorrow." Sidra gave Sapphire a small smile. "I'm kinda tired right now and could use a good night's sleep."

Amos finally managed to close his jaw before tapping his chin. "Now that Basilius is defeated, won't you be safer?"

"I'm not sure." Sidra looked shocked. "I didn't know he had been *defeated*. What does that mean exactly?"

Jaxon filled her in. "He's dead. Killed by an Angel in a battle we were in against him and his Demons. We were only a small part of the fight, and two of my Dragons are still with our Goddess as she tries to heal them."

"I see." Sidra looked thoughtful for a moment, popping a piece of chicken into her mouth and sighing. "I'm not entirely sure who is behind sending the Demons after me. I'd thought it was this King of Hell, Basilius, but if he's dead you'd think they would have stopped. Hmm, I wonder who it is that's so desperate to get their hands on me."

"Whoever it is, we'll deal with them," Jaxon said firmly as the thought of her being in danger caused his heart to hammer in his chest.

"I don't want anyone here to be at risk because of me." Sidra looked around at all of them. "I see you're strong warriors, but I think I'll have to move on soon."

"No." Jaxon shook his head. "We'll find out who's behind it and take them out. That should solve the problem."

"Jaxon," Sapphire said, leaning forward, "I'm not sure that's a good idea. We've got a lot of people here to look after."

Jaxon glared over at her. "Most of which will soon be able to rejoin society. Basilius was behind the hunting of Witches. With him gone, things should settle down, and if Cassius Allarde holds true to his word, he's offering sanctuary to any Witches that want it."

Skar sneered, his perfect white teeth shining against his dark skin. "That's going to take time, boss, we can't just throw everyone out of their homes here. We don't even know if anybody *wants* to leave. They might want to stay here, and if they do, then we have to protect them. It is our way."

"I'm pretty darn sure that when they know it's safe outside these confines, they'll want to go in search of their loved ones." Jaxon sighed. "But of course we will look after any that wish to stay. I'm just saying that things are about to change for everyone. Us included."

"I'll stay for the time being but if there's any threat to the people here then I'll leave." Sidra smirked. "I can get away easily enough now that I don't have a baby to worry about."

Jaxon gritted his teeth, forcing himself to calm down before he stood. The thought of her leaving sent shocks of panic rushing through him. "We'll find somewhere for you to stay for now."

Sidra leaned her head back so she could look him dead in the eye. "I'm staying with you."

"What?" Jaxon shook his head. "No, not possible."

"Why would you want to stay with Mr. Grumpy Pants?" Sapphire grinned. "I have a spare room you can use."

"No." Sidra cocked her head to the side. "I have a feeling that I have to stay close to this one. I tend to listen to my *feelings* so although I expect it to be a tad unpleasant, I'm staying with him."

"This is ridiculous." Jaxon stomped toward the door. "My home isn't set up to cater to a woman."

"Do you have hot water? A bed or sofa I can sleep on? If yes to those two things, then everything's fine with me. I've spent the last few months in the damn forest and anything with a roof over my head is a luxury. So, Jaxon, Master of the Guild of Dragon Warriors, I'll be staying at your place until it's time for me to move on. Or until I figure out what it is about you that's sent my sixth sense into overload."

Jaxon saw her chin jutting out defiantly, her eyes locked on his with steely determination. His heart stuttered in his chest as he gave in. "All right, but don't expect me to entertain you. A roof over your head and a bed to sleep in, that's all you'll get from me."

"That's all I was expecting," Sidra replied calmly.

Sapphire rose, her face a mask of astonishment. "Well, I guess I should go get you some clean clothes and toiletries. He'll not have anything fit for you to use."

"Thanks." Sidra lowered her head, focusing on the food on her plate. "I'll finish this and check on the baby, then if someone can point me toward his place that would be great."

"I'll wait for you and take you over," Bliss whispered.

Sidra nodded once before starting to eat just as Em appeared back with the baby in her arms. The child was sound asleep, bathed, and dressed in pink clothes. "She looks content," Sidra commented as Em stopped next to her.

"She is." Em held the child protectively against her breast. "She's nice and clean, had several bottles of formula, and promptly fell asleep. I've got a crib set up in my room and I'll keep her for a day or two until we decide what to do with her."

Sidra eyed Em closely. "But she'll be well taken care of?"

"Of course." Em scowled at Sidra. "There are some childless couples here who would be ecstatic to adopt her. I will vet them and then I'll meet with Jaxon to decide who gets this little bundle of joy."

"Really?" Sidra asked.

"Yes, really. Even if there were no couples without children that wanted to adopt, we have our fair share of families who would be willing to help. She'll be loved and cherished, don't think she won't."

"I'm glad." Sidra reached up, her finger tracing the sleeping child's face. "She's had a tough start and I don't even know her mother's name or anything about her to pass on when she's older. All I know is that I think she was a Witch and I can sense magic inside this little one too."

"We'll make sure she's given the best we have to offer," the old woman emphasized.

"Would it be all right if I checked in to see how she's doing tomorrow?"

Em nodded. "Of course. I'm usually here so drop by anytime. I'll bet I have a lot of new helpers tomorrow when they see this beautiful babe. But for now, I'm heading home to get her settled in her crib. You lot," Em made eye contact with everyone present, "make sure to clean up after yourselves. If I arrive in the morning to a mess, I'll make sure you are dealt with."

"We will." Sapphire chuckled. "I'll make the twins wash up when everyone's done."

"What? No, no, wait a minute, we did it the last time," Amos grumbled.

"We'll do it," Aric replied curtly.

"Bro, why do you always give in so easily?" Amos scowled at his twin.

"It's a few dishes, Amos, no need to get worked up." Aric shook his head at his brother.

"Exactly." Sapphire grinned at Amos who flung his arms up in the air dramatically.

"Fine! We'll do the dishes, again."

"That's a good boy." Em laughed as she walked to the door where Jaxon still stood then stopped and turned back, addressing Sidra. "And I'd like to see your beast tomorrow too. I caught a glimpse of one when I was a child and the memory is still fresh in my head as if it were yesterday. Yes, lass, I want to see your Unicorn tomorrow, you'll make a very old woman happy to reveal such a sight."

Sidra gave Em a smile. "I'll let you know when I'm going to transform. It'll be in the morning once I've rested."

"Have a hearty breakfast to give you plenty of energy." Em chuckled as she left.

"I plan on it," Sidra said to her back.

"So, Sidra, that's a unique name. I've never heard it before." Sapphire raised an eyebrow in query.

"It means Star Child," Bliss said quietly.

"Does it?" Sapphire turned to Bliss.

"Yes," Sidra responded. "I guess my parents had a bit of a laugh about that."

"Well, I guess if your dad's a freaking Angel then you'd need a special name," Amos snickered.

"I think they thought it suited me, especially as Dad took Mom to one of the Angel realms to give birth. He said it was the safest place for her and as she survived, I presume he was right."

Bliss let out a gasp. "He took your mother to an Angel realm. Is that even allowed?"

"Probably not." Sidra shrugged. "But he wasn't one for following all of the rules, hence my conception in the first place."

"Awesome!" Amos grinned.

Skar shook his head. "I can't quite get my head around all of this but I'm anxious to see your Unicorn tomorrow. I'll be up bright and early but please don't do anything until I arrive."

"Training again?" Sapphire asked.

"Of course." Skar smirked as he rose, handing his empty plate to Amos. "Here you go, lad, remember and leave things nice and tidy or Em will have your guts for garters."

"I know." Amos' shoulders drooped. "I hate washing up."

"I'll wash, you dry," Aric said as he disappeared into the kitchen.

"Duty calls." Amos picked up the remaining dishes and followed his brother. "See you tomorrow for the great unveiling."

"So, Sidra, what do you need for staying with our lord and master?" Sapphire sneaked a cheeky grin over at Jaxon.

"I'm afraid I have nothing," Sidra spoke quietly. "I did have a pack but I lost that when I found the baby. We had a close call with the Demons who'd killed her mother so I just grabbed her and ran. Basically I don't have a thing to my name."

"No worries." Sapphire stood up. "I'll go to the stores now and get you some stuff and drop it off in a little while."

"Thank you." Sidra waited until Sapphire had pushed past Jaxon then turned to Bliss. "I'm sorry I called you two faced earlier. It was uncalled for."

"Thank you." Bliss smiled. "I understand that you may have felt uncomfortable with what I did."

"Yes." Sidra turned to eyeball Jaxon. "But if *he'd* told you to do it, then it's not your fault."

"Even if he hadn't asked me I would still have been able to read you when we shook hands."

"That's all by the by now. Hopefully your *Master* won't order you to read me again."

Jaxon huffed out in annoyance before leaving, slamming the door behind him for good measure. *"What the hell is she thinking wanting to stay with me?"* he thought as he quickly made his way home. He suddenly remembered the living room looked untidier than a run-down hovel and he wasn't about to give *her* the satisfaction of commenting on it.

In fact, if he was being honest, he wanted to impress her. Weird. He'd never felt the need to impress anyone in his life before. Well, apart from their Goddess, Zeeandra.

CHAPTER NINE

Sidra's eyes stayed on the door long after Jaxon slammed it. Her mind going into overdrive at the feelings coursing through her. Confused and annoyed in equal measures, she jumped when Bliss reached over and tapped her arm.

"Are you all right?" Bliss asked concern in every syllable.

Sidra shook her head. "Truth is I have no idea. I don't know what's going on but I have a feeling that man is going to be important to me. In what way, I have no clue, but I'm not happy about it at all. He's cranky, sullen, and ill-tempered and yet, something inside me is urging me to stay close to him."

Bliss smiled. "He's not so bad. He's got a lot of responsibility on his shoulders, keeping everyone here safe. Jaxon is kind and considerate, not just tough and hard. I think maybe he is feeling something too and it's knocked him off-kilter."

"Possibly," Sidra relented. "Then again, maybe he is just a grouchy git."

"Git?" Bliss frowned.

"Yeah, my mom used to use it a lot and I guess it stuck. Not entirely sure of the proper meaning but it seems to fit the high and mighty Jaxon."

"He's not like that at all." Bliss laughed. "He just takes his duty seriously and trying to keep this lot in line can be a hard job, trust me on that. The twins alone are enough to give anyone a headache."

Sidra snickered. "Yeah, they do seem a handful, especially the talkative one."

"Aww, Amos is just high-spirited, his job is important to him and he works very hard." Bliss sighed. "He and Aric work in tandem and it's amazing to see them fly together."

Sidra smirked as she whispered, "You like him, don't you? But which one? Amos or Aric? I'm not entirely sure."

Bliss blushed scarlet, her eyes dropping to the table. "No, shush, they might hear you."

"Sorry." Sidra cocked her head to the side, sizing up the shy woman opposite. "Do you go on missions?"

"Hmm, no, not really." Bliss blushed even redder, if that were possible. "Well, not on any where there's a chance of any fighting being involved. I'm not what you'd call a typical Dragon."

"I can sense that." Sidra could feel the gentleness inside Bliss. "I suppose you've never hurt anyone, or anything, in your life. Have you?"

Bliss shook her head. "No, not intentionally anyway."

"Hey," Sidra tried to lighten the young girl's obvious distress. "That's not a bad thing, Bliss, there are far too many that take joy in hurting others."

"I know." Bliss' hand covered her heart. "It hurts me inside, but I worry when most of them are out on missions and I'm here with just a few others left to guard the camp. If we were attacked, I'd die if my weakness caused them harm."

"It's not weakness," Sidra said forcefully. "It's a gift."

"I don't think the others see it that way." Bliss sighed.

"I can't comment on them because I don't know them, or how they perceive you. But, Bliss, I think if it came down to it you'd stand up and fight for those in your care. I understand you don't believe that but I sense it."

"Really?" Bliss asked wide-eyed.

"Yes, really." Sidra lowered her voice. "I've got several gifts and one of them is reading people. Kinda like you do, but I tend to see inside their souls, and although I can feel the turmoil in you, I think you worry needlessly."

"I hope you're right," Bliss admitted. "I've never been in the position where I had to fight and it scares me just thinking about it."

"That's what shows how much you care." Sidra nodded toward the door. "I'm a little tired, and I know I must smell like the back end of a donkey, so could you take me to Jaxon's, please? I could really do with a shower."

Bliss jumped up. "Oh, I'm sorry, I've been holding you back. Come on and I'll take you."

Sidra followed Bliss out of the hall. "Hey, no need to run," she quipped as Bliss jogged along.

"I've taken up too much of your time as it is and I've got a couple of teenagers living with me at the moment. I should get back and check on them."

"Teenagers?" Sidra asked.

"Yeah, they were brought in a day or two ago," Bliss said sadly. "Their parents were killed but the twins managed to save the kids. A boy and a girl, they're still at the quiet stage, but I'm trying to help them cope and Skar is going to teach them some self-defense. I think it will help them, especially the boy. He's full of anger and pent-up rage so sparring with Skar is probably just what he needs."

"Good idea," Sidra agreed. "If I can help in any way just let me know. I'll be happy to help."

"Thank you," Bliss replied.

"I've not exactly had a lot of interaction with kids but I have a few powers that may help." Sidra looked thoughtful for a moment. "I can *calm* people with touch so that might help. I'll have a think tonight and see if any of my other little *foibles* will help. I've not had much of a chance to test everything I can do so it might be a hit and miss."

"I appreciate that." Bliss slowed her steps. "I think anything we can do for them now will help them to recover better. I'd hate for them to have nightmares for the rest of their lives."

"Nightmares? Are they having those?"

Bliss nodded. "So far, yes, the girl, her name's Lara, she barely sleeps and when she does she wakes up screaming. Lucas, her brother, he pads around for hours in his room and I know it's because he's scared to go to sleep. I have some of my concoctions that I could give them to knock them out but I don't want to do that. I'm slowly earning their trust and I wouldn't want to blow that by doping them up. At the same time, I know they need rest so it's a catch twenty-two situation."

Sidra tapped her chin. "If they don't have a good night's rest tonight then I'll see what I can do to help them. I'll be up front with them, Bliss, I'll tell them I can possibly help them rest, but I can't guarantee no bad dreams. How does that sound?"

"Wonderful." Bliss clapped her hands. "Thank you."

"My pleasure." Sidra noticed they'd come to a complete stop, asking, "How far?"

"Oh, it's right here." Bliss pointed to the cabin next to them. "I hope you know what you're doing. Jaxon can be a little gruff and don't even try talking to him in the morning before he has his coffee. That is a complete no-no."

Sidra chuckled. "I'll do my best not to annoy him, though I still can't figure out why I insisted on staying with him. Just a feeling inside, ya know?"

Bliss smiled, nodding. "Yes, I get those all the time."

"Glad it's not just me." Sidra grinned. "Oh well, I guess I should get in and showered. I'm so tired I might just fall asleep while washing."

"That's silly." Bliss shook her head. "You'd fall down."

With that, she turned and walked away leaving Sidra looking after her with disbelief. "Wow." Sidra turned, knocked on the door once and opened it to find Jaxon with an armful of towels.

"Oh, you're here. I was just putting fresh towels in your room."

She closed the door, holding her arms out. "That's okay, I'll take them."

Jaxon handed them over. "Your room is down the hall first door you come to, and it has a small bathroom with a shower. There's a larger bathroom next to it with a tub and a shower, then my room is next to that."

"Thanks." Sidra glanced around, taking in the lounge and kitchen area, surprised to see it tidy.

"Do you want anything? A coffee or a drink?" Jaxon asked, seemingly reluctant.

His tone set her hackles rising, and she snapped back at him before storming away. "No need to go out of your way for me. I'm fine."

She was sure she heard him curse as she slammed her room door. Sidra leaned her back against the wood, knocking her head a couple of times. "What the hell am I doing here?" she muttered to herself before peeling her body from the door, fiddling to find the light switch.

Her eyes barely registered anything in the room, her focus was on getting into the bathroom and having her first hot shower in weeks. Using her foot to kick the door open and her elbow to switch the light on, she was pleasantly surprised to find a nice, clean, if rather bare, room. All white with a toilet, sink and a larger shower than she'd expected.

"Yes." She sighed as she placed the towels down on top of a laundry basket, quickly turning on the shower. Steam soon started to fill the room causing her to almost moan in anticipation of finally getting herself clean. She knew her hair must be a mess and that was just the start, she longed for the warmth of the water to cleanse her, so much so she almost tore her clothes off and threw them on the floor. Hopefully Sapphire would have dropped off some things for her by the time she'd finished showering. If not she'd just sleep naked. She was exhausted and the thought of slipping into a clean and warm bed was a dream come true.

The hot water enveloped her and she couldn't stop the groan of pleasure that fell from her lips. Using the soap and shampoo that were available, Sidra scrubbed herself so vigorously that her skin grew red, a soft bubble of laughter erupting from her throat as she relished the new found freedom from the fear that she'd been under for months. "Thank you," she whispered to whatever force that had the Dragons rescuing her.

She wasn't used to receiving help from anyone, most "threw her under the bus" as soon as they realized Demons were hunting her. To have a group of people she'd only just met tell her they'd help keep her safe was something new, and she had to admit she liked the thought of staying in one place for more than a few days. The only fly in the ointment was Jaxon.

Why she was drawn to him puzzled her. He'd been downright grumpy and definitely not friendly, but he'd insisted she stay. Why? Was it possible he felt some weird connection like she had? Sidra shook her head and muttered, "Strange," as she pondered her decision to stay with him.

Reluctantly leaving the shower, she towel dried her hair before wrapping one around herself. She noticed a new toothbrush and toothpaste sitting on the shelf above the sink and almost squealed with delight. When she'd lost her pack, she'd lost her own toothbrush and her mouth felt like the bottom of a trash can. Disgustingly filthy. She tore the wrapping off the brush and liberally spread toothpaste on it. Sidra grinned as she looked in the mirror, furiously brushing her teeth. "Heaven," she mumbled as she took a few minutes to clean her entire mouth. After rinsing, she wiped around the sink to make sure it was nice and clean.

Once she'd made sure the bathroom was spic and span, she headed back to the bedroom, looking forward to sleeping in a bed. She noted the bed seemed to have been newly made up with clean sheets and the comforter on top looked thick and warm. "Nice." She yawned, pulling the cover back. She let her towel drop to the floor, deciding to just slip in and sleep naked, and that's when the bedroom door opened.

Her eyes widened as Jaxon stepped inside, a large pack in his hand. Sidra scrambled to grab the towel, holding it in front of her as she yelled, "What the hell are you doing?"

Jaxon stopped dead, inhaling sharply as his eyes raked her body before landing on hers. His face changed, one eyebrow raising as he dangled the pack from his hand. "Sorry, I was just bringing you the things Sapphire got for you."

Sidra could hear his breathing picking up as he stared at her and she could feel her own quickening. A tug in her stomach causing her to take a step toward him, her heart hammering in her chest as her thighs clamped together, tingling. "Thank you." She reached to grab the pack.

Jaxon's free hand snapped forward, reaching for her wrist and pulling her toward him. Caught by surprise, Sidra stumbled, falling against his large body. "What the hell?" she managed to gasp as he dropped the pack, his other arm encircling her waist.

Jaxon gazed down at her, confusion on his face. "I—" was all he got out before he tugged her closer.

Sidra couldn't take her eyes from his lips, her own opening as she reached up on her tiptoes, their mouths a hair's breadth apart. Jaxon groaned, closing the distance between them, his lips meeting hers in a searing kiss.

Sidra stiffened, for the briefest of moments, then her hands slid up and around his neck, holding him firmly in place. Her brain screaming at her to stop but something else entirely seemed to be in control. She couldn't have pulled away if her life depended on it. Jaxon's mouth devouring hers with a kiss that literally left her legs like jelly.

His strong, thick and powerful arms kept her upright and tightly against his body. One hand slid down from behind her neck, his fingers caressing her naked back before cupping her ass and drawing her even closer. She could feel his hardness digging into her belly, her heart rate picking up speed at the revelation of how aroused he was.

Sidra's body was out of her control, her thighs clasped together to try and stem the feelings that were engulfing her sex. She was shocked when she moaned into his mouth as desire overtook her entirely. Her brain screamed at her that this was meant to be. She couldn't understand it but then again, she barely gave it a rational thought, acting on instinct alone. Jaxon growled as she pressed herself closer and she wasn't sure which of them was more out of control.

His hands roamed freely over her body setting it on fire as his tongue invaded her mouth. She met it with hers, tangling together, her mind a haze of desire. She'd never felt these feelings, ever. She'd only had sex a few times but nothing compared to what was happening to her body now. It seemed to come alive under his touch. Jaxon seemed to be similarly affected, his actions growing more frantic as he yanked her toward the bed. He briefly broke contact, his eyes filled with lust mixed with mystification.

His voice was hoarse as he mumbled, "I don't know what's happening."

"I'm the same," she gasped. "But it feels *right*, Jaxon."

"Yes," he huffed before covering her mouth again with such passion that she thought she'd pass out from the exquisite feelings running rampant through her system.

Again he pulled away, frowning. "This isn't a good idea."

Sidra nodded, a cheeky smirk on her face and far more confidence in her voice than she felt. "I agree, but you started it, big guy. You can't walk away and leave me all riled up."

Jaxon nodded toward the bed.

She complied, getting onto the soft mattress, her eyes gazing up at him as he undressed with a speed that had her head whirling. His body being revealed did nothing to dampen down her excitement. Strong, hard muscles covered him entirely, his thighs almost as thick as her waist. His jeans dropping to reveal them, and his manhood. Her eyes widened when she saw it for the first time. A small whimper escaping her and she wasn't sure if it was due to fear at the size or anticipation of him sinking inside her.

His dark eyes scoured her body, his mouth tugging up at the side as she bit her lip. He stepped to the side of the bed, his cock standing proud, his chest heaving. "Are you sure about this?"

Sidra tried to think but all she could do was feel and she nodded up at him.

He mirrored her, nodding once. "Be sure, Twinkle, 'cause once I join you there in that bed I'm not sure I'll be able to walk away."

"Twinkle?" Sidra asked confused.

"Yeah, Twinkle Toes." Jaxon chuckled. "I always called the Unicorns from my youth that 'cause they were always so graceful and beautiful."

"Hmm." Sidra shook her head. "I'm not so sure 'bout that."

"Too bad." Jaxon joined her in the bed, leaning over her and gazing down at her, a cheeky sparkle in his almost black eyes. "You'll always be Twinkle to me."

Just as she was about to argue, he lowered himself, trapping her beneath him as his mouth latched onto hers again. Sidra became lost in the intense feelings he elicited from her with his expert ministrations, and soon they were both rising to heights that were downright impossible.

He was gentle at the same time as being firm, tender and fierce, with an intensity she'd never before experienced. Sidra was certain she was going to black out as an earth-shattering orgasm completely overtook her. Her body shook, her heart stuttering in her chest, pleasure overwhelming her utterly and entirely.

Jaxon's roar of pleasure was like an exquisite orgasmic aftershock, the weight of his body on hers making her feel the safest she'd felt in her life. For a brief moment, she dreamed of being protected forever. With Jaxon at her side, she was certain he'd shelter her, guard her, and care for her with every fiber of his being.

The feeling lasted only a moment as Jaxon cursed, jerking back and glaring down at her. "I'm sorry." His voice was full of unadulterated anguish as he leaped out of the bed, grabbed his clothes, and ran.

"What the fuck?" Sidra cursed, anger overtaking her as tears stung her eyes.

CHAPTER TEN

Jaxon dressed as he stumbled to the front door, flinging it open and rushing out into the darkness. "What the fuck just happened?" he asked aloud as he tried to get distance between him and Sidra.

Skar's voice caused him to jerk around. "You okay?"

He hadn't seen Skar, his dark skin hiding him in the shadows as Jaxon pulled on his t-shirt then buttoned his jeans, his face heating with embarrassment. "To be honest I'm not sure."

"Wanna talk about it?" Skar asked as he fell in beside Jaxon.

"Not sure about that either." Jaxon took a huge breath in, letting it out slowly, trying to calm himself.

"Well, why don't we just take a walk and if you want to talk we can."

"Sure," Jaxon murmured.

They walked right out of camp, onto the middle of the adjoining field, each step calming Jaxon's thundering heart. Skar remained silent until he stopped and turned to face Jaxon. "So, boss, what's going on with you and the Unicorn?"

Jaxon exhaled, his mind in turmoil as he turned to face his friend. "We had sex."

Skar grunted, his hand shooting up to hide his mouth and Jaxon realized the "grunt" had been a muffled laugh. "So why were you running from your own cabin, half naked?"

Jaxon almost snarled as anger, doubt, and indecision enveloped him. "Because I have no idea how it happened and I'm Master of the Guild. I've never had sex within this camp. Not once."

"Okaaaaaaaay, so tell me, Jax, how could you not know *how* it happened?" Skar cocked his head to the side, an incredulous look on his face, one that Jaxon saw even in the darkness.

"Well, I know *how*, as such, but I've no idea how we got there." Jaxon ran a hand through his hair. "I took her the pack that Sapphy had dropped off for her. I went in and she was there, just out of the shower, her hair wet as well as her body and she'd dropped the towel and something inside me took over. Skar, I've never felt anything like it before. I couldn't control myself. What kind of leader am I if I can't even control my sexual urges?"

Skar shrugged, which annoyed Jaxon greatly, taking a moment before he replied. "Something was going on between you two from the start. We could all sense it, Jax. I've been trying to figure out what it is and here you tell me that you've had sex and you couldn't control yourself." Skar paused. "I assume she was agreeable?"

Jaxon stepped back, outraged. "Of course she was! I'd never force myself on a woman."

"Hey, I'm just trying to figure this out." Skar held his hands up before him, raising an eyebrow. "And, I'm wondering if, and don't bite my head off, that she's your mate? Your Destiny?"

"What?" Jaxon asked, his voice rising in shock. "Don't be stupid. There's not been a Dragon that's found their Destiny for centuries."

"Doesn't mean she's not yours." Skar smirked. "There's gotta be a time when we start to meet them again, Jax. If not then we'll die out. I know some Dragons that have fallen for a human, Witch, or even a Wolf, but they never produce children. Only our Destiny can have our babies. Maybe she's yours."

"My Destiny?" Jaxon's breathing grew labored at the thought. "But I'm Master of the Guild, no Warriors have a woman, destined or otherwise."

"There are no rules against it." Skar grinned. "I'm feeling more and more that this might be what's going on."

"No." Jaxon shook his head. "She couldn't be. Could she?"

"Only one way to find out for certain." Skar raised an eyebrow. "Contact the Goddess and ask her."

"Damn it." Jaxon paced back and forth. "What if she is? What am I supposed to do with a woman to care for?"

"Love her," Skar said simply.

"I'm not sure I'm capable of that," Jaxon admitted.

"Jax," Skar chuckled, "I'm pretty sure if she is your Destiny then you'll not have much choice in the matter."

"Fuck!" Jaxon cursed loudly.

Skar stepped over. "Now I know you're thinking along the same lines. You rarely swear, boss. So, why don't you mind-link with Zeeandra and put yourself out of this misery of not knowing."

"Will you hang around?" For the first time in his life, Jaxon felt scared of what he would find out.

"Sure I will." Skar walked a few paces away. "I'll give you some privacy."

"It's not as if I'm gonna invite you into the conversation," Jaxon joked.

"I know, but truth is, I don't want to be standing too close in case you go all nuts on me." Skar laughed as he continued to put space between them.

Jaxon took a deep breath before opening a mind-link with their Goddess. *"Zeeandra, do you have time to talk?"*

She replied instantly. *"Took your time, Jaxon, I've been expecting your call."*

"Really?" he asked, anticipation causing his stomach muscles to clench.

"Yes, really. So, what can I do for you? Or shall I just go ahead and answer your question?"

Jaxon shook his head to clear it. *"Is it true? Have our Destinies been activated again?"*

"They were never 'deactivated' but they are special beings and don't usually come around that often." Zeeandra sighed. *"With everything that's been going on, it's only added to the problem. Making them even rarer."*

Jaxon's heart sped up. *"Does that mean there is now more than one out there?"*

Zeeandra laughed. *"Jaxon, really, that's what you want to ask me?"*

"Well, no, not exclusively, but it would be nice to be able to tell my Warriors that there are Destinies out there waiting on them."

"Spit it out, Jaxon, I want to hear you ask it."

Jaxon looked over to where Skar waited, taking a moment to ask the question that would change his life from this moment on. He finally plucked up the courage to voice the question he was desperate to know the answer to. *"Is Sidra my Cinneamhain? Is she my Destiny?"*

"Jaxon, my most loyal Dragon, I don't think I've ever felt happier because, yes, she is your Destiny."

Jaxon's legs wobbled, almost giving way, Skar rushing forward to catch him. His eyes sought Jaxon's, the question clear for him to see. Jaxon nodded once as he tried to concentrate on Zeeandra. *"Why didn't you tell me? I didn't know what was happening to me inside. I felt confusion and fear, and damn it, I've just ran out on her because of it."*

"Jaxon—" Zeeandra's voice was chastising and firm. *"Are you questioning me?"*

"No, of course not," Jaxon quickly responded. *"My apologies, Goddess, I'm just shocked and out of sorts."*

"Apology accepted. Now, go and make things up with Sidra. She is as confused as you are and it is up to you to explain things to her."

"I'm not sure how to do that. She is not Dragon, she might not understand."

"Then you must make her understand, Jaxon. She will be in grave danger in the future and you have to keep her safe. Your child's life depends on it."

Jaxon felt his legs give way again, Skar's strong arms the only thing keeping him upright at the shocking revelations. *"My child?"* he managed to croak.

"Yes, my brave Warrior, your child. Your seed is taking root as we speak, and Sidra will soon realize that she is pregnant." Zeeandra sniggered. *"I trust you to make amends for your appalling behavior before that happens or you may have a tough time ahead."*

"My Goddess," Jaxon's voice hitched. *"Will I still be Master of the Guild?"*

"Of course, why would you ask such a thing?"

"I've not heard of a Master that had a woman by his side."

Zeeandra chuckled. *"I am Goddess over all Dragons, Jaxon. I decide what can and cannot be. You have served me well for many years and there is no other better suited to the position. You may have to make adjustments to suit your new life, but that is dependent on you placating Sidra's ire. Go, now, before it is too late."*

Jaxon grabbed Skar's shoulders, holding himself steady for a moment. *"I will, thank you, my Goddess, for this gift."*

"My pleasure, oh, before you go, I have news regarding Terigan and Allyssa."

"Yes?" Jaxon held his breath waiting to find out if Terigan had survived.

"They'll be on their way home tomorrow."

"That's wonderful news, I'll let everyone know."

"I thought that would make you happy, however, a word of warning. Keep your guards posted and alert, I sense danger coming your way."

"Noted." Jaxon felt strong enough to move away from Skar. *"Thanks for the warning."*

"Goodbye for now."

"Bye." Jaxon started laughing, his whole body shaking as he processed what he'd been told. Skar reached over, shaking his shoulder hard.

"Are you going to let me in on whatever's got you in this state?"

Jaxon nodded, working hard to control himself. "Good news, my friend. Terigan and Allyssa will be returning home tomorrow."

Skar pumped his fist in the air. "That's fantastic. I can't wait to see them and tell everyone. I think this calls for a party, don't you?"

"I'm afraid that'll have to be put on hold." Jaxon looked back toward the camp. "We might be in for some trouble so could you double the guards and tell them to stay alert?"

"Will do." Skar turned to jog back to camp, got about fifty yards then stopped, shouting over his shoulder. "What about Sidra?"

Jaxon's smile split his face. "She's mine."

"Really? Wow, that's wonderful news." Skar frowned. "Pity bout no party though. We could've had a double for Terigan and Allyssa's return and your linking to your Destiny."

"Maybe later on, when we're certain everything and everyone is safe." Jaxon started to run, overtaking Skar in seconds. "For now I've got to go and build some bridges. See you in the morning, Skar."

"Yeah, yeah, rub it in, why dontcha. You've found your forever, the rest of us just have to keep praying for ours."

Jaxon laughed, raising his arm and waving as he sped across the field. Urgency ran through him, adrenaline kicking in, a burning need to reach Sidra and make things right coursing in his veins. He only hoped she'd listen to him as he apologized for being such an ass earlier.

Shoving his door open with more force than necessary, he ran inside, stopping abruptly when he saw Sidra's backside in the air, her head poking into his fridge. Dressed in tight yoga pants and a t-shirt, she looked delectable as she jumped with fright at the door slamming against the wall, turning around quickly. Her face closed down when she saw him and he knew he had a lot of work to do to repair things between them.

Closing the door gently he kept his eyes on hers. They looked red, as if she'd been crying, and his heart stuttered in his chest with regret. "Sidra, I'm sorry about earlier."

She interrupted him, her chin jutting out defiantly. "Nothing to apologize for. It was just sex."

Jaxon stepped closer shaking his head. "No, it wasn't. I've never had sex here; it was something far more than that."

"What?" Sidra's face was covered in disbelief. "You've not had sex in your own home?"

"No." Jaxon took another step closer. "Not just here in my cabin, but not within the confines of the camp. I've never had sex with anyone here, ever. But that's not what I was meaning. I'd like if you'd sit down so we can talk."

Sidra glowered at him, her body tense as she grudgingly went to the table and sat down. "I'm not sure you have anything to say that I want to hear right now."

"I know, and I'm sorry for running out on you, but the truth is I was shocked and upset, I let my feelings get the best of me." Jaxon slowly walked over to join her, sitting opposite so as not to crowd her. "My behavior was deplorable and I can't apologize enough."

"Yeah, so you said," Sidra said quietly.

"Maybe if I explain then you'll understand."

"I doubt it," Sidra snorted. "I'm not really in the mood for placations, big guy. You made me feel rather shitty and I don't tend to forgive easily."

Jaxon ran his hands down his face, anger at himself boiling under the surface. "I was a jerk. I know that."

"Yes, you were," Sidra said, her face guarded as she watched him.

"I'm Master of the Guild and I've always held myself above the others. I try to lead by example and I've never behaved like that in my life, but the truth is, I panicked. I was feeling things I'd never experienced before and I didn't know how to process what it was. I'm a fecking eejit, that's what I am."

Sidra frowned. "Eejit?"

"Yes, an eejit." Jaxon shrugged. "It's a Scottish word for a great big fool of the highest order."

"Oh, I see." Sidra nodded. "Well then, I agree, you were totally an eejit."

"Yeah, I'm well aware of that." Jaxon leaned forward, his elbows on the table. "Can I ask you a question?" Sidra nodded curtly. "I've felt something since we first met, have you?"

Sidra's eyes flitted away for a second. "I guess so. No idea what though."

"I see." Jaxon gave her a small smile. "Have you ever heard of Dragons finding their Destiny?"

"What? No. What're you talking about? Like fate or something?" Sidra looked confused as she stared over at him. He noticed her body wasn't quite as tense as it had been to start.

"Not exactly." Jaxon sighed, trying to figure out how to tell her the most important thing he'd ever spoken. "A Dragon's Destiny is a person. One that is their 'other half' sort of thing. Our Goddess, Zeeandra, is in charge of all of this and although some Dragons may have strong feelings for a woman, or man, and make a life with them akin to marriage, they can't have children. Only Dragons who find and link with their Destiny can reproduce. It's been centuries since that's happened though."

"That's odd, and excuse me, but how are you supposed to thrive as a species if you can't have kids?"

"We've been busy trying to survive in the turmoil of this world. It's not just the inter-species war that's been a factor. The human realm has been at war against each other for far too long and we've been doing our bit to try and help. However, since the species war we've been busy trying to protect those that were in need. Mostly Witches but others too. We'll take in anyone that is in need of our protection, regardless of species."

"I understand that but surely you need to procreate?" Sidra scowled. "Plus, isn't it unfair, cruel even, to not allow any of you to find a true-love?"

"We don't question our Goddess, but trust that she knows what is best for us." Jaxon realized they were getting off topic and tried to steer it back to them. "So, Dragons have one and only one Destiny awaiting them."

"What's this got to do with the pathetic way you acted earlier?"

"As I said, you've affected me and I wasn't sure what was going on. All I knew was that I'd lost control of myself and I *never* lose control. So, I panicked. Like a virgin Warrior in his first battle with a horde of Demons coming his way. I did the unthinkable, I ran."

"Jaxon." Sidra shook her head, her eyes flashing with anger. "I'm not exactly happy at being cast in the same vein as a horde of Demons and I still have no clue what you're trying to say."

"I'm saying you're my Cinneamhain."

"What language is that and what does it mean?" Sidra cocked her head to the side, her guard dropping even more.

Jaxon reached over and ran his fingers over the back of her hand. When she didn't pull away he smiled. "It's Gaelic and it means you are mine. My Destiny. We are destined to be together, Sidra, and everything I've been feeling is because of that. I'm hoping you've been experiencing the same."

Sidra now jerked her hand away, scooting her chair back. "Whoa, wait just a minute. I'm not sure where you've got that idea but this is ludicrous. I'm not a Dragon and I'm damn sure not accepting this crap just so you can get me back into bed."

He held his hands up to try and calm her. Sidra's anger seeming to roll off her in waves. "Please, wait, hear me out."

"I'm listening but I can assure you that we're not having sex again, Jaxon. Not happening, buster, so don't even try and worm your way back into my bed."

Jaxon couldn't help the grin that spread on his face. His Destiny was feisty and he liked it very much. When she glowered at him he wiped the smile from his face. "I've already checked with Zeeandra. She confirmed it. Sidra, you *are* my Destiny and I am yours. There is no getting away from it."

"What? How? Did you go see her or did she come here? You've not been away that long so how can you have seen her?"

"Dragons can mind-link to each other and we can talk to each other telepathically. I spoke to her earlier and she confirmed it."

"Mind-talk? Damn, that's rather scary. I wouldn't want anyone inside my head." Sidra raised an eyebrow. "You can't read my thoughts, can you?"

"No." Jaxon shook his head. "We can't really read other Dragons thoughts either. But we can converse in our heads and we do get a 'sense' of feelings and emotions, that's all. I won't be able to read your every thought, so you don't have to worry about that."

"So, this Goddess of yours, Zeeandra, she told you that we're supposed to be together?" Sidra almost choked out. "We don't even know each other, apart from that hot sex session."

"Hot?" Jaxon smirked, enjoying the way her face blushed red.

"Shut up!" Looking daggers at him and waving a hand around in frustration. "I'm not denying it was nice, but to spend the rest of my life with you, now that's not something I'm prepared to agree to anytime soon."

"You don't really have much choice in the matter," Jaxon enlightened her. "Now that we've met, the feelings within will grow stronger with each passing hour. Soon we will be so drawn to each other that we won't be able to resist. Then we'll have to 'link' ourselves and we'll be like that until our deaths."

"Link? What the hell does that mean?" Sidra started to look panicked, her eyes darting to the door.

"Please, don't be alarmed." Jaxon tried to calm her down. "I suppose you could say it's like a human wedding, or a Wolf bonding ceremony. We acknowledge our Destiny and our love for one another. It can be done publicly or privately, it doesn't really matter. Whatever you feel comfortable with."

Sidra shook her head violently. "No, no, and hell no! I've known you for less than a day and you're talking about binding us together. Not happening. I mean it, Jaxon. This is all . . . too much. Yup, too much to take in and I'm not discussing this any further."

Jaxon wanted nothing more than to pull her into his arms and bend her to his will. He kept tight control of himself, knowing she'd flee if he made any move on her. His stomach fluttered as he imagined the child that was barely taking root in her belly, barely managing to refrain from mentioning that fact.

Sidra stood, still shaking her head. "I'm not talking about this anymore tonight. I'm going to bed, alone, and you better not even try and come into my room or you'll get a nasty shock, Dragon."

"I wouldn't dream of it." Jaxon stayed in his seat. "I hope you rest well, Cinneamhain."

"Don't call me that!" she exclaimed as she stormed away.

Jaxon exhaled, whispering to himself. "I hope she's in a more agreeable mood tomorrow."

He waited until he heard her door closing firmly before rising and making his way to his own bed, doubting he'd get much sleep. With everything rolling around in his head, he guessed he'd be awake for a long time in the night ahead.

CHAPTER  ELEVEN

Sidra tossed and turned for hours, eventually falling asleep when exhaustion took her over into darkness.

That's when the dreams started. Unsettling in the extreme as she ran from an unseen pursuer, her belly sticking out in front of her, heavy with pregnancy. Her heart beating almost out of her chest as she sped away from danger, trying to keep her child safe from the unseen threat. Terror encompassed her as her legs started shaking from the effort to keep ahead of whatever was chasing her, a scream erupting from her throat as she thrashed around in the bed.

Strong arms grabbed her and she punched and fought to be free. A loud "Ouch, that hurt," brought her fully awake. Her eyes flew open to find Jaxon sitting on the bed trying to hold her still.

His concerned voice whispered, "Hey, it's okay, you're dreaming. Wake up, Twink, you're safe."

"Shit!" she gasped, the feeling of terror slowly subsiding as his arms held her close.

"Are you all right?" Jaxon asked, his eyes filled with worry.

Sidra took a few steadying breaths before she could answer. "I think so. It was a scary dream."

"I'd gathered that." Jaxon still held her close, causing her heart to speed up for a very different reason. "Want to tell me 'bout it?"

"Hmm." Sidra felt a blush creeping up her face. "I was being chased by something and I couldn't run fast enough to escape because, well, I was heavily pregnant. Weird, huh?"

Jaxon lost all color in his face as he nodded. "Yeah, weird."

Sidra could feel his apprehension grow as she studied his face. Fear, anxiety and concern rolled from him. "Why are you so worried? It was just a dream."

"I don't like to see you suffer." Jaxon tried to smile, his lips barely lifting. "Even if it's only a nightmare."

"Well, I'm fine now so you can let me go." Sidra wiggled to be free of his embrace. The touch of his arms around her making her feel things she definitely didn't want to.

Jaxon seemed reluctant to release her, but when she continued to squirm he finally let her go. "If you're sure you're all right?"

"I'm good, thanks." Sidra pulled the cover up to her chin, using it as a shield against the pull of his magnetism. "You can leave now."

He rose, still staring at her as he backpedaled to the door. "I'm only a shout away if you need me."

Sidra smirked. "I'm a big girl now, Jaxon. I can sleep all by myself."

He nodded once before disappearing out the door. Sidra noticed he didn't close it fully and smiled at his thoughtfulness. Giving herself a stern reprimand when she realized she was thinking of him in a far better light than before. *"Stop it, you silly woman. Remember he walked out seconds after having his wicked way with you."*

Sidra snuggled back into the bed, relishing the warmth and comfort, closing her eyes and trying to fall back asleep. Her thoughts still on the tall, rugged Jaxon as sleep pulled her deep into its grasp.

Jaxon paced back and forth in his room, which suddenly seemed far too small. He felt confined and trapped as thoughts of Sidra's nightmare flew around in his head. *"What if it was a*

premonition rather than just a dream?" he thought over and over, his determination to keep her safe growing by the second.

He resolved to meet with his Warriors in the morning and alert them to the possible danger. Although, if she were heavy with child in the dream then maybe they had time on their hands. *"Bugger that. I'm leaving nothing to chance,"* he thought, throwing himself onto the armchair next to the window.

Jaxon knew sleep would not return for him, so he settled himself into the chair and ran through everything he had to do when the sun rose. First and foremost was making sure Sidra was safe at all times and if that meant assigning someone to her then that's what he'd do. He doubted she would be happy about it, but then again, she didn't need to know. The Guild was rather adept at staying hidden when the need arose, and he'd use those talents to the fullest to make sure his Destiny was safe.

Finding his Cinneamhain was the most wonderful feeling he'd ever experienced, and at the same time making him the most fearful in his long life. The mere thought of anything happening to her had his heart going into overdrive and adrenaline releasing into his system. So much so that his hands started to shake and tremble.

Giving up any pretense of rest, Jaxon decided to go for a run, dressing quickly and quietly leaving his room. He stopped outside Sidra's door, smiling when he heard her even breathing, interrupted by a few soft snores. It was still a couple of hours to sunrise so he could get in a good workout and be back in plenty of time to shower and have coffee made for her waking.

Jaxon grinned at that thought. Thinking of doing such a mundane task actually brought him joy. *"Things are going to change around here,"* he thought as he carried on and out of the cabin.

Jogging to warm up, Jaxon soon found himself on the edge of camp. He took a moment to stretch out his muscles then sped away into the distance. If he ran to the surrounding forest, through it, circling around to the mountains and back again, he'd have a good hour or more of running. A good run always calmed his mind.

On and on he ran, focusing on nothing more than putting one foot in front of the other. His breathing only slightly labored as he completed the route. Not quite ready to stop, he circled the camp once more, ending up in the large landing field. Jaxon stopped to stretch out his muscles again and as he started to slowly jog in place, he heard the unmistakable sound of Dragon wings.

Looking skywards in the darkness, he made out two large beasts descending. His heart soared when he finally managed to recognize Terigan's and Allyssa's beasts as they came in to land. As soon as their feet touched the ground, both transformed, Terigan rushing toward him.

"Jaxon, I didn't expect to find you here but I'm glad I did." Terigan stopped before him, his head cocking to the side and staring intently. "What's wrong? I could sense something going on with you hours ago so did Lyssa, so we set off earlier than planned to get here."

Allyssa joined them, her face masked with worry. "Is everything all right?"

"Hey you two." Jaxon looked them both over intently, looking for any signs of their previous wounds. "First things first, how are you both? Terigan, you had us worried."

Terigan wagged a finger at Jaxon. "We're fine, and stop delaying, Jax. Tell us what the hell's going on."

Jaxon couldn't help the smile that erupted. "Yes, everything's fine. In fact, it's better than fine. Something amazing has happened and at first I wasn't sure what was going on, hence the confusion and worry, but I spoke to Zeeandra and she confirmed something."

Allyssa stepped forward, poking him hard when he paused. "Tell us!"

"I've found my Destiny and she's right here in the camp. She was the woman Zane was sent out on a mission to find. It was touch and go as she had Demons hunting her and I took some of the boys to help out." Jaxon shook his head, still not believing he'd found his Destiny. "She's a feisty thing and also something that's not been around in a long time."

"What?" Terigan asked confused. "What's that supposed to mean?"

"Let's put it this way, her father was an Angel, not a Fallen, a pure Angel." Jaxon waited and saw realization dawn on Terigan's face while Allyssa frowned, looking between them.

Terigan shook his head. "No, really?"

Allyssa poked Jaxon again. "All right, I'm obviously missing something. Care to enlighten me?"

She looked even more puzzled when Terigan slapped his back then burst out laughing. "I can't believe it! I wonder what your kids will turn out like. That's a pairing I'm pretty damn sure has never happened before."

Allyssa stamped her foot, exclaiming, "Will someone please tell me?"

Jaxon straightened, his chest puffing out. "She's a Shifter, a very special kind, probably the only one around at this time"

Again, Allyssa stamped her foot. "Will you just tell me already? Or I'm gonna burst."

"She's a Unicorn." Jaxon chuckled as her mouth fell open in shock.

"A Unicorn?" Her eyes squinted, shaking her head in disbelief. "You're joking. Right?"

"No." Jaxon shook his head. "I'm not joking, Allyssa. Her name is Sidra and she's the most exquisite thing on this earth. Although she's not entirely convinced of things yet, but I'm working on that."

"Dang." Allyssa clapped her hands. "When do I get to see it? What color is it? White? Yes, must be white. All Unicorns are white, aren't they?"

Jaxon tried his best to keep up as she fired questions at him. "In the morning, no idea yet and I don't think all of them are white. I saw one in my youth and I remember it as being a silver color, but it was so long ago that might be wrong."

"Wow." Terigan smiled like a lunatic. "Your Destiny, that's not something I was expecting. Does that mean there are others out there? It's been so long since we heard of a Dragon finding theirs, I'd kinda given up hope."

"I know," Jaxon agreed. "Truth be told I was a bit of an ass because I didn't know what was happening to me. Luckily, Skar intervened and told me to talk to Zee. When she confirmed what Sidra was, I can tell you I was shocked to my core. I'm pretty sure Skar had to hold me up, my legs were so weak from the news."

Terigan stared intently at Jaxon, raising an eyebrow. "There's more though, isn't there?"

Jaxon had hoped to wait and tell his Warriors at the same time but his friend knew him too well. "Sidra is, apparently, in some sort of danger that Zee warned me about so I'm getting everyone together after breakfast to set in place some security for her. I doubt she'll be amenable to that, especially as I haven't told her what Zee said, but we're good at hiding ourselves so it shouldn't be a problem."

Allyssa gasped as she shook her head. "No, no and no again. That's not the way to start your life together. Lying to her will not do you any favors, Jax. You need to talk to her and tell her everything."

Terigan apparently agreed. "Sorry, my friend, but she's right. You don't want to muck things up any more by lying. If she finds out, she'll be angry and upset and rightly so in my mind."

Jaxon sighed. "I guess I was looking for the easy option."

"Nothing easy about keeping your Destiny safe and if you start off by lying to her, shoot, she may just decide to up and leave." Terigan shook his head. "I assume that's not what you want, so, go ahead, organize security, but I think you should also talk to her and tell her what Zeeandra said."

Allyssa nodded. "Yup, that's what you should do. I know I'd be angry as hell if the person I was to spend the rest of my life with started off by lying to me."

"What is this?" Jaxon huffed. "Some kind of 'intervention'? Yeah, it's 'Make sure Jaxon isn't an idiot' time."

"Your words, not ours." Terigan laughed. "But seriously, you know nothing good comes from lies. Never has, never will."

Allyssa frowned, tapping a long fingernail on her chin. "Hmm, not sure about that. I mean, if a girl asks that age old question, 'Does my bum look big in this?' then I assure you a well worded lie can save a *lot* of grief."

Shaking his head Jaxon chuckled. "It's nice to have you two home again. I've missed you both."

"What?" Terigan raised an eyebrow. "I thought Amos would keep you amused in my absence, boss."

"That lad would try the patience of a saint," Jaxon moaned. "He's a livewire and I'm just happy Aric is there to calm him down at times."

"He's so cute though." Allyssa patted her heart. "If we're 'outed' now and go out into the big bad world, we'll have to keep an eye on him, or he may be whisked away by some hot girl."

"I'll tan his ass if he does." Jaxon scowled.

Allyssa punched his arm. "Hey, he's young and he's not had much of a chance to just be a man. You should cut him some slack, Jaxon. He may be a joker but he's a damn fine Dragon and works his firm little tushy off. He's always the first to volunteer for things and never shirks his duty."

"I'm aware of that, but we still need to be careful, Allyssa." Jaxon waved his arm in an arc. "Out there is still dangerous and he might be led astray by someone for reasons other than a night of passion. Now it's known about our existence, I suspect there may be people with nefarious intentions trying to get their hands on a real live Dragon. I don't want the boy hurt, or worse. We cannot let our guard down, not anytime soon anyway."

"Oh," Allyssa looked worried, "I hadn't thought of that. Shoot, you don't really think we might be under that kind of threat?"

"Yes," Jaxon sighed, "I do. It's been mulling around in my head and I do think we *may* be in danger. I could be overreacting, but somehow I don't think so. Just look at what's gone on these past thirty years or so. One species against the other, always looking for ways to get the upper hand. If there are still beings out there with delusions of grandeur, then what better way to hurt others and take over than by having a Dragon on their side? I hope that's not the case but I'm a little jaded after everything I've witnessed and I won't allow any of you to let your guard down."

Terigan started back toward camp. "I agree but right now I'm exhausted so I'm off to bed. I'll catch up on anything I need to later, if that's all right?"

Jaxon followed, his feet dragging at the thought of the conversation he was going to have to have with Sidra. "Sure, rest and I'll see you later. Again, I'm glad you're well and back home. You had me more than a little concerned, Terigan. Try and not do that again, please?"

Chuckling over his shoulder, Terigan carried on. "Yeah, I'll try real hard not to get myself almost killed, boss. You can trust me on *that*."

Allyssa groaned. "Lame, Terigan, even for you."

"Hey, I'm just saying it how it is." Terigan picked up speed. "I'm dying to sleep in my own bed. See ya later, guys."

"Later." Allyssa waved, keeping pace with Jaxon.

"So, tell me, what's she like?"

Jaxon paused, his thoughts focused on Sidra, smiling. "She's fiery and definitely got a mind of her own. She was running from Demons and she stopped to rescue a baby, which then stopped her from transforming and escaping as she would normally. Even when they were closing in on her and the child, she refused to leave it. She's pretty damn brave."

"Jeez, that must've been scary for her. Is she okay?"

"Yes." Jaxon nodded. "She took it all in stride and was still bolshie when we landed and transformed. She's definitely not a typical woman, that's for darn sure."

"Good." Allyssa laughed. "She'll need her wits about her to keep you in your place."

"What?" Jaxon squinted down at Allyssa. "I'm not quite sure what you mean by that."

"You're rather intense, Jax, and you scare a lot of people with your demeanor. So, if she's that brave to stand up to Demons, then she'll be able to stand up to you too."

"I don't scare people."

"Maybe not intentionally, but you kinda do." Allyssa shrugged. "You are always so focused on missions, safety, and rules that you sometimes forget to just be a man."

"Hmm." Jaxon raised an eyebrow. "I guess that's right, but I certainly don't mean to scare anyone. Well, not anyone that doesn't deserve it."

"Exactly." Allyssa waggled a finger at him. "You sometimes don't 'turn off' your Master head and you can come across as being gruff and severe. I hope your Destiny can bring out a softer side to you, though I think she may have a battle on her hands on that score."

Jaxon's eyes widened as Allyssa snickered before jogging away. "See you later, boss. I have a date with my nice big tub. I've missed her."

"Her?" Jaxon muttered. "Who thinks of a tub as a her?" Shaking his head, he realized he was almost at his cabin. Steeling himself for the argument he knew would come, he went inside. Jaxon started the coffee machine going before heading off to his shower, hoping that the conversation between him and Sidra didn't end up with him losing his temper.

One thing about himself he was well aware of; he didn't take it well if someone disagreed with his decisions. After all, he was Master of the Guild and his word was law.

CHAPTER TWELVE

Sidra's nose twitched, waking to the luscious smell of freshly brewed coffee, her most favorite thing in the world. Stretching her arms above her, she remembered the previous evening, and her nightmare. Jaxon's strong arms comforting her brought a smirk to her face, then a frown as she remembered him leaving her after they'd had sex.

"Damn it." She groaned as she rose and let her nose lead her to the kitchen, and the divine coffee. "Hmm." She grabbed a mug, pouring until the dark liquid was almost touching the rim. Sitting at the table with her elbows resting on the smooth surface, her hands cupping the mug, she inhaled deeply, a soft moan of pleasure rumbling up her throat.

She jumped when she realized she wasn't alone, Jaxon leaned against the counter to her side. He looked too damn hot in a pair of leather trousers that hugged his thighs far too well. Sidra felt a blush creeping up her face as she took in the sight of Jaxon dressed for battle, taking a sip of her coffee before she said anything. "You off to war?"

Jaxon's head fell to the side, his hair not yet bound behind his neck, tumbling over his shoulder. "No, just a usual day of work. I've got some important things to attend to today but I'd like to speak with you first."

"Don't let me keep you." Lowering her eyes, she drank more of the precious coffee, trying desperately to ignore the growing attraction inside her.

"You're not." Jaxon opened a cupboard, retrieving a huge mug, which he filled. "What I need to do today is partly to do with you."

"This is great coffee." She tried to focus as her eyes strayed to his leather covered ass.

"Yes, I fly to Columbia to get it. There are still some small coffee farmers producing it." Jaxon turned, his eyes boring into hers before sitting next to her.

Sidra shuffled, trying to gain some distance between them. "Well, I'm glad you do. Go get it that is. It's wonderful."

"I'm glad you like it." Jaxon smirked. "It's one of my favorites."

"That's some mug you have there. Don't you get caffeine jitters drinking that much?"

Again he smirked, causing her stomach to clench unbidden. "No, Dragons have a very high metabolism so I need a good load before it affects me in any way. I usually have a couple of these before I start the day."

"Jeez, I'd be bumping off the walls if I drank that much."

Jaxon drank down almost all of his coffee in one go, setting his mug on the table and spearing her with his eyes. "Sorry to interrupt the small talk, but I have more important business we need to discuss."

"Really?" she asked curtly, feeling out of sorts every time she was around him, annoyance at that fact simmering inside.

"Yes." Jaxon reached for her hand, but she snatched it away, spilling some coffee in the process. He ignored it, only raising an eyebrow at her act of defiance. "I tried to explain what we are to each other. The importance of that is not in question and I'd like to apologize again for my behavior last night. I'm sorry I acted like—"

"An ass? An idiot? Or what about a big fat jerk?" Sidra snapped. "Oh wait, you were all of those and more."

"I know I was." A pained expression on his face as he nodded. "I'm sorry, I don't know how many times I'll have to say that to make it up to you, but if it's a hundred, a thousand, then I'll do it. I'm sorry, truly sorry, for acting like that."

Sidra tried not to react to the pain she heard in his voice. She tried to keep herself firm against his apologies. She failed. "If you ever act like that again then I'm outta here, Jaxon, I mean it. I'll be gone before you can even blink an eye and you will never find me again. I promise you that, buster."

"Thank you." Jaxon let out a long sigh. "I promise you, I won't ever do that again. I can't promise I won't be a jerk though. Apparently, I can give out the wrong signals or so I've recently been told."

"Ya think?" Sidra snorted.

"So, about what we spoke about last night. What I told you of your importance to me, being my Destiny. Have you had time to think about that?"

Sidra nodded once. "Yes. I can't say it's something I'm entirely sure about but I can't deny there's definitely some kind of pull between us."

"That will only grow stronger the longer we are together. Soon, my Cinneamhain, you will not be able to deny what we are to each other." Jaxon reached again for her hand and this time she allowed his fingers to entwine with hers. His thumb ran small circles on her skin as he smiled. "I look forward to getting to know you,

Sidra, and I hope I'm not a disappointment to you."

"Disappointment?" she asked, confused.

"I am merely a Dragon whilst you are one of the rarest creatures ever created. I'm shocked that we've been paired together but I'm excited too. I can barely think of anything else and that is definitely not like me. I usually focus on work, the camp, and keeping the Guild on its toes. I think I'm going to have a, now what is that saying Sapphire uses? Oh yes, I'm going to have a very steep learning curve, when it comes to having a woman by my side."

"First thing you need to do is get me some decent shampoo and conditioner. That stuff in my room is atrocious." Sidra barely contained her smirk as his eyes flew open.

"Conditioner? What's that? Never mind, I'll ask Sapphy to get you some."

Sidra chuckled. "Yes, she'll know what to get me, or, and here's a thought, why don't you point me in the direction of where you keep your stores and I'll pick some up for myself?"

"I can do that." Jaxon straightened up, a serious look now on his face. "I've got something else that I need to talk to you about that's probably going to scare you."

Sidra frowned. "Not sure if you're aware or not, but I've been running from Demons for several years. Not a lot scares me, bud."

"In that case, this conversation may go much smoother than I'd thought." Jaxon leaned forward, closing the distance between them, his hand gripping hers. "I've reason to believe that you may be in danger and as Master of the Guild, I have to take your safety seriously. I'm going to have some security put in place, now wait a minute."

He held up his hand as her mouth shot open. "Hear me out. I promise you won't have anyone dragging behind you. Dragons are extremely skilled at being around and at the same time hidden. You won't feel as if you have a bodyguard joined to your hip but this is something that I need to do. Not only to protect you but to ensure the safety of the camp as a whole. If you're a target then we need to take steps to minimize the danger to everyone, you included."

Sidra did something she usually didn't—she kept her mouth closed. She tried to process what he'd said, thinking on Em and the baby causing her to think of doing what she always did: run.

Jaxon shook his head. "Don't even think about it."

"What?" she asked innocently while trying to think where she could go.

"You're not going anywhere." Jaxon held her hand firmly in place. "I've spoken to our Goddess about this and I've put some thought into the situation. You stay here and we'll keep you and everyone else, safe."

"This is a large camp. I'm sure you have a lot of people here that could get hurt." She tried to tug her hand free but he had it in an iron grip. "You have to put the needs of the masses against the needs of one. That's common sense."

"Not here." Jaxon shook his head again. "We look after everyone. Trust me, this is not the first time someone we've rescued has had people coming after them. We took care of those that dared to harm anyone under our protection, harshly, and we'll do the same now. The only thing we're not clear on is the when, hence me putting in place security for you. It could be days, weeks, or even longer, Sidra. I've just found you and you are not leaving."

Tears stung her eyes as she fought for control. Nobody had looked out for her, offered her help, since the death of her parents. The unfamiliar feelings running rampant through her as Jaxon's voice softened.

"Sidra, my Cinneamhain, I won't be alone in keeping you safe. I know, for a fact, that each and every one of my Dragons will be by my side in this. Trust me, they'll keep you and everyone else safe."

She swiped at her eyes with her free hand, fighting back the urge to fall into Jaxon's arms. She'd never felt that way before, even with her mom and dad. It was alien to her, she was more prone to pull away, but he scooted his chair closer, his free arm circling her shoulders.

"You can rely on me, Sidra, for anything and at any time." He leaned forward placing a kiss on her temple. "I promise I'll always be here for you, but you have to promise me something. Don't ever run from me. It would kill me and I'm not quite sure how I'd react. Not very well, I think."

"I'll try." She relented, allowing her body to lean toward his. "This is all very strange and new for me. It's going to take some getting used to."

"I understand that but we are destined for each other, nothing can change that, so please trust me to keep you safe."

"I've spent the last few years not relying on anyone but myself so that's gonna be hard too, big guy. I just don't want anyone in the camp to suffer because of me."

Jaxon nodded. "I get that, but things will be changing here pretty soon. Many of the people we have here are Witches and now that the threat to them has lifted, I'm sure many of them will want to leave in search of friends and family. The camp might be a tad empty pretty soon."

"Oh, I hadn't realized that."

"I'll be having a meeting with my Warriors after breakfast and then I'll be getting the word out that it is, relatively, safe to leave."

"Breakfast, now there's something I've missed lately." She gave him a small smile and the resulting twinkle in his eyes caused her heart to stutter in her chest. Damn, he was good looking even when stern and serious, but with that twinkle he was downright gorgeous.

"Why don't we head over and grab some?"

"I need to get dressed." She reluctantly stood up, the feeling of safety his embrace produced surprising her.

"I'll wait here for you." Jaxon picked up his huge mug. "I'll have some more coffee while I wait."

Sidra shook her head as she went back to her room to see what clothes she had available to her. She was pleased to find some jeans, panties, and tops. Unfortunately, there were no bras, but a little note from Sapphire saying she'd take her to the stores later to pick up some more things, including bras, because she hadn't known her size for that or shoes. "Thoughtful," she murmured as she dressed, tugging on her old battered boots and then trying to do something with her long hair.

Again, Sapphire had attended to that need, including a brush and some bands so she could tie her hair up. Sidra looked in the mirror as she put her hair into a high ponytail, noticing she had a kind of *glow* to her skin. "Strange," she said aloud as she moved her face around, checking from all angles, and seeing said glow everywhere.

Shaking her head, she went out to find Jaxon washing up their mugs. His back taut as he leaned over the sink. A sigh escaped her as she took in his magnificence, to which he looked over his shoulder, smirking.

"I'm almost done." He rinsed the mugs and put them down to dry, turning fully toward her. His eyes raked across her and she wished she'd put on a larger, baggier top. "You look delicious."

"I'm hungry." She changed the subject, striding to the door. "I hope there's bacon."

"There's always bacon." Jaxon grinned. "And it's cooked every which way imaginable so you're sure to find your favorite."

"Crispy." Sidra almost moaned at the thought of hot, crispy bacon.

"There's lots of crispy bacon. It happens to be my preference too."

"Sapphire left me a little note saying she'd take me to the stores to get some things that she couldn't—" Sidra felt herself blushing. "Stuff she couldn't guess on sizes."

"That's a pity." Jaxon reached for her hand, linking their fingers as they walked.

"What?" she asked confused.

"I suppose it means you'll be wearing a bra later and I've gotta say, I do like the way that t-shirt is hugging you right now."

Sidra gasped, tugging her hand free and crossing her arms in front of her. "I can't believe you just said that! I'm not wearing a bra because Sapphire didn't know my size and the one I had, well, it's only fit for the trash. Now I'm going to have to go back and put something else on."

She turned to return to the cabin, Jaxon grabbing her before she'd gone more than a couple of steps. "I'm sorry, lass, I didn't mean to upset you. You look fine and trust me, anyone else ogling your chest is going to end up on their ass very quickly."

"Hmm, I'm not sure you putting someone on their ass would help the situation." Sidra huffed. "And what the hell is a lass? Em used that too and I've never heard it before. Well, I don't think I have."

"Em spent time in Ireland when she was young and I grew up in Scotland. Lass is used frequently in both those places, it's used when talking to a young woman, or girl. Lassie is also used but I tend to use the shortened version, especially after that TV show came out about the collie."

"What's a collie?" Sidra frowned, more confused.

"It's a type of dog and there was a show made with one and it was called Lassie." Jaxon laughed. "I guess you're far too young to remember that. You were probably born after the war had already started and everything had gone to hell in a handbasket."

"Yes," Sidra nodded. "I've never watched a TV show or what are those other things called? Movers?"

"Movies." Jaxon snorted. "Movies not movers and I can remedy that for you. I've got a large collection of DVDs and we can watch one tonight if you want?"

Sidra stopped at the door of the mess hall, quirking her eyebrow. "Oh, I see what you did there. You totally distracted me, sneaky."

"Me? No, I'd never do something like that." Jaxon kept a straight face as he opened the door.

Sidra paused, trying to decide whether to go back and change. The smell of food wafting from the open door made up her mind. Stepping inside she inhaled deeply, her mouth watering as the scents assailed her. Looking around she saw it was quite busy, with lots of people dotted around. She grew nervous, never having been amongst so many before.

Jaxon's hand landed on her lower back, guiding her inside. "Come on, I can see Sapphire. We can sit with her."

"Okay." Sidra allowed him to lead her to a table off to the side where Sapphire sat, together with Bliss.

"Morning," Sapphire greeted them quietly, Bliss giving a small smile as she chewed.

"Morning." Sidra sat down. "Thank you for the clothes 'n stuff. I really appreciate it."

"You get my note?" Sapphire whispered.

"Yes, and if it's okay, I'd like to do that as soon as we've eaten."

"Sure." Sapphire nodded.

"Don't be too long, Sapphire." Jaxon's tone had lost any friendliness, all business as he spoke. "I want everyone at a meeting in half an hour. Try and not be late."

"Me too?" Bliss asked.

"Yes, you too." Jaxon pointed to the food laid out. "Sidra, why don't you go help yourself? I'll get mine in a moment."

Sidra didn't wait to be told twice, rushing to heap a plate with food. She took a glass of orange juice returning to the table as Bliss stood.

"All right, I've just got to go check on Lucas and Lara and then I'll be right over."

"Fine." Jaxon got up to get his own food. "Can you make sure everyone knows not to be late? I've already told them but I don't want anyone forgetting."

"You mean the twins, don't you?" Bliss smiled. "I'll let them know."

"Good." Jaxon's face hardened. "Tell them if they are late I'll make them spar with Skar and me for two hours."

Sapphire chuckled. "They definitely won't be late if you tell them that."

Bliss agreed, "I know. Nobody wants to spend time sparring with you and Skar."

"Why not?" Sidra asked as Bliss left.

"Because," Sapphire leaned over the table, "those two would kick their asses to hell and back. I've been on the receiving end of this *punishment* and I can tell you I hurt like a bitch for days."

"I see." Sidra munched on the crunchy bacon, barely holding back a groan of delight. "This is good with a capital G."

"Yes, I know." Sapphire finished off her own as Jaxon returned.

His plate piled high with a mound of food so high that Sidra's mouth fell open. "That's the normal for our guys," Sapphire enlightened her. "In fact, we all eat a lot. Our metabolism runs fast so we've got to keep ourselves stocked up on calories. It's wonderful to sit and eat a huge bar of candy and know it won't be going straight to my ass."

"I can't remember the last time I had candy, so I've not really had that problem." Sidra giggled. "I'd kill for a home-made chocolate cake. My mom used to bake it for me, though I have no idea where she used to get the chocolate. I suspect my dad had something to do with that part. But, I've not tasted anything sweet in forever."

"I'll see if I can grab you some later." Sapphire shook her head, sadly. "I think I'd curl up and die if I didn't have my treats and just wait until Em makes one of her meringue desserts. They are to die for."

"I look forward to them." Sidra drained her juice. "I'm finished, can we go to the stores now?"

Jaxon frowned. "If you hang on I'll go with you."

Sidra collected her plate and glass. "I'm a big girl, Jaxon, and I am *not* having you there while I pick out underwear. I'll be fine."

His eyes speared Sapphire. "Keep a watch out, she may be in danger and I need everyone on point."

"No worries." Sapphire followed Sidra to take her dirty dishes to the collection point, talking over her shoulder as she went. "I'll keep an eye out and I promise I won't keep her long."

"Fine," Jaxon sighed. "Bring her to the clubhouse when you're done at the stores. I want to keep her close."

"Will do." Sapphire waved as she and Sidra walked away. "And don't worry. We'll be fine."

They both heard him huff out, "Bloody better be."

CHAPTER
THIRTEEN

Jaxon paced back and forth in the Guild headquarters. The large cabin set at the very back of the camp; separate from all other buildings. It was made up of several rooms, one being a weapons store, a small office that Jaxon used for paperwork, and this, the main meeting room. Skar, Terigan, Allyssa and Bliss were already there and although nobody was late, yet, Jaxon was growing annoyed.

His satellite phone buzzed in his pocket. He snatched it out, answering curtly. "Jaxon."

He was only slightly surprised when he heard Cassius Allarde's voice on the other end. "Jaxon, Cassius Allarde here. I wonder if you have a moment to speak with Rose. News of your camp has broken and to say she is excited is putting it mildly."

Jaxon ran a hand through his hair, he'd been expecting this call and dreaded it. "Sure."

He heard Cassius hand over the phone, telling Rose to stay calm and not get her hopes up. "Jaxon, it's Rose here. We know about you helping Witches and, well, my mom was taken away when I was a child and I'm just wondering. Is she there?"

Jaxon sighed, not wanting to have this conversation at all, but especially not now. "Rose, I'm sorry, but I've already checked and there's nobody here with your mom's name. I'm truly sorry."

He heard her sigh, or was it a sob, he wasn't sure, but her tone was filled with sadness when she spoke again. "Ahh, I see, well thanks anyway. It was worth a shot."

"Yes, and I really am sorry that I couldn't give you better news." Jaxon felt bad for crushing the ray of hope he knew she'd had.

"That's okay, not your fault, Jaxon." Rose sighed. "Sorry to have bothered you."

"No bother at all, Rose."

"Thanks, gotta go, lots of stuff going on here."

He knew she was lying. She wanted the conversation to end because she was close to tears and he felt even worse. "Bye."

Ending the call, he returned his phone to his pocket, his mood even worse than it had been before.

Terigan sat on the edge of a desk, his leg swinging as he eyed Jaxon. "You're a little on edge, Master."

Jaxon turned, his title being the norm within these walls. "I am."

"No shit," Skar quipped.

Jaxon threw a filthy look Skar's way before continuing with his pacing. Allyssa shrugged and Bliss sat quietly behind one of the free desks. She rarely joined in these meetings as she didn't usually go out on missions, and she looked decidedly uncomfortable, nibbling on a fingernail. Allyssa patted Bliss' back as she made her way to Jaxon.

"Master, why don't you sit down?"

Jaxon spun around, scowling. "I'm fine."

He saw Allyssa was about to argue when the rest of the Dragons who were in the camp arrived. Several were still out on missions but Jaxon would mind-link them in on the conversation. "Good, you're all here so let's get started."

Sidra hovered at the door so he motioned her inside. "Just take a seat," he told her as she walked to the rear of the hall.

Once she was sitting down, Jaxon raised an arm to silence the conversations going on around him. Mainly it was the twins joking but they shut up when he took control. "I don't want any interruptions but there'll be time for some questions when I'm finished."

Everyone nodded so he plowed on. "First things first. The main threat to Witches is gone, so, Allyssa and Amos, I want you two to speak to everyone here and let them know that. I also want you to find out if they want to leave. They may well want to go in search of friends and family but I don't want people just leaving without us knowing about it. You can tell them we'll be organizing groups to leave, starting in two days. We'll give them safe passage to the main highway but after that they'll be on their own. Emphasize that it would be prudent for them to travel in groups, just in case, and we'll be organizing that in due time."

Amos nodded, Allyssa raising her hand. Jaxon nodded. "Master, if some don't want to wait, or go in groups, what should we say? We can't force them to do what we know is best."

"If anyone insists on leaving before, or alone, then reiterate what I've said but, as you say, we can't force them. Make sure they understand the need to let us know if they're leaving, so we can update our records though. I also think it would be a good idea if they could let us know the general area they're hoping to travel to. That way, when we start getting calls about this, then we can pass on that info."

"Calls?" Allyssa frowned.

"Yes," Jaxon sighed. "I'm expecting them to start soon. Once word gets out about our little haven here, then people will soon be wanting to find out if their loved ones are here. Many just vanished and although we rescued them, they left people at home. So, those individuals will want answers and to see if the person they thought was dead is actually alive and safe here."

"I hadn't thought of that," Allyssa said quietly. "I'll make sure we've got an up to date list to use for anyone that's trying to find someone."

"Thank you." Jaxon inclined his head. "Now, onto something else. I spoke with Zeeandra and she's advised that there could be a threat headed our way, coming after Sidra. So, first thing I'll let you know is that Sidra is my Destiny, and yes, our Goddess has confirmed this."

There was more than one gasp before voices started talking over one another. Mostly congratulations, but several curse words flew around as everyone's eyes turned to stare at Sidra whose face turned red as she exclaimed. "Wow. Way to make me feel uncomfortable."

Jaxon raised his voice, trying to calm the rabble. "Okay, enough, focus people."

It took a few moments before silence resumed. Jaxon focusing on his next words. "So, as you can guess I'm a little worried at the thought of something, or someone, coming for my Destiny."

"We'll keep her safe," Amos shouted out.

"That's what I'm planning." Jaxon glanced at Sidra, noticing her unhappy face. "Sidra doesn't particularly like what I'm about to do but we don't have a choice. Not only is she my Destiny, but she is unique and there's probably no others of her kind out there. So, that alone is reason to keep her free from harm. I want a Rota set up so that she has at least one of us looking out for her during the day. She's staying at my cabin so I'll have her under my care in the evenings and overnight."

Skar stepped forward. "I'll get that set up and let everyone know what day is theirs. We've got another couple coming back in from missions in the next few days so that gives us some wiggle room."

"Thank you," Jaxon said, gratefully. "A bit of good news for you all . . ."

Jaxon stopped abruptly when Zeeandra appeared next to him, dressed in a flowing red silk dress and a huge smile on her face. She nodded to him, "I hope I'm not interrupting but I'd like to speak to you all." She paused, looking at Jaxon who nodded. "As you are now aware, Sidra is Jaxon's Destiny, and I know you'll be as happy as I am for them both. However," she paused again, looking out over the assembled Warriors, "she is not the only Destiny out there. I am overjoyed to announce that there are others waiting for their Dragons to find them. Soon, there will be the joyous creation of new Dragon life and we can rejoice that others will find their Destiny, love, and peace. I wanted to pass on this information myself and I'll be travelling to every Guild camp to pass on the news. I sincerely wish that all of you find happiness, but alas, that may not be the case. Some of you still have a long time to wait, while others will find theirs soon. I want all of you to have patience and wait for fate to put your Destiny in your path."

Jaxon grinned widely. "Thank you, Zeeandra, I was just about to tell them. It is an honor to have you here within us."

"My pleasure." Zeeandra smiled. "I have to go now, but remember my Dragons, there are many more Destinies out there. All that remains is for them to be found."

Zeeandra turned, giving Jaxon a glorious smile, and disappeared as voices fought to be heard over one another, chaos erupting in the room. Jaxon raised his voice. "All right, calm down."

He waited, and when there was silence he carried on. "As our Goddess has confirmed that Sidra is not alone, and that there are other Destinies out there just waiting to be found, I can't tell you how relieved I was to hear that news. After all, we've had no live Dragon births in a very long time and I'd begun to despair on that front. To hear that there are other Destinies was like a great burden being lifted from my shoulders, and I hope you feel the same way. However, it doesn't mean we stop doing our jobs. We are still Warriors in the Guild so we will continue doing what we've always done and hope that some more find your own Destiny soon."

The mood in the room had lightened dramatically, smiles and grins abounded. Amos fist pumped and jumped around. "This is freaking awesome! Looks like I might not have to wait 'til I'm an old man to find mine."

"Excuse me?" Jaxon strode over, eyeballing the young man. "Was that a dig at me?"

Amos' grin disappeared, his face sobering as Jaxon glowered down at him. "Sorry, Master, no that was definitely not aimed at you."

"Better not have been." Jaxon crossed his arms. "Because if you think I'm an 'old man' we can go and do some training right now. One on one."

"No." Amos held his hands up, backing away. "You're absolutely not old. I was not referring to you in any way, shape, or form."

Jaxon snarled at Amos who turned tail and ran for the door. "I've gotta go, lots to do. Come on, Bliss."

Bliss scampered after him, shooting careful looks at Jaxon. She wasn't used to their meetings and appeared scared so he gave her a quick wink that brought a smile to her face. Terigan patted Jaxon's back. "Congratulations, my friend."

"Thanks." Jaxon held out a hand toward Sidra who blushed and shook her head. "Come here, I want to introduce you."

She slowly made her way forward, Terigan and Allyssa crowding around. Jaxon held her hand, pulling her to his side. "This is Sidra. Sidra, this is Terigan and Allyssa."

"So happy to meet you," Allyssa chuckled. "You'll have your hands full with this one."

Sidra shook the offered hand, only nodding, before Terigan stuck his hand out. "Lovely to meet you and I hear you're rather special. I hope we'll all get to see your beast soon."

"Yes," Sidra acknowledged quietly. "I'll be going to check on the baby I found and then I'll be transforming. I'm not used to going days without changing so my skin feels a little itchy weird."

"Itchy weird?" Jaxon asked, perplexed.

"Yeah," Sidra confirmed. "I get kind of a weird feeling if I leave it too long between shifts. Makes my skin feel as if it's itchy but not itchy, it's a weird kind of feeling."

"I see. Well, why don't I take you to see Em and the little one and then we can meet everyone in the landing field in half an hour?"

"Sounds good." Sidra nodded before tugging Jaxon's head down to whisper, "I'd like to go and change first." She held up a large bag as she poked him in the ribs. "You know, that thing we were talking about earlier."

Realization dawned on Jaxon and he fought to keep the smirk from his face. "You can do that at Em's."

"Okay." Sidra held out the bag. "Make yourself useful and take this, please. It's heavy."

Terigan roared with laughter as Jaxon took it from her. "What?" Jaxon scowled. "It *is* heavy." He shook it around. "What on earth have you got in here?"

"Boots mostly." Sidra shrugged. "I couldn't decide on which ones to get so I took a few."

Jaxon shook his head. "I'm pretty sure there's more than 'a few' in here. It weighs a ton."

"Aww, not strong enough, big guy?" Sidra joked, holding her hand out. "Give it back and I'll carry it."

"No." Jaxon grabbed the bag more firmly. "Let's get going because I'm pretty impatient about seeing you in your other form."

"Me too." Kat joined in, having been silent until then. "Sorry, I'm Kat and I was a little late as I was on duty."

"I didn't see you arrive," Jaxon admitted.

"Good." Kat smirked. "That was the plan."

"I knew you were working so it wasn't a problem," Jaxon huffed. "I'm not an ogre so you didn't need to sneak in."

"I heard what you'd said about what would happen to anyone being late." Kat stepped back. "I'm too darn tired to spar with you today."

"That was mostly aimed at the twins, and you know it," Jaxon retorted.

"I wasn't taking any chances." Kat smiled down at Sidra. "So, here I am and it's lovely to meet you and I definitely can't wait to see a freaking Unicorn."

"I just hope none of you are disappointed." Sidra nibbled her bottom lip for a brief moment. "Dad used to say I wasn't like other Unicorns but as I've never met, or even seen one, I have nothing to compare to."

"I'm sure you'll be magnificent," Kat encouraged.

"We'll see," Sidra replied, hesitantly.

"Let's go," Jaxon urged, eager to see his Destiny's beast surging to the surface. "Em is at home with the baby and she's expecting us."

"She is?" Sidra queried.

"Yes, we told her last night, remember?"

"Oh, yes," Sidra said.

"Then let's be on our way." Jaxon placed his free hand on her back, ushering her away.

"See you later," Kat called at the same time as Allyssa, causing both of them to laugh.

Sidra reached for Jaxon's hand. "I hope the baby is all right. I'd hate for anything to happen to her after everything she went through."

"She'll be fine," Jaxon stated firmly. "Em would have known if there was anything seriously wrong with the child and under her care the baby will thrive. I'm certain of it."

"I like your confidence."

"I've known Em a long time and I know she'll be looking after the girl better than anyone else." Jaxon swung the heavy pack. "How many pairs of boots have you got in here? It feels like a sack of coal."

"I'll admit there's a few." Sidra glanced up at him, her eyes wide with excitement. "I've always had a thing for shoes but never had the chance to have more than a couple of pairs since my parents died. So, I'm taking the opportunity to try some on and I'll keep a couple of pairs I like. If that's okay? Sapphire said it was, but if it's not, then just say it and I'll take them back."

"Of course it's all right." Jaxon waved the bag again. "If you want we can go back later and get you some more and if there's anything you want then just let me know. If we don't have it in the store, then I'll go and find it for you. I mean it, Sidra, anything at all."

"Really?" She looked up at him, her eyes twinkling. "Because I love to read and I lost my last book ages ago."

"You enjoy reading?" Jaxon chuckled. "So do I. We've got quite the library here. It's in a side room at the mess hall. I'll show you it later. Also, Bliss is absolutely hooked on reading and she has quite a collection of e-readers already loaded with books. I'll ask her if you can borrow one."

"E-reader? What's that?"

"It's an electronic device that has books preloaded on them. They were all the rage before the war. I'm afraid you don't have a choice of what's on them, it's whatever the previous owner had already bought and downloaded and they need to be recharged every now and then, but that's not a problem here."

"That sounds amazing. I've not come across one of those. I only had what dad used to bring me, he called them 'the classics' but after they died and I had to move on I would keep an eye out for any books I could find. I've read some really fabulous stories, as well as some that had me laughing at how funny they were."

Jaxon ran his thumb over her hand, enjoying the feel of her skin. "You won't lack for reading material here, but again, I can source them from some of the larger libraries in the big cities."

"I can't wait to curl up and read." Sidra smirked. "Only thing that would make it even better would be if I had some chocolate and wine to go along with the book."

"Done." Jaxon smirked back at her.

"Oh my, I've died and gone to heaven." Sidra's free hand flew to her heart, patting it gently. "I'm all aflutter with excitement."

"I am too, but mine is because I'm desperate to see your beast."

"Soon," Sidra replied. "Just need to check on the baby first."

"I know, but doesn't stop me from being wound up just thinking about it." Jaxon stopped, gazing down into her upturned face. "I can't begin to put into words how I feel. I'm not good with that stuff, Sidra, but I want you to know that I'll always look after you, keep you safe, and love you 'til my dying breath."

He saw her grey eyes shining, unshed tears pooling until a drop broke free, running down the side of her face. She quickly swiped it away, taking a deep breath in. "I'm not sure what to say, other than, I think you're a whole lot better with 'that stuff' than you believe."

"You don't have to say anything right now." Jaxon leaned down, pressing a soft kiss on her lips. "I know this is all strange for you. The whole Destiny thing, and I'll try and take things slow so we can get to know each other better. But, my beautiful lass, I need you to know how deep my feelings for you are. As far as I'm concerned, you are the most important person alive, and I'll worship the ground you walk on from here on out."

Sidra's fingers grabbed his leather jacket, holding on tight. "Yes, it is strange, but what's stranger is that with every passing hour my feelings for you seem to be growing stronger. I'm not quite at the stage you are but, Jax, I'm getting there."

"That's because we are near one another." Jaxon leaned down farther, his forehead touching hers so he could look into her gorgeous eyes. "When fated Destinies are near then their love grows until there is no doubt in either of them. That's one of the reasons I'm not letting you go anywhere, my beautiful lass. I want you beside me at least until we've taken our vows."

"This is all a bit scary, for me anyway." Sidra's hand moved to caress the side of his face. "In a good way though."

"You'll be taken care of here, baby, I promise."

"Thank you." Sidra smiled. "It's been a long time since I felt as if I belonged anywhere, or felt safe, even remotely. The more I think about this place, the more I feel 'at home', ya know?"

"Yes." Jaxon smile mirrored hers. "I looked for almost ten months for a place to set up but as soon as I found this spot I knew it was going to be the right place. It has a special energy and atmosphere that seems to help people settle."

"I agree, it is a very special spot and I'm looking forward to seeing more of it."

"I can show you later, for now, why don't we go check on that wee girl?"

"Sounds like a plan." Sidra stepped back, Jaxon taking her hand and leading her inside Em's cabin.

CHAPTER FOURTEEN

Sidra's face beamed as they left Em's. Her happiness at seeing the happy, clean, and well fed baby, and Em's obvious love for the child, had been a great relief. Jaxon had stayed silent, sitting with a coffee and cookies as Sidra fired question after question at Em.

What surprised Jaxon was that Em allowed her to. Normally the old woman would've put anyone talking to her like that firmly in their place. But the old woman had answered each question with a smile, even managing to send a quick wink in Jaxon's direction. It was obvious Em was placating Sidra and being extremely polite when her usual reply would've been scathing and curt.

He'd patted Em's shoulder as they left, whispering a quick, "Thank you." Sidra appeared far more relaxed now that she knew the child was going to be well looked after. Her spirit happier and even playful as they made their way to the landing field, after dropping off the pack full of boots at their cabin.

"She's really nice, isn't she?" Sidra grinned as they walked hand in hand.

"Who? Em?" Jaxon paused to weigh up his next words. "I suppose she is, but I have to say she was being especially nice today. I don't want you to get the wrong impression of her, but usually she is not quite so civil toward someone who questions her actions, like you just did."

"You know what? I think it's because she knew I would've taken the child back if I hadn't been happy."

Jaxon stopped, shocked. "What? What would you have done with her?"

"The baby?" Sidra asked and when he nodded, she shrugged. "I would have looked after her until I could find a suitable place for her. But, and this is what I'm very happy about, Em has that all under control and her love for children is clear for even a blind man to see."

"I like the kids in the camp, and I've even held a babe or two in my time. I love that unique baby smell, it's like nothing else on earth." Jaxon started toward the field again, shuddering as he went. "But I know they're a lot of work and, jeez, they cry an awful lot and have you up a dozen times through the night. And don't even get me started on what comes out of them. Not just one end, both! But I guess that comes with the package of being a parent."

Sidra laughed, tugging on his hand. "What is it about babies that makes grown men so damn weak? You're all the same, especially about the diaper changing."

"It's disgusting." Jaxon made a face showing his revulsion.

"So you don't want kids?" Sidra sneaked a look at him.

"I didn't say that." Jaxon shook his head. "Truth is I've always wondered what it'd be like to hold my own child in my arms. I'm just aware how much work they are, and come on, who likes changing a dirty diaper?" He shuddered dramatically. "I've been told it's different when it's your own so I guess I'll just have to wait and see on that front."

"I just don't get it—" Sidra chuckled. "How something so small can turn men into gibbering idiots and have them running for the hills. I'm pretty sure you've seen far more sickening sights in battle."

"Yeah, I suppose, but it still gives me the collywobbles." Jaxon shuddered for effect.

"Collywobbles? What the hell is that?"

Jaxon chuckled. "A word from my Scottish heritage. It's kinda hard to explain though but I'll try. You know that feeling when you're very scared and your stomach is full of butterflies? It's a little like that."

"Ah, I see." Sidra stopped dead. "Shit."

Jaxon's head spun around, looking for a threat. "What's wrong?"

She pointed to the field, and the throng of people that had gathered. "Jaxon, I think the whole camp's turned up."

"I think you're right." Jaxon could barely see the field for the people in front of them.

"I can't do this. Not with that many people around."

Jaxon pulled her to his side, his arm circling her waist. "I think you've got the collywobbles."

"Ya think?" she snapped up at him.

"It'll be okay, honey, they're all anxious to see your Unicorn. You can't blame them really. Almost everyone alive thinks they don't exist so the chance to see one is something they'll not want to miss."

"It's too many."

Jaxon felt her shiver, tightening his grip on her. "What if I come with you and I transform too. Once we've both morphed we can just up and fly away."

"I'm not sure, Jax, can't we just leave?"

"Look at the people who've come out to see you, Sid, they're all waiting and it wouldn't be nice to leave them there."

"I can *see* the people, I'm not blind," Sidra snapped.

"You're nervous." Jaxon turned her into his body, his free hand lifting to stroke her face. "I can feel it and it's understandable, but nobody here will hurt you. They just want to see your Unicorn and I have to say, I'm as anxious as they are. Take a breath, honey, a nice deep breath. Yes, that's it. Now hold it for a count of three and let it out slowly, yup that's right, and again. Good, you're going to be fine. Trust me."

"You'll stay with me?" she whispered, her eyes locked with his.

"I will," he confirmed. "I'll hold your hand right up until you tell me to let go for your transformation. All right?"

"I suppose." Her hand reached up to her face, taking hold of his. "Don't leave me."

"I promise." Jaxon leaned down, kissing her softly, his lips covering hers in a brief caress.

Sidra was the one to break the kiss, pulling back to shake her head at him. "Distraction tactics, huh?"

"You can call it what you want. I just wanted to feel your luscious lips beneath mine." He winked at her, stepping back quickly as she moved to punch his arm. "Hey, no abuse is allowed here. We have very strict rules about that kind of thing."

"Abuse? Yeah, right. You probably wouldn't even feel it." Sidra's tone dripped with sarcasm.

"So, shall we do this?"

"I guess so." Sidra held her hand out and he linked his fingers with hers. "Probably best to get it over and done with or folks will always be hanging around to see if they can catch me morphing."

"You're probably right." Jaxon squeezed her hand. "All right, let's go and do this."

Sidra held her head high, looking straight ahead, as he led her towards the crowd. He held a hand up, waving it around as he shouted. "Clear a path, now."

Miraculously, the way in front of them opened up enough for them to walk straight through and onto the field. "We'll need to go far enough in to give my Dragon the room to manifest."

"Okay," Sidra murmured, chewing her bottom lip.

"A little further." They walked on and then he stopped. "This is far enough. Remember, I'll hold on until you decide to change and then just let me know. Okay?"

"Sure." Sidra glanced back at the people who were now spreading out around the field. "That's a lot of people."

"Yes, it is but not one of them has any ill will toward you. They're just excited and curious, that's all."

Sidra nodded. "I know. I suppose we should do this. So, I'm going to change and then you change too and we can go for a fly around."

"Yes, I can't wait to show you the mountain range. It's magnificent."

"Sounds good. Okay, Jax, you can let me go."

Jaxon released her hand and stepped back, giving her plenty of room. His eyes glued to her as he waited on her transformation. He didn't have long to wait, his rate of breathing increased as a silver shimmer encompassed Sidra. It was so bright that his hand flew up to cover his eyes, and then he saw the moment his beautiful woman disappeared. The bright light decreased centimeter by centimeter to reveal the most breathtaking sight he'd ever seen.

The Unicorn that was exposed quite simply took his breath away. It was the size of a large horse and had four legs and a tail, but that's where the similarities ended. The beast shone radiantly, its tail swishing back and forth looked like a trail of spun silver. Its mane was pure white and fell around the beast's neck in great waves and the horn that stood proud between its eyes glistened in the daylight.

If that wasn't enough, and he could clearly hear the gasps and exclamations from the people around them, a pair of luminous wings opened either side of the beast. Jaxon gasped, his eyes taking in every inch of Sidra's beast.

"By the Goddess, you are the most beautiful creature I've ever laid eyes on."

She replied by stamping one of her front hooves against the ground, moving away a little as her wings unfurled even further. They were large but looked so flimsy that Jaxon worried at their capability to lift her into the air.

"I guess I'll find out soon enough." He chuckled, putting more distance between them before transforming himself.

His Dragon appeared quickly, letting out a roar as its wings beat to launch it skyward. He kept his eyes on the Unicorn, watching as its own wings gracefully flapped and lifted the beast into the air. He hovered for a moment, allowing it to catch up, and then he took off toward the mountains. His heart full of awe and wonder as the Unicorn sped up, flying side by side with his Dragon toward the range.

Jaxon soared higher, Sidra keeping pace as they left the camp behind. Putting on a burst of speed, he flew up and over the Unicorn, before retaking his place at her side. To say he was surprised that it appeared capable of great speed was an understatement. Its wings looking far too fragile to keep her in the sky, far less the pace they were maintaining.

He could only hazard a guess that magic played a part in its capabilities. Without thinking, he used his mind-link. *"You are miraculous and astonishingly beautiful."*

"Why thank you, kind sir."

Her reply sounded clear in his mind, his beast's head swiveling to stare at her. Had he imagined that? *"Sidra, you can hear me?"*

"Yes." She sounded surprised. *"How is that possible?"*

"No idea." Jaxon let out a bellow of joy. *"But it may be because you are my Destiny and we are fated to be as one. Other than that, I have no clue as I've only ever been able to communicate with Zeeandra and my fellow Warriors."*

"This is how you speak to one another?"

"Yes, but we can only mind-link properly with blood-bound Guild Warriors and Bliss. I can't talk to just any Dragon although we can get a sense of moods from non-Guild members. This is the first time I've spoken to anyone other than my Warriors."

"Well, it's kinda cool, dontcha think?"

"Yes." Jaxon swooped up and over the Unicorn again. *"It's amazing. I wonder if we'll be able to do it when we transform back. I hope so."*

"Hmm, Jax, I know we're talking but you can't read my mind or anything creepy like that. Can you?"

"No. I assure you I'm not inside your head, my stunning and amazing Unicorn."

"That's good, 'cause I definitely don't want anyone, not even you, in my brain. A girl's gotta have some secrets."

"I wouldn't like it either," Jaxon admitted. "I sometimes have information from Zeeandra that is strictly private and confidential. So, if we were inside each other's head then I'd need to let her know."

"Of course."

"So, what do you think of the mountains? Aren't they stunning?"

"Yes, they are. I can see the practicality of them, protecting the camp, but I also see great beauty and solitude. There's plenty of places to land and have time to yourself, if you're in the mood for that."

"Exactly." Jaxon had known she would get what he loved about the range. "I frequently come here to chill and get away from things. It always calms me and then there's the cavern with our healing waters that is beyond words. I can't describe it adequately, but I'll show it to you soon."

"Okay. Hmm, Jax, do you think the crowd will be gone by now? Is it safe to return?"

"Yes, I'd think so, why?"

"Don't tease me but I really want to go and try on the boots I got from the store."

Jaxon's beast shook as he laughed, although it came out more like snorts and bellows. "Okay, lass, we'll go back now."

"Thank you."

Sidra's Unicorn swept around, heading back to camp. Again, Jaxon was amazed at the speed with which she could fly as he beat his own wings furiously in a bid to catch her. He did, but only just before they landed with her Unicorn curling her wings into the sides and disappearing completely from view.

"How do you do that?"

"Do what?"

"There's no trace of your wings, honey."

"Oh that, I dunno, they just go when I don't need them. It's always been like that but I don't know the ins and outs of it. I've not exactly had anyone I could ask about anything Unicorn related, ya know?"

"I guess not." Jaxon waited, wanting to witness her transformation before morphing himself. He didn't want to miss a second of seeing her in her beast form or of her changing back to human.

Jaxon watched intently as her form shimmered for a second before the light around her intensified, forcing him to squint as he tried to witness the very moment she changed. The glare intensified, blinding him for a split-second and when his vision cleared Sidra stood before him, dressed as she had been before.

"Damn it!" he exclaimed, changing quickly and walking over to her.

"What?" she asked perplexed.

"What what?"

"You said 'damn it' and didn't sound too happy. What's wrong?"

"You heard that?"

"Yes," she said, staring at him worriedly.

"Sid, I was still in beast form. How did you hear that?"

Sidra looked puzzled. "I'm not sure but I sure as heck heard it and you've still not told me what upset you."

Jaxon picked her up, twirling her around with glee. "Hold on a second." He placed her back down, his hands on either side of her face, speaking to her using his mind-link. *"Darling, can you hear me?"*

Her eyes widened then she smiled, answering, *"Loud and clear."*

"That's amazing." Jaxon laughed happily. "I'm overjoyed that we have that link, honey. It means if you are ever fearful, in danger, or just want to talk, then I'll always be there for you."

"Can I use it if I'm lying in bed and want you to bring me a snack? Or if I fancy some deer and I want you to go find me one? Or is that an abuse of the power?"

Her eyes twinkled up at him, a cheeky smirk on her face. Jaxon picked her up again, this time bringing her lips to his. *"You can do all that and more. Anytime, for anything, my sweet lass."*

"Wow, you've created a monster. I'll be using this all the time! Just think, I can talk to you when we're surrounded by people and they won't have a clue."

"Exactly." Jaxon motioned with his head as Sapphire and Bliss joined them.

"That was out of this world," Bliss sighed. "Your Unicorn is, well, I have no words. It was astonishing to see it."

"She's a bit excited." Sidra smiled at Bliss.

"Thank you. Not many people have seen it."

Jaxon stifled a laugh, barely.

Sapphire was nodding furiously. "A freaking Unicorn. To find out they exist is thrilling enough, but to see one is outta this world. And here I thought Dragons were the most amazing creatures ever. Damn, girl, you rock."

Jaxon saw Sidra blush and took the opportunity to add to it. *"I can't wait until we're alone. I want to kiss you until you can't breathe and have you calling my name so loud the entire camp hears you."*

Sidra's face burned scarlet, her head spun around and she opened her mouth to speak then closed it. Sapphire was quick off the mark, eyeing Jaxon curiously. "What's going on?"

"Nothing," Sidra gasped.

Jaxon remained silent and then Sapphire seemed to figure it out. "You can't, can you?"

"What?" he asked innocently.

"Don't be coy, boss, can you and Sidra mind-link?"

Sidra started to leave. "Sorry, but I need to go and sort out my belongings."

Jaxon shrugged. "Gotta go."

Sapphire tried to stop him. "Wait, Jax, tell me, can you two talk through your link? Come on! I've gotta know."

"No, Sapphire, you don't have to know." Jaxon carried on after Sidra, leaving Bliss looking confused and Sapphire angry.

"But I do!" Sapphire shouted. "Come on, boss, tell me. It's a security issue."

Jaxon stopped, whirling back around. "Just what the hell do you mean by that?"

Sapphire jogged over, closely followed by Bliss. "Master, what I mean is that Sidra may be at risk, and if you and she can communicate via the mind-link then, if the need arises, we can use that to our advantage in any type of dangerous situation. The rest of us need to be aware of that fact. Don't we?"

Jaxon pondered for a moment. "I'll take your concerns on board and will let you know my decision tomorrow."

"What decision?" Bliss asked, looking totally lost.

"Whether to answer Sapphire's question. Or not." Jaxon about turned and went after Sidra who was now entering camp.

His heart sped up as he thought on the way he wished to spend the evening with his Destiny. If she allowed, then he'd make darn sure he showed her exactly how much she meant to him and the pleasure he could give.

CHAPTER

FIFTEEN

He screamed as realization dawned. He'd lost the damn Unicorn, again. "Imbeciles, total fucking imbeciles."

He turned to face the cowering Demon before him. "Tell me again how she got away this time? I mean, she was burdened down with a repulsive child, and she couldn't just fly away. With a horde of Demons on her tail and a babe in her arms, she *still* managed to escape. How the fuck is that even possible?"

The slithering Snake Demon lowered her head, trembling before him. "I'm sorry. I don't know how they managed to allow her escape because all of them were killed. When I arrived only one was still alive, but he was almost burnt to a cinder and died immediately after I found him. He didn't have a chance to say anything to me, Draven, Sir."

"Burnt? Hmm, that puts a different light on things, doesn't it, Sarff?"

Draven turned around, flicking through pages of his beloved Grimoire. "I suspect the tales of

Dragons are true and that they were the ones to aid in her escape."

"That would certainly explain the devastation I came across." Sarff raised her head. "The area was decimated, fierce fire had struck in several places, and each Demon had been obliterated. I only found parts of them scattered around the clearing."

"Yes, definitely Dragons. Now, Sarff, how do you propose we tackle this? Suggestions?" Draven looked pointedly at her. "You *are* my right-hand girl. So, tell me, what should we do?"

"We need to locate her first and see if it will be possible to sneak her away from her protectors. It will be a difficult task, but with the right planning, it should be achievable. I'm certain of it."

"Good, good, my thoughts exactly." Draven clapped his hands, causing her to jump. "Can you send out some scouts to garner her whereabouts and we can take things from there? Hopefully, if we keep an eye on her we will be able to whisk her away."

"Yes, Sir, I'll do that now." Sarff bowed her head, looking up at him through her dark lashes. "It may take some time though, before they get the information."

"I'm aware of that." Draven stepped down from his altar and ran a hand through her black hair. "I'm sure you can keep me entertained while we wait."

"Of course." Sarff leaned her head into his touch. "It would be my honor."

"Fine, go and send your spies and then make yourself presentable in my chamber. I'll join you soon."

"Shall I wear the black lace?" She asked, her voice a soft murmur of hope.

Draven tapped his chin, turning away toward his beloved book. "No, I think the red one and set out some of my toys. I think you deserve some punishment for allowing this bitch to escape us once again."

"If that's your wish."

"It is." Draven turned, scowling down at her. "Now go before I decide a harsher price should be paid."

Sarff bowed low, backing out of the cavernous room.

"Fuck!" Draven picked up a cup, throwing it violently across the room to crash on the floor. "I'll get my hands on you, bitch. If it's the last thing I do, I'll get you and then my plans will come to fruition and nobody will be more powerful than me. *Nobody!*"

His voice reverberated around the room, knowing his dream, his goal, his desire, was almost within his grasp.

Sidra stretched her arms up, her body tired but sated. Jaxon had shown her exactly how he felt, lavishing her body with his touch, kisses, and love. Her muscles ached after the workout he'd given her, a smile on her face as she thought on the moment he'd gently pushed inside her.

She'd grabbed his hair roughly, tugging at his lips and grinning up at him. "I won't break, Jax. No need to be so gentle."

His worried frown had been adorable as he murmured, "I don't want to hurt you."

"You won't, but I might hurt you if you treat me like fine china." She'd darted forward, nipping his bottom lip, and the groan that escaped him caused her desire to rocket. "If you don't take me hard, right now, I'm going to make you pay, big guy."

"Really?" he asked playfully.

"Yes, really." Sidra lay back down, smiling up at him. "In fact, I think I may have to make you beg if you don't do as you're told."

"Beg?" he scoffed. "I've never begged in my life, darling."

"There's a first time for everything," she'd retorted, pushing her hips up toward him.

"You sure?" he'd asked, pulling out of her so that only the tip of him remained inside.

"Damn straight I am." She gasped as he thrust into her. "Now that's more like it."

He laughed, for a moment, before his arousal took over and they'd spent quite some time getting to know one another's bodies. She found out how much he loved it when she ran her lips down his cock, teasing him mercilessly by flicking her tongue over his tip, but not quite taking him inside her mouth.

She'd moaned with utter abandon when he'd flipped her over, taking her from behind and angling her in such a way that he hit something inside her that caused her to see stars. Yes, he definitely knew how to make a woman happy, and she was certain that she'd done the same for him.

His bedroom had surprised her, expecting it to be drab and utilitarian, and instead it was bright and cheerful. The colors he'd used were yellows and greens, and looked as if nature had been brought inside. The bed itself was huge, apparently hand-made by Jaxon and Skar. It was impressive and beautiful, with carvings along the headboard that had the most intricate of details on the beasts of the world. Wolves, bears, eagles, and even a Dragon were sculpted into the wood. It looked as if it would have taken a heck of a long time to do, but he'd assured her that it had taken only a week.

There was a massive walk-in closet with one side taken up by weapons of every shape and size. He'd shrugged when she raised her eyebrow pointedly but agreed he would make room for her things. "Too right you will." She'd shaken her head, laughing. "Boys and their toys."

His attached bath was almost as large as her bedroom had been, with an immense shower that took up about a third of the area. Jaxon had grinned saying he knew plenty of ways they could make use of it, and she didn't doubt him for one second.

He lay next to her, lightly snoring, with her body snuggled within his embrace. She felt happy, of course, but something else too, something more. She couldn't quite put her finger on it, but the nearest she could get was content.

She'd never felt that way before, not even before her parents had been killed and her life had gone to hell in a handbasket. Nope, she'd always felt *uneasy* growing up, as if she knew there were things to come that would shatter her world.

That happened when she saw her father being killed. Something she'd thought impossible. He was a freaking Angel. He shouldn't have been taken from her. But he had, and in the most brutal of fashions. She swore her heart had been ripped out that day and then realized only half had gone when her mother was also killed.

Since then she'd just been trying to survive and she'd been doing not too bad a job of it until she'd found the baby in the forest. She knew the second she picked the child up that together, they stood no chance against the Demons, and they'd probably die but she couldn't leave it. Nobody could, right?

Jaxon's arms tightened around her, his mouth whispering into her ear. "Are you okay, lass? I sense turmoil inside you."

"I'm fine." She turned to gaze up at him. "I was just thinking how my life was before."

"I'm sorry you lost your parents." He nuzzled her neck. "But I promise that you're safe here."

"I know that and thanks." She ran a finger down the side of his face. "I realized earlier that I feel safe here, content is more apt. I know this is all weird Dragon shit, but this Destiny thing is real. I feel it, Jax, deep inside."

"I'm glad you're recognizing that, it makes things a lot easier." Jaxon kissed her gently. "We have to organize our ceremony, which is more for others than for us. By the time a couple get to that stage they're usually already linked."

"Are we linked?" she asked.

"I would say so, after all, we can mind-link, and I'm absolutely certain of my love and devotion to you."

"I love you too." Sidra said the words properly for the first time, tears filling her eyes.

"Hey, my sweet lass, why are you crying?"

"I've been alone for so long and now here I am, with you and I guess it's a little overwhelming."

"You'll never be alone again, Sidra. That's a promise I make with my oath as Master of the Guild. It's one I will never break, ever."

"You can't say that." Sidra smiled sadly. "My father was an Angel, Jaxon, and he was taken from me, as was my mom. So, although I know what you mean I also know that nothing is certain in this apocalyptic world we now live in."

"Hey." Jaxon smirked. "I'm a Dragon, much tougher to put down than a mere Angel."

Sidra snorted. "Yeah, you keep telling yourself that, buster."

"As far as the rest of the world goes, it's being dealt with." Jaxon lifted her chin with a finger. "Cassius Allarde has an army behind him and he's a good man, an honorable man, even if he is a darn Vampire. He's working hard to bring order to the chaos that now roams the earth and it may take some time, but I don't doubt he can do it."

"If you have faith in him then I guess I should too, but it's hard, especially when there's this supposed threat coming for me." Frowning up at him, she tried to put her fears into words. "I'm not scared for me. Well, yes, I am, of course I am, but I don't want anyone else being hurt just because I'm here. That, by the way, takes in you and your Dragons. I'd hate for any of them to be injured, or worse."

"Sidra, you need to understand about us and the Guild." Jaxon lay on his back, pulling her so she was on his chest. "We're bound by an oath to protect those in need. It doesn't matter if they are human, or any kind of supernatural being, if someone needs our help then we give it. Freely and with pleasure. It is who we are and we live by this code every single day. We've lost Dragons, we've had Dragons being badly wounded, but we would never shirk our responsibility. If we did, even once, then we would not be worthy of being a Guild Warrior."

"You lot are like Knights in Shining Armor. I wish there were more of you around."

"There are." Jaxon smiled. "We have Dragons in Europe, and in Asia, Africa, and just about every continent out there. Admittedly, some of the branches are small and only have a few members, but now that the Goddess has confirmed that there are more Destinies out there then it's only a matter of time until our numbers increase."

"So, am I getting this right? Every Dragon is a Guild member?"

"No, honey." Jaxon shook his head. "It takes years of training to be admitted to the Guild and there are some Dragons who are just not interested in joining. We even have a few 'bad apples' but we tend to keep a close eye on those and if they step out of line we round them up and take them to Zeeandra for punishment."

"Really? What does she do?"

"She is really into rehabilitation but if that doesn't work and the crime is serious, then she'll execute them."

"Damn," Sidra gasped. "I can see that there's more to your species than I first thought."

"Much more." He smirked. "There's more of us out there than you'd realize but they tend to keep to themselves and it's mainly couples who found their Destiny long ago. Some of the younger males are also around on their own. Mainly 'sowing their wild oats' so to speak, but most of them find their way to us in the end."

"Like Amos?" she giggled. "I'll bet he was wild when he was younger."

"Actually, no." Jaxon corrected her misconception. "He's all talk and he and Aric have been training for more than ten years to join us."

"Ten years?" she gasped.

"Yes." Jaxon nodded. "The training is long, harsh and takes a hell of a lot of commitment. It's not for the faint of heart and sometimes, though rarely, we have to deny admission."

"What happens to those?"

"Sometimes they go away for a few years and come back when they're more focused, but usually it's because they're one of the 'bad apples' I was telling you about. That means we keep tabs on them and if need be, we take them to Zeeandra if they're caught doing wrong. Even Dragons not within the Guild are held to our Goddess' rules and first and foremost is that we do not harm humans."

"Ever?" Sidra questioned. "What if the human is doing wrong? Say you caught one, or a group, killing people or raping a child, what would you do then?"

"That is a clear cut case for us." Jaxon's face grew serious. "They would be dealt with harshly, usually ending with their death. Our

Goddess has a code of conduct and one of the main ones is 'do no harm to others.'"

"I see." Sidra nodded. "Good. I'm glad because let's be honest, there's not a hell of a lot else that can be done with people like that. It's better that they are removed from society so they can't harm anyone else."

Jaxon laughed. "Many years ago, before the war, there were places called prisons. The humans would give wrongdoers a trial and if convicted they would be sent to prison, sometimes for the rest of their lives. These prisons were overrun and held hundreds of thousands of people. That's how they used to deal with that type of scum."

"Wasn't that a drain on resources? I presume they had to have staff to look after these prisons so who paid for that?"

"My point exactly," Jaxon huffed.

"Nuts." Sidra shook her head, before running a hand up Jaxon's muscled torso. "Enough about that. I'd like to hear about your Scots heritage. I've only ever met one other person that was from there but I found it hard to understand him. His accent was atrociously bad and I used to just nod and pretend I knew what he was saying."

Jaxon chuckled, laying his own dormant accent on thick. "Aye, I ken whit ye mean."

Sidra prodded him. "That's it! What the heck does ken mean?"

"Roughly translated that's, yes, I know what you mean." Jaxon thought back through the centuries to the hard life he'd lived in Scotland. "It's centuries since I lived there, though I've been back to visit now and again. It was a hard life back then as it's a harsh environment without modern housing and stuff. But I loved my time in Scotland, it's one of the most beautiful places on earth. When the heather is blossoming all across the Highlands, it's a sight to see and I do miss it sometimes."

"Maybe you'll return again soon." Sidra placed her head on his chest, her breaths tickling his skin.

Jaxon sighed. "Not anytime soon. We've got far too much work to do here."

"I don't wanna move but I'm afraid I have to." Sidra tried to wiggle out from Jaxon's grip.

"Why?"

"I'm freaking starving." Sidra's stomach backed her up by rumbling loudly. "Hear that? Proof positive."

"I guess I should take better care of you." Jaxon released her, getting out his side of the bed. "Do you want to eat here or in the hall?"

"In the hall if that's okay?" Sidra started to pull on her clothes. "I might get a glimpse of

Lucky if Em's there. Hmm, I wonder if she'll change her name. It's not exactly a good name for a little girl."

Jaxon disagreed. "I think it fits perfectly. She was damn lucky you found her."

"It just sounds more like something you'd call a pet." Sidra frowned. "I think she should be called Bella because she's so damn cute."

"Bella's good too but I still prefer Lucky," Jaxon said as they left the bedroom.

"I'll see what Em thinks," Sidra said as they left the cabin, making their way to the mess hall.

They'd barely made it half way when Jaxon stopped, his body tensing and his head cocking to the side. "What's wrong?"

"Shh." He held up a hand, a look of concentration on his face.

Sidra watched and waited, fear lapping at her insides.

CHAPTER  SIXTEEN

Jaxon's heart almost stopped when Skar contacted him through their link. *"Boss, we got trouble."*

He could hear the concern in Skar's voice, and replied immediately. *"What's up, Skar?"*

"Demons!" Skar shouted. *"More than one, on the mountains. Looks like some kind of scouting party."*

"Who's available?" Jaxon barked back.

"I've got Amos and Aric with me and Kat and Sapphy are on their way. Zane is on guard duty but I've told him to stay put in case any more appear."

"How did they get there without Zane seeing them?" Jaxon's anger grew at the thought of Demons being so close to camp.

"They materialized, Jax, he couldn't have done anything any sooner than he did. As soon as he sensed them he alerted us."

"He didn't fucking alert me!" Jaxon retorted angrily.

"That's because we told him not to. Jax, you and Sidra were having some alone time and I told him to contact me, Kat or Sapphire, if there were any

problems. Don't take it out on the boy because you're angry."

"Fine," Jaxon huffed, pulling Sidra with him towards the food hall. *"I'll get Sidra into the mess and then I'll join you. I want them taken alive, if possible, so we can find out who's behind this."*

"All right." Skar disconnected and Jaxon looked down into Sidra's white face.

"It's okay, lass, Skar and the others have it covered, but I need to leave you for a little while. I won't be long."

Sidra nodded. "Is it because of me? Whatever's happening, is it because I'm here?"

"I honestly don't know yet, honey." Jaxon pushed the door open, ushering her inside. He spied Bliss and Terigan, grabbing Sidra's hand he led her over to them. "We've got a bit of a situation. Can you two look after Sidra until I get back?"

Terigan pushed his seat back, standing quickly. "I'll come with you."

Jaxon shook his head. "No, I'd rather leave Sidra with you, my friend. I need to know she's safe."

"What's going on?" Bliss asked, wide eyed and looking more than a little scared.

"I don't have time to talk now." Jaxon pulled Sidra close, kissing her quickly. "I won't be long. Have something to eat and I'll see you soon."

"Yeah, right. As if I'll be able to eat now," Sidra groaned as he turned to leave.

"Try, for me. This is just something I need to go and check out. I won't be long."

Sidra shook her head. "All right, try and get back soon, please."

"I will, lass." Jaxon gave her a forced smile and walked away.

He heard Terigan's calm voice as he rushed away. "It'll be fine. Probably one of the youngsters saw a bear and think we're under attack when really it's just looking for somewhere nice to hunker down."

Terigan smiled at her, and added. "Animals can tell when rain is on the way and so can Dragons, and I'm telling you, rain is just around the corner."

"Really?" Sidra frowned. "I'm not entirely sure I believe a word of that."

"Oh it's true." Bliss nodded. "We can predict the weather and rain is certainly coming. Though, to be honest, I would've said we had a few days until it got here. The bear, if there is a bear, is probably just looking for somewhere dry."

"Hmm." Sidra looked over to the door Jaxon had disappeared through. "If it's just a bear then why is he running out of here as if his pants are on fire?"

Bliss sniggered, her hand covering her mouth as Terigan sat back down. "Because he's just found you and even a stray bear will have him jumpy. He wants to make sure you, and everyone else here, is safe, so he'll pop over and check things out for himself."

Em appeared at Sidra's side, holding the baby. "I thought you might want to see Lucky. She's coming along a treat and I've got three couples who've approached me about adopting her."

Sidra's attention was drawn to the gurgling baby. "She's adorable." She held her arms out. "Can I have a cuddle?"

"Of course." Em handed her over.

"She looks so much better." Sidra cooed down at the smiling child. "She's got color in her cheeks and she sure as heck smells a lot better."

Em laughed. "Indeed. She was a tad ripe when she arrived."

"I'd run out of supplies for her and to be honest I was despairing of how long she'd last without formula."

"She's a strong one, that's for sure." Em patted Sidra's shoulder. "You saved her life, sweetie, she'll always be grateful for that."

"What?" Sidra asked confused.

"I'm making it a stipulation that whoever takes her they'll tell her about her start in life. And the woman who saved her. In fact, I'm considering changing her name too. I think Sidra would be a fine name for her, don't you?"

Sidra's throat closed, a lump the size of a mountain appearing, as tears formed in her eyes. It was Bliss that broke the silence. "That's wonderful, Em, I think that's a beautiful name for her."

"Me too," Terigan said quietly.

Em opened her arms and hugged Sidra, as well as the baby. "You're a strong woman with a heart as wide as the Mississippi, honey, and I'm glad you've found your Destiny. I wish nothing but the best for your future and Jaxon's."

"Thank you," Sidra managed to whisper before Em pulled away.

"Now, let's get you something to eat. I've got some fabulous things on offer tonight, so come on and we'll get you a nice big plateful." Em lowered her voice, whispering conspiratorially. "I've also got some chocolate cake that's not long out of the oven. Do you like chocolate?"

Sidra grinned. "Now, what's that saying? Oh yeah, does a bear 'you know what' in the woods?"

"You know what?" Em chuckled. "You mean shit, does a bear shit in the woods, and yes, they do, my dear, yes, they do. So, I'll keep you a nice slice of my rather tasty cake for after."

"Thank you." Sidra followed behind, her mind so focused on Em and the thought of tasting chocolate again, that she forgot Jaxon's hasty departure.

Terigan watched her go, using the moment to check in with Jaxon. *"Boss, what's going on?"*

"Demons," Jaxon replied and Terigan fought not to let his concern show on his face.

"You sure you don't need me?" Terigan would much rather be there with Jaxon.

"No, Skar and a few of the others are here. Thanks, Terigan, but I really do need you to look after Sidra for me. You know how important she is and I could leave her in no better hands. Plus, I don't want her even more worried. If you leave now she'll know something is definitely wrong."

Terigan sighed. *"Okay, if that's what you need, I'll make sure she's safe but Em's got it covered right now. She's tempting her with her famous chocolate cake."*

Jaxon laughed. *"Tell them to remember and keep me a slice. I'll get it later and once we've got these*

Demons in our control, I'd like your help in interrogating them. I'll tell you when that's done. For now, I've got to go."

"All right. Be careful, boss, Demons are nasty and full of surprises."

"Tell me about it."

As Jaxon cut their link, Bliss' hand landed on Terigan's arm. "Is everything all right?"

"Sure." Terigan smiled, trying to allay her fears, everyone always looked out for Bliss, knowing how sensitive she was. "Nothing to worry about. Now, do you think we can manage to sneak a slice of cake?"

Bliss grinned. "I hope so."

Skar's Dragon hovered, appearing to just be checking things out, as Jaxon ran full speed out of camp. As soon as he was free of the buildings, he morphed without breaking stride and taking to the air a moment later, he disappeared from view. *"Where are they?"* he asked, using an open link between the Dragons already airborne.

"Right behind camp, settled down on an outcrop, but they're not doing anything other than watching,"

Kat answered. *"We're keeping an eye on them but so far they've not moved."*

"How many?" Jaxon barked, fear swirling around in his guts.

"Three," Sapphire answered. *"And they have no clue we're here, we're all cloaked and Zane is making sure no more Demons are in the area."*

"Good. Stay cloaked and I'll be with you in a few minutes. Remember, I want them taken alive."

"Yeah, we heard you, but that won't be easy." Kat voiced everyone's concern. *"I'm not sure how we do that."*

"Quickly and with our talons," Jaxon answered. *"If they don't know we're here then we set up a line and we go in one after the other, pick one up and hold that fucker until we can get back to camp. We then drop them on their heads and knock them out."*

"Will that work? What if they just disappear like they appeared here?" Sapphire asked, doubt in every syllable.

Jaxon tried to allay her concerns. *"Not every Demon can do that. I'm guessing that only one of them has the ability and brought the rest with him. If this is just a scouting party, then I'm sure they wouldn't send their strongest, these will be lower class Demons. Lower class means less powers, or that's what I'm hoping."*

"I hope you're right," Sapphire replied.

"*I only need one,*" Jaxon reiterated. "*If I get my hands on one, then we should be able to find out who's behind this. And if he doesn't talk voluntarily then I'll persuade him. Last resort is we let Bliss have a go at finding out why they were sent here.*"

Skar agreed, "*One is all we need. I'll be right there with you, boss, and between us I'm pretty damn sure we'll make them talk.*"

"*Thanks.*" Jaxon heaved a sigh of relief. Skar could be one scary mother when the mood took him. Even more menacing than *he* was, and that said something. Jaxon was terrifying when angry.

"*Okay, Sapphire, I can see you.*" Jaxon saw Sapphire's Dragon, with Kat's right beside her, hovering over an outcropping about mid-way down the mountain. Amos and Aric flew higher, keeping an eye on everything from their vantage point.

"*Gotcha.*" Kat let him know they saw him and Skar. "*So, who's going first?*"

"*Let me do a fly-by. I want to see what's what.*" Jaxon's wings slowed, not wanting to alert the Demons by noise or a downdraft. He glided over the outcrop, his beast's eyes carefully scanning below. "*All right. I see them and they are spread out on the outcrop. I want this done with precision, people, there's no room for error and I want each one of those dirty Demons in our talons. I'm going in first,*

229

I'll take the one on the left, farthest away from us. Skar, I want you to be right on my ass and grab the middle one. Kat, you come in behind Skar and get the one on the right. Sapphire, I want you as back up in case one of us miss. If we do, then get your ass down there and grab our targets. Okay?"

Skar's response was immediate. *"I'll be so close to your ass I'll know what you've had for dinner, boss."*

"I'll get mine, don't you worry 'bout that, Jax," Kat said with more than a little bite.

Sapphire chuckled. *"I've got them all in my line of sight, I'll stay just in front and a little above them. If any of you miss, and by the way if you do you're getting me a new pair of shoes, I'll grab their ass."*

"I won't be getting you anything, sweetheart, that Demon's ass is mine." Skar's tone was grim which pleased Jaxon greatly.

Skar was on a mission and he would not fail. He never did. None of them did.

"I'm getting into position. Fall in, Dragons. Amos, Aric, stay where you are and keep an eye on things. If you see any more Demons then let us know."

"Copy that," Amos replied quickly.

Jaxon soared up and off to the side, his eyes locking with his target. Nothing, absolutely nothing would stop him from sinking his talons into that despicable being.

He saw Skar and Kat get into position behind him and he waited for a brief moment until Sapphire took up hers. *"All right, let's do this. On my mark, three, two, one. Go!"*

Jaxon beat his wings furiously, picking up speed within a second or two, sweeping down, furling his wings in at the last possible second to allow him to fly nearer the outcrop. His legs stretched down, his talons opening and fiercely snatching his allocated Demon by the shoulders. He allowed his razor sharp claws to dig in, piercing the Demon's skin and embedding deep in its muscles. The high pitched, blood curdling scream that erupted from it was soft music to his ears. He barely stopped himself from bellowing in victory, careful not to alert the other two Demons as to what was happening.

He needn't have worried, two more shrieks of pain sounded almost immediately. Spinning his long neck around, he saw both Skar and Kat with their Demons held firmly in their claws. *"Good work you two. Amos, Aric, Sapphire, get down to the field and transform, be ready to grab these spies as soon as we drop them. Skar, Kat, I think about a twenty-foot drop should do it, don't you?"*

Kat's voice dripped with sarcasm laced with anger. *"I think twenty-five, just to be on the safe side, boss."*

"*Personally, I think thirty. They're Demons, they'll take a bit of knocking out.*" Skar chuckled.

"*True. Thirty it is. Let's go and give these three a headache.*" Jaxon swooped down over the camp, heading to the large field at the other end, hell bent on getting answers from the sniveling Demons in their grasp.

CHAPTER

 SEVENTEEN

Sarff sat crossed leg, her eyes closed as she used a spell to *see* through the eyes of the Demons she'd taken to the mountain range surrounding the Dragons camp. She had known where it was, had for some time, but she wasn't stupid and kept that juicy piece of information to herself.

She tried to focus on the spell linking her to the Demons, but her mind wandered to Draven over and over again. Cursing herself for allowing him to trick her, which resulted in her precarious position now. How he'd managed to enslave her, she still wasn't clear about, but enslaved she was.

"Fucking slimy bastard," she cursed, shivering as she recalled the punishment he'd doled out to her earlier. She hated him. With every single fiber of her being, she hated him. When, not if, the opportunity arose she'd take great pleasure in bringing him down. She only had to find a way to do that. She had to, soon, because if he laid his dirty hands on her again she knew she'd go insane.

She jerked as the landscape changed in her mind. The Demon she'd been channeling no longer sat looking down over the camp. No, he seemed to be struggling and high in the air. His head lowered and Sarff's own stomach churned at the sheer drop down to the ground. "What the hell's going on?" she murmured, waiting to see if she could figure it out.

The Demon was flying through the air. That much was obvious, but how and why? She couldn't understand and then he seemed to be falling, the ground rushing up to meet him very fast indeed. Sarff waited but a moment later, as the ground dashed up to meet him, everything went dark. "Damn fool's been knocked out. Did he fall?" she mused, trying to make sense of it. "Nope, he was flying at first and that can only mean one thing, the Dragons caught them."

Sarff smiled, her mind working overtime at this piece of news. "Might be my chance," she muttered, getting up and dressed. She had been sitting naked, allowing her body to heal after Draven's abuse but now she had to move. Quickly, or her opportunity may disappear.

"You can do this," she told herself over and over, knowing it was now or never.

If Draven suspected what she was about to do, he'd kill her, but not until she begged for him to do so. He was a sadist of the highest order and she could take no more, shivering in disgust at the thought of his hands touching her skin, again.

No, she'd do whatever it took to ensure he never laid a finger on her ever again.

Jaxon waited until the Demons were securely tied up, using rope spelled by their strongest Witches. "I'll be back shortly. Keep an eye on them and let me know if they wake up. I want them separated, one in each room so they don't know what's happened to the others."

"Will do." Skar roughly picked one up and opened the door to the cellar of the Guild house. "I'll pop this one down here, Aric, take one into the meeting room, and Amos, you keep an eye on this one here. I won't be long, boys."

"Will do," the twins answered together.

Jaxon left them to it, knowing they'd do their job, so he went in search of Sidra. *"Hey, honey, are you all right?"* He used their link to find out where she was.

"Hi, you, I'm fine, just finishing up some chocolate cake. Is everything okay?"

"Yes, just some business." Jaxon didn't want to worry her unnecessarily. *"I'll be there shortly. But first, I need to find Terigan for a brief chat."*

"Oh, he's here."

"Good, I'll be there in a second."

Jaxon started to jog, stopping at the door to the hall and composing himself. He didn't want to give anything away when he entered. Seeing Sidra, still with Terigan and Bliss, he went over, walking casually with his hands in his pockets. "Hi."

Sidra jumped up, hugging him fiercely. "Are you sure you're okay?"

"I'm fine, just Guild business." Jaxon hugged her back, before kissing her, pulling back he grinned. "I can taste the chocolate. Fancy grabbing me a slice and keeping it for later?"

"Sure." Sidra frowned. "Does that mean you're not finished?"

"Afraid not, lass, I've still got some work to do and I need Terigan." Jaxon raised an eyebrow at his friend. "You free to come help me with something?"

"Yeah," Terigan replied, casually, obviously aware Jaxon didn't want Sidra upset. "I've finished my cake so I'm happy. Where we going, boss?"

"Just to the Guild hall." Jaxon released Sidra. "Bliss, wonder if you could do something for me?"

"Of course." Bliss nodded.

"Sidra likes to read so could you loan her one of your e-readers and show her how it works?"

"Really?" Bliss beamed at Sidra. "I love reading and I've collected a ton of them. I'd be happy to lend you whatever you want."

"Thank you, Bliss." Jaxon stepped away. "I'll not be too long, honey, if you want to stay with Bliss until I'm free, I'll come get you there."

"Sounds good to me." Sidra looked behind her toward the kitchen. "I'll grab you some cake first though."

"Thanks. See you two later." Jaxon turned and walked slowly away.

Terigan beside him whispering, "I assume we're going at a snail's pace so as not to alert Sidra?"

"Aye," Jaxon said out the side of his mouth.

"Oh oh." Terigan frowned. "You just said, aye, you must be really upset if you're using your old tongue."

"What?" Jaxon pulled the door open, eager to be away from Sidra's sight. "Did I?"

"Yeah, you did." Terigan patted his shoulder. "I assume you managed to capture a Demon?"

"Three, we caught all three." Jaxon sped up, jogging toward their hall.

"Three? Damn it, that's good going. We'll get answers, Jax, one of them will break."

"They better tell us who sent them, because I am not in the mood to play nice."

They found Amos standing guard over his Demon, giving it a kick to try and wake it up. "This one is out for the count, boss."

"Skar, Aric, are either of your Demons awake?" Jaxon asked quickly.

Aric answered first. *"Not awake, no, but showing signs of coming around."*

"Mine is, I poured a pail of water over him." Skar's news meant Jaxon and Terigan headed straight down to the cellar.

"I'll be back," Jaxon ground out, his anger growing at the intrusion of his sanctuary by Demons.

"Hey, I've seen that film, you sound just like him," Amos joked.

"What?" Jaxon spun around.

"Nothing, boss, sorry." Amos lowered his head at the angry glare from Jaxon.

"Just keep your eye on him." Jaxon nodded toward the unconscious Demon tied to a chair. "If he wakes let me know through our link. Do not say anything to him, not a word. Got it?"

"Yes." Amos nodded furiously.

Jaxon shook his head at the youngster then disappeared to join Skar. He was looking forward to getting some answers and he'd do whatever it took to get them.

As he and Terigan entered the cellar, Skar gave a brief nod of acknowledgment. His friend leaned against the wall, arms crossed, and scowling at the Demon before them. Jaxon strode over, kicking the tied feet of the being who'd infiltrated their camp. "What's your name and what the hell are you doing here?"

The Demon looked terrified, its eyes flitting between Jaxon and Skar, then back again. He shook his head, almost moaning a reply. "I can't say. I want to, really, but if I do, my life won't be worth living."

Jaxon's anger grew, a growl rumbled through his throat. "And you think it'll be worth living if you remain silent? I can assure you, *Demon*, that we don't take kindly to being spied on. Do you really want to make us any angrier than we already are?"

Skar pulled his massive body from the wall, pouncing forward, showing his teeth in a grimace. "Can I, boss? Please tell me I can."

The Demon pulled back, terrified. Jaxon smirked evilly. "Oh, I don't know. Maybe we should give him some more time before I let you eat him."

"I'm *hungry!*" Skar snarled grotesquely.

"What?" The Demon's eyes almost bulged out his head. "You wouldn't."

Skar leaned forward, making a show of sniffing the Demon. "He's not the best I've had, but he'll do for now. Come on, boss, just a little nibble to keep me going."

Terigan joined in, circling the Demon menacingly. "He's got plenty of meat on him, boss, we could just take a little. It wouldn't kill him, you could still question him."

Jaxon stepped back, giving the other two plenty of room to terrify the Demon. "If you're not going to answer any of my questions, then I'm leaving. I'm sure once your friends see what's happened to you, that it'll loosen their tongues."

"What? No, don't leave me with these two." The Demon shrieked fearfully.

"Last chance," Jaxon snarled. "First, what is your name?"

"Billy," The Demon hurriedly answered.

Skar laughed out loud, shaking his head, as Terigan grabbed the Demon's hair and pulled his head roughly back. "What did you just say? Billy? Are you shitting us? What kind of name is that for a Demon?"

Billy tried to nod but failed as Terigan held him tightly. "Yes, that's my name. I'm quite a young Demon, only a few hundred years old and I read stories of a human gunslinger from the Wild West, Billy the Kid, and I took his name. There's nothing wrong with the name Billy. I like it."

"For a human no, for a Demon, not so much." Skar chuckled. "How do you expect to instill fear in people with the name Billy?"

"I don't," Billy replied. "I don't like scaring anyone. I'm what you'd call a lover not a fighter."

Jaxon couldn't believe what he was hearing. "Are you playing with us? Because I'm telling you here and now, if you are, I'll rip your fucking insides out myself."

"No, honest." Billy whined. "I've spent my time here in the human realm 'cause I hate all the fighting and vicious Demony things. I don't think I've ever killed anyone in my life. Oh wait, yeah, there was that one time in Vegas but that was an accident."

"Enough with the babbling." Jaxon growled. "Demony things? Jeez, what the hell have we got here?" He shook his head at Skar and Terigan.

"No idea, boss, but I'm still hungry so if he's not gonna give us the information we need, can I just eat him already?" Skar snarled, showing his teeth once again.

"You don't really do that? Do you?" Billy shrank back from Skar's vicious growl, his eyes darting to Jaxon. "Dragons don't eat people, do they?"

"Answer my damn questions, boy!" Jaxon released part of his beast, roaring loudly.

"Please don't let them eat me," Billy sniveled. "Okay, I'll talk, but then I guess you can just kill me 'cause I'll be dead anyway once they know I've talked."

"Let's do this simply," Jaxon barked out, fed up with the prattling. "First, why are you here?"

"To keep watch on the Unicorn lady." Billy went to carry on but Jaxon held up his hand.

"Answer my questions only, no more blathering."

Billy snapped his mouth shut, nodding. Jaxon sighed. "Are you here to hurt her? Were you sent for that purpose?"

"No," Billy replied quickly.

"So, you were just to watch her?" Jaxon frowned.

"Yes, we were told to watch and alert Sarff if the Unicorn lady was ever vulnerable."

"Vulnerable? That means you were here to hurt her and who the hell is Sarff?" Jaxon's anger grew again at the thought of the Demons looking for a *vulnerable* Sidra.

"No, no! We were not to hurt her. Sarff made that very clear." Billy's voice rose so that it sounded like a scared girl's. "Sarff is in charge of all of us lower Demons. She tells us what to do, where to go, and basically runs our lives. She told us if we harmed Unicorn lady that she'd skin us alive, literally."

"So is this Sarff that wants to harm Unicorn lady?" Jaxon refused to supply the enemy with Sidra's name.

"No." Billy looked terrified and confused at the same time. "She's enslaved to Draven and it's him that wants her. I don't know why and I've no idea what's so important about her. Well, apart from the fact she's a freaking Unicorn which is awesome, of course, but I . . ."

Jaxon held up his hand and Billy clamped his mouth shut. "Billy, okay, so Sarff is who tells you what to do, but Draven tells Sarff what to do? Right? Nod if the answer is yes."

Terigan released Billy's hair and he nodded. Jaxon started to pace. "What kind of Demons are they?"

Billy frowned. "Sarff is a Demon, a snake one, but Draven isn't a Demon."

"Then what the hell is he?" Jaxon barked.

"I thought he was a Witch, but he gets real angry if anyone calls him that. He says he's a Wizard, but I don't know what the difference is.

Anyway, he's really powerful and he managed to trick Sarff somehow and now she's enslaved to him but he treats her badly, like . . ."

Jaxon felt as if his head was going to explode. "Enough! I've told you, answer the question and stop babbling."

Billy looked around at all three of them, his fear radiating off him in great waves that cloyed the air around them. Skar looked at the Demon. "So, *Billy*, what does Draven want with the Unicorn?"

"I don't know."

Terigan grabbed his hair again, tugging roughly. "Tell us."

"I don't know! I only do as I'm told and it's only ever Sarff that tells me what to do."

"How do you contact her?" Jaxon prodded.

"I don't." Billy's eyes spun around in terror. "Please, I'm telling the truth. She uses magic to see through our eyes and if she wants to contact us, she does so through a freaky mind speak thing. But she only uses it to give us more orders, nothing more."

"Can you speak to her through this link?" Skar spat out, his anger clearly showing, which seemed to scare Billy even further.

"No." He tried to shake his head but Terigan still held his hair firmly in his grasp.

Jaxon pondered on what they'd learned. *"Terigan,"* he needed to know something, *"go and find Em and ask her what the hell's the difference between a Wizard and a Witch."*

"Will do." Terigan released Billy's hair and stormed away.

"Tell me about the other two Demons who were with you. Are they more powerful than you? Because, I've got to say, Billy, you don't seem all that powerful to me," Jaxon scoffed.

"No, we're all about the same, and none of us is what you could call powerful. We're kinda on the lowest level Demon wise."

"Good to know." Jaxon passed that information along to Aric and Amos.

"What are you going to do with me?" Billy's eyes darted around as if looking for an escape.

"Not sure yet," Jaxon replied. "Skar, why don't you go and check on the other two, see if their story backs his up. If it doesn't then I'll allow you to eat this fucker alive."

"No!" Billy yelled as Skar quickly left.

"Shut up." Jaxon kicked out at Billy's feet. "Or I may just eat you myself. Not another sound, or else."

Billy fell silent, his eyes pleading with Jaxon who leaned against a spare desk in the corner. "I'll just wait here and see what Skar finds out. I hope for your sake you weren't lying."

Billy opened his mouth. Jaxon shook his head, waggling a finger. "Nope, not one word."

Jaxon settled to wait on both Terigan and Skar, hoping against hope that they could unravel who this Wizard was, and how to defeat him.

If he had to tear Draven's head from his body, Jaxon knew he'd do it, and not give it another thought. His Destiny's safety was all he cared about.

CHAPTER

EIGHTEEN

Sidra couldn't contain her excitement as Bliss explained the concept of an e-reader. The collection of them in Bliss' cabin was extensive, tons of the devices set up in a bookcase. "Wow, how many do you have?"

"I've lost count." Bliss shrugged. "A lot. Every time the guys go out on a mission they keep their eyes peeled and if they see one they snag it for me. If I go out on a supply run, I usually manage to grab one or two as well."

"And how many books are on each one?" Sidra found it hard to comprehend that the devices, some very small indeed, held a cornucopia of books inside them.

"It depends." Bliss picked a bright pink covered device from the top shelf. "This is one of my favorites. It's got almost a thousand books on it and some of my favorite authors. Hmm, I wonder if any of them are still alive. What do you think?"

"A thousand books on that little thing?" Sidra gasped in surprise.

"Yes, and there's a full collection of books from Tracey Jane Jackson, she's one of my favorites. She's got several series but the one I've read over and over is her Cauld Ane series. It's amazing!" Bliss beamed as she handed over the device.

"Cauld Ane, what the heck is that?" Sidra asked, looking at the screen of the device that Bliss had turned on.

"Oh, it's a fabulous series, but I don't want to spoil it for you so just read it and let me know what you think. It is romance though. Do you like romance books?" Bliss sighed, patting her heart. "Her heroes are so hot and yummy."

Sidra laughed. "Yes, I like romance, I like most kinds and I'll be sure to read it and let you know what I thought."

"Yes, please do." Bliss nodded to one of her comfy sofas. "Why don't you get comfortable and I'll get us a glass of wine."

"Sounds good to me." Sidra held the e-reader carefully, scared she would break it somehow."

Bliss must've noticed as she giggled. "Oh it's fine, Sidra, I've dropped so many devices I'm amazed they're not all smashed to smithereens."

"I don't want to damage it." Sidra sat down, pleasure rippling through her at the thought of having books on tap. "You said the guys look for them when they're on missions. Do you not go out on missions?"

"No—" Bliss looked a little embarrassed. "I'm a Dragon, and I've lived here since Jaxon set up the camp, but I'm not a Guild Warrior."

"I see." Sidra didn't see at all. She'd thought all the Dragons here were Guild Warriors.

"It's okay, I know it sounds weird, and it is, kinda." Bliss brought over the wine. "I started training years ago but there's a lot of things I'm not very good at. Like hurting people. So Jaxon and I had a long talk and we agreed it would probably be better if I stopped training and just lived with them as a member of the Guild but not a Warrior. They're like my family and I couldn't live without them, but I'm definitely not Warrior material. I help in other ways, like the kids I've got staying with me at the moment. I love children and usually look after new additions if their parents aren't here, or not able to do it themselves. Plus, I have that little gift, you know, where I can touch someone and see things about them. Jaxon uses that when he needs to as well."

"Where are the kids?" Sidra looked around, only now seeing trainers lying by the doorway and jackets slung over the back of a chair.

"They're in their room watching some DVDs." Bliss lowered her voice to barely a whisper as she sat down next to Sidra. "I have enough room for them to have their own but they won't sleep apart. They're having a really tough time just now, but we'll get them through it."

"It's so sad that they had to see what happened to their parents. I know how that feels and it sucks big time," Sidra said with feeling. "If I can help, just let me know."

"I might take you up on that." Bliss patted Sidra's knee. "If anyone can relate to them, it's you."

"I'll do whatever I can," Sidra said before wiggling the e-reader. "So, any more on here that I should check out?"

Bliss' eyes lit up. "Yes, tons, but one I'd recommend is an author called Eden Elsworth. She writes a series called the Real World series and it's about a human world where they have no idea about other beings, like Witches, Faera, and something that's called a Halfbreed, which is half Vampire. It's wonderfully exciting and she writes so well you feel as if you're right there."

"Halfbreeds, huh? I guess I'll check those ones out too." Sidra sipped from her wine, enjoying her time with Bliss. After their rocky start, she was realizing that she and Bliss could become firm friends and looked forward to getting to know the Dragon even better.

Sidra leaned back, relaxing, when Bliss suddenly jumped up. "No!" Bliss yelled a second before a person appeared before them.

"Stay where you are or I'll hurt those two upstairs." The green-eyed woman pointed a finger at Bliss then Sidra. "We wouldn't want them hurt now, would we?"

Bliss shook and at first Sidra thought it was from fear, but the steely glint in her eyes told Sidra it was anger. Bliss sneered at the woman. "I don't know who you are, but you better get your skinny ass out of here before I tear you apart."

Sidra gasped at the venom spouting from Bliss. Her entire being thrumming with energy but the strange woman only shook her head. "I'm not alone, Dragon. I have two more standing right outside their bedroom door. One noise from down here and they go in and well, let's just say, that would *not* be good for those kids' health."

"I'll find you, if you harm a hair on their heads, I'll find you and rip *your* head clean off."

Sidra slowly rose, placing a hand gently on Bliss' shoulder to try and calm her. Sidra eyed the woman coldly. "Who are you and what do you want?"

"My name is unimportant, but I'll give it to you, mainly so *you*," she nodded to Bliss, "can pass it on to the Master, it's Sarff, and if you hadn't already guessed, I'm a Demon."

"Jaxon will punish you severely for coming here but you didn't answer. What do you want?" Sidra remembered at that moment about her link. *"Jax, I'm with Bliss at her place, and we've got an uninvited guest who's turned up. I think we need your help."*

"I'm here for you." Sarff pointed to Sidra with nails painted blood red. "If you come quietly, with no fighting or trying to escape, then I'll leave the children in peace. But you only have until I count to three to get your ass over here."

"Sid!" Jaxon sounded terrified as he spoke to her. *"Stay there, I'm on my way, I'll be one minute, one minute, baby."*

"I don't have a minute," Sidra told him quickly.

"Now!" Sarff shouted. "One, two . . ."

"Okay, I'm coming." Sidra stepped forward, Bliss trying to hold her back. "It's okay, Bliss, I'll go with her. We can't risk the kids being hurt."

"Sidra . . ." Bliss' voice broke as tears filled her eyes.

"That's a good girlie." Sarff grabbed a tight hold of Sidra's arm. "Tell your Master that I'll be keeping this little lady until he agrees to help me."

"What?" Bliss looked angry and confused at the same time.

"I suppose he's already got information from the Demons I sent earlier so tell him, I need him to take out Draven, and then I'll return the Unicorn."

"Wait," Bliss held out her hand. "I don't understand."

"He will." Sarff smiled coldly. "Tell him if he doesn't destroy Draven, then I'll destroy his little pet. I'll be keeping an eye on things and if he does as asked, then I'll return her with not a hair on her pretty little head harmed. I will not contact any of you again. Once this is done my business with you is over."

"I'm sorry, Jax." Sidra's heart broke at being taken from him, his yell through their link breaking off halfway through as she felt her body fold in on itself. Every single cell felt as if it were being torn apart and put back together again with glue. The dark magic being used to transport them causing her to feel so disoriented that as soon as she felt solid ground beneath her feet, all she could do was lean over and retch.

She lost her dinner, and her cake, as she puked onto the stone beneath her. Sarff's disgust was obvious, the Demon's voice echoing through the dim cave as she said, "Eeeeew, that's revolting."

Sidra slowly felt herself "settling" and she straightened to glare at Sarff. "You know he'll kill you. Don't you? You can't be that stupid to think he won't come after you."

"All I care about is Draven's demise," Sarff scoffed. "Once that happens, I'm free to return to my own realm and I'll never come back to this shitty place again."

Sidra focused on her inner magic, courtesy of her father, ready to blast the woman before her. Sarff shook her head. "I wouldn't do that if I were you. This cave has been magic-proofed. If you attempt to do anything, it will bounce back against you, so I guess you'll be attacking yourself. Isn't that funny?"

Sidra slowly prodded with her magic and found what Sarff said to be true. Annoyed and angry she whirled around. "Okay, so I can't blast you to pieces but I can sure as hell whip your butt."

Sarff giggled like a maniac. "Oops, sorry, no can do, honey. Although I would enjoy a little one on one with you, I have other things to attend to. Enjoy your solitude and let's hope the Dragon can save your beautiful booty."

Before she could even take a step toward Sarff, the Demon had disappeared. "What the fuck?" Sidra cursed, looking around her for a way out and trying to contact Jaxon.

"Jax, honey, can you hear me?"

Nothing. *"Jaxon, please, can you hear me? I'm in a cave but I don't know where. Can you hear me?"*

With no response, Sidra's shoulders slumped, unease creeping inside as she realized she was somewhere only Sarff knew. If she wanted to, the Demon could leave her to rot. "Calm down," she told herself, speaking aloud to break the utter silence. "Okay, check out your surroundings and see what there is." Taking a deep breath, she focused on the area around her.

What she found was basically a room made of stone, with no windows, and no door. A bundle in the corner turned out to be some hastily thrown down sleeping bags, a crate of bottled water, and a ton of energy bars lay next to them. "At least I won't starve," she said as she continued inspecting her prison.

Although it was a cave, and obviously underground, it wasn't entirely dark, a soft glow from the ceiling let her see her way around, but wasn't bright enough for much else. She found two empty metal pails, the accompanying toilet tissue soon explained what they were for.

"I hope I'm not in here long enough to have to use those," she muttered angrily.

Sidra went back to the sleeping bags, finding several, she reached out, only then realizing she still held the e-reader in her hand. "Thank goodness for small mercies," she laughed, at least she had something to help her pass the time. She focused on the sleeping bags, sorting them so they were layered and relatively comfortable to sit on.

Settling down, she switched the e-reader on and sat back to read. Her subconscious praying that Jaxon would find her soon. She wasn't sure how long she could stay in the dark hole before she lost her sanity.

Jaxon roared as he tore out of their hall. "Everyone to Bliss', Sidra's in danger."

He was out the door a split-second later, Skar, Amos and Aric stampeding after him. As they ran full-speed through the camp, he saw Terigan exiting the mess hall. *"Terigan, get to Bliss', they're in danger."*

Terigan about turned, his long legs speeding toward Bliss' cabin. It was his friend who got there first, having a head start, but Jaxon was in the door mere moments later. His heart stopped when he saw Bliss pacing back and forth, swearing like a fishwife. He was certain he'd never heard such language from her lips but more importantly, Sidra was nowhere to be seen.

"I'll fucking kill the bitch! How dare she come into my home and threaten those kids! I'll kill her. I'll rip her apart with my bare hands!"

Terigan grabbed Bliss by the shoulders, holding her in place. "Tell us what happened."

Jaxon felt sick, his insides in turmoil as Bliss explained, her voice laced with anger and loathing. "A fucking Demon appeared, right there!" She stamped her foot, pointing to the fireplace. "She said there were two more upstairs and if we tried anything they'd hurt the kids."

Said kids were now standing pale-faced and trembling at the bottom of the stairs. Jaxon nodded to Amos. "Get them out of here."

Amos went over, silently leading the terrified children out as Bliss carried on, her anger seemingly increasing with every word. "She said to tell you her name is Sarff and that if you destroy someone called Draven, then she'll release Sidra. If not then she'll kill her. Who the fuck is she and who is Draven? I want to kill them both for this. Who the hell threatens *kids*?"

Jaxon couldn't stop the groan of pain that escaped him. Skar stood at his side and grasped his shoulder firmly. Jaxon took a deep breath, trying to clear his head. "Sarff has been enslaved by a Wizard named Draven. She obviously wants her freedom and thinks this is the way to get it. Since Draven is the one who's been hunting Sidra, she thinks we'll be willing to do that."

"I see." Bliss' anger seemed to disappear, her legs shaking and if Terigan hadn't caught her, she would've fallen.

"Sit down, sweetie, you're going to feel strange with the adrenaline pumping through your system." Terigan placed her on the sofa, talking softly down at her.

Tears started to fall from her stricken eyes. "I'm sorry, Jaxon, I was going to attack but when she said the kids would be hurt I couldn't. I couldn't let her hurt them. I'm useless, utterly fucking useless."

Jaxon felt her pain, her sorrow, and her still simmering anger. "It's not your fault. It's mine. I should've left a guard, but from what you say, it wouldn't have mattered. We wouldn't have allowed the children to be hurt, Bliss. That was the right call to make."

"What do we do? We need to find her and get her home." Bliss was frantic, her hands starting to shake from the adrenaline rush.

"I'd already planned on trying to find this Draven." Jaxon paced back and forth. "Now we have to do it as quickly as possible and since he was planning on kidnapping Sidra and doing goodness knows what with her, well, his fate was sealed as soon as I heard that. So, Warriors, we need to have a mission brief and decide how we do that."

"What on earth's going on?" Em's voice interrupted them. The old Witch stomping in, she sat next to Bliss as soon as she saw her. "Bliss, are you all right, honey?"

"No," Bliss sobbed. "I let them take Sidra."

"Let isn't the word I'd use." Jaxon shook his head. "You had no other choice, but now we need to find Draven and I think you can help."

"Help? How?" Bliss perked up. "I'll do anything, Jaxon, anything at all, if it helps us save Sidra."

Em patted Bliss' shoulder. "I'll look after Lara and Lucas, you go and do what you've gotta do."

"Before we go, can someone please explain why this Draven guy is hell bent on being called a Wizard?" Jaxon asked, still confused about that point. "I thought a Witch was a Witch, regardless of sex."

"Yes, they are," Em agreed. "I've only ever known one other man who called himself a Wizard and he was not a nice person. His soul was black and he dabbled in the dark arts, using them to enslave other beings, including Demons, to do his bidding. He came to a sticky end though after his eye caught a rather comely Demon and he tried to do the same to her." Em grinned wickedly. "She was a Fire Demon, small, and beautiful, and many misjudged her powers. Her name was Nicola Blaze and she burnt that ass to hell, serves him right, but that's the only Wizard I've known."

"So basically we're dealing with a Witch with ideas of grandeur," Jaxon said quietly.

"Yes and no." Em stood, staring seriously up at Jaxon. "Anyone that deals with the dark side of our art is dangerous, very dangerous, Jaxon. Be careful, boy, or you could be in a lot of trouble."

Jaxon nodded. "Thanks for the warning, but tell me, Em, if I rip his head from his shoulders, will that kill him like any other being?"

Em chuckled, nodding as she walked away. "Indeed it will, but you've got to get close enough to do that, Dragon, and he won't make it easy for you."

"I'll find a way," Jaxon stated with complete confidence.

"I'll keep the kids with me for now. Don't worry about coming for them later, Bliss, I've plenty of room for them."

"Thank you, Em." Bliss gave the old woman a smile before turning back to Jaxon, her voice firm and her eyes cold. "So, how do I help?"

"Follow me, there's some Demons I'd like you to meet." Jaxon turned on his heel and strode away, not allowing the fear inside to take over. No, he was on a mission and he'd carry it through to the bitter end and get his Destiny back where she belonged: in his arms.

CHAPTER

NINETEEN

Bliss glared at Billy, the look on her face not one Jaxon had ever seen before. He pointed at her as he explained to Billy what they were going to do. "This is Bliss, and she's a Dragon with a few expert talents. One of which is getting inside your head and finding out where this Draven has his little lair. So, Billy boy, sit back, relax and let her do her thing."

"Sit still," Bliss snapped. "I want all the information I can gather and if you try and fight it, I'm more than capable of making this extremely painful for you."

Jaxon frowned, not aware she could do that. It wasn't something she'd ever done and she'd certainly never voiced that before. *"You can do that?"* he queried, interested to know either way.

"Yes, I can, I've just never had the occasion to do so. Today just might be my first time."

"I think he'll be cooperating, Bliss, he seems far too terrified to do anything else. After Skar threatened to eat him alive, he kinda caved."

"Eat him? Why would Skar say something so gross?"

Jaxon kept the smirk from his face. "To scare him into talking."

"Oh, I see, okay, well I'm ready, let's get started."

Billy started to shake as Bliss stepped closer, his eyes wide. "I won't fight you. I *want* to help. I do. Hells bells and buggery, if I help you take out Draven then all of us are free. It's what we all dream about."

"Whatever," Bliss snarled. "Just stay still and I'll try and not scramble your brains while I'm in there."

Jaxon turned away, not able to stop his lips tugging up this time. Skar was in the corner and raised an eyebrow. "Looks like we've been losing out on a great interrogator, boss."

"Yeah, looks like," Jaxon answered, sobering his face before turning back to Bliss and Billy.

"Please, miss, I won't do anything to stop you doing what you have to do, but I'm just wondering what it is you want to know."

"We want to find Draven and when we do we're going to go for a little visit," Jaxon growled, worry eating away at his insides.

"Why didn't you just ask me?" Billy said innocently.

"What?" Bliss looked at Jaxon, raising an eyebrow.

"Didn't we?" Jaxon asked, looking at Skar who shrugged.

"No, not directly." Billy shook his head. "I've already told you stuff so I'm a goner anyway so giving up Draven is something I'll gladly do. He's despicable and evil, cruel and nasty, so I'm happy to tell you where he is. Or rather, where he usually is."

"So tell us," Jaxon spat out, angry that they hadn't asked this simple question first.

"His place is near the Rockies, just outside Boulder. It's a huge old building on its own land and it's got a wall surrounding it to stop anyone getting in. It's got spells all around the wall so if you're going in that way I'd be careful if I were you. He doesn't spend a lot of time in the actual house though, nope, the creepy shit stays in his cavern underneath, which was built into the rock foundations. It's got his main room that he does spells 'n shit in, and a few bedrooms, as well as a room he uses for punishment. He does like to dole out punishment whenever he can and it's always painful, bloody, and sadistic. I can show you on a map, if you'd like?"

"Yes, we'd like you to do that." Bliss turned away. "Doesn't look as if you need me here anymore, but I would like to be kept in the loop on this one, Jaxon."

"I can do that." Jaxon nodded to her, still seeing the anger flashing in her usually serene eyes.

"When you're dealing with Sarff, I'd like to be involved. I know I'm not a Warrior, but I could be useful."

"I'll think about that and let you know." Jaxon was surprised at her request and would have to decide whether or not to allow her to be included. Not something he'd make a snap decision on, especially when it coincided with the safety of Sidra.

"Skar," Jaxon turned to his friend. "Can you go up and bring down one of our maps that covers that area?"

"Be right back." Skar disappeared and Jaxon turned his attention back to Billy.

"So, if you're going to Draven's, as I said he stays in his cavern and you get there through a door under the stairs." Billy squinted, as if he was thinking. "I usually go in the back door, but I guess you'll be going in the front. So, there's a staircase right opposite the door, if you go to the left of the stairs, you'll find a few doors set underneath. It's the third one along from the front. Yes, definitely the third. Once through it, you go down steps for ages, but just keep going and that brings you to the cave. If he's not there then he'll be in one of the rooms adjoining it and if he's in the punishment room, all you'll need to do is follow the screams."

"Thank you." Jaxon cocked his head to the side. "That's information that we definitely needed."

Jaxon stared at him for a moment or two. "So, Billy the Demon, what do you propose we do with you?" Jaxon slowly circled him, Billy's head swiveling and trying to keep a watch on him.

"Well, Sir, there's not a lot to be done really. I'm enslaved to Draven so if you release me I have to try and make my way back there. Unless Sarff comes to transport us back, then we'd need to trek back ourselves. It's not something I want to do, believe me, I hate the bastard, but I'd have no other choice. Unless, of course, he's killed and then I'd go home to my mom. I know she'll be worrying about me 'cause I've not been able to talk to her for weeks. Not since I was tricked."

"Tricked, yes, you've used that word several times but how am I to believe you?" Jaxon shook his head. "Demons aren't exactly known for their honesty and tell me, Billy, where is your mom? I don't suppose Demons play happy families, do they?"

"Hey, don't dis my mom! I won't let you do that. She's good, for a Demon anyway, and she's never hurt a fly. She might steal food every now and then but that's about it."

"You expect me to believe that?" Jaxon snorted rudely.

"I don't give a flying fig what you believe but my mom is kind and loving. She's already adopted another two kids 'cause their parents were killed in that battle a while back. Basilius didn't give folks a choice, it was go to the battle or be killed by his guards. We lost some friends who had never fought anyone in their lives. Jeez, they wouldn't know *how* to fight, so my mom has taken a couple of their kids in and she's looking after them. We're not all bloodthirsty assholes you know."

Bliss stepped forward, "May I?" she asked Jaxon.

"Sure, let's see if he's telling the truth, or not."

"I'm not lying." Billy jutted his chin out. "Do what you need to do, lady."

Bliss placed her fingertips on either side of his temples, her eyes closing in concentration. Jaxon kept watch, in case she needed him, but no, after only a moment she pulled away. Her eyes locked on Billy's, shock at first, then compassion. "He's not lying and he's never hurt anyone, Jaxon. Draven did indeed trick him, with promises of food and shelter for the orphans. Unfortunately, Billy didn't read the small print which enslaved him to Draven for one hundred years before the man had to actually do anything for the kids."

"Told ya." Billy smirked.

"So, if we let you go, you'd have to try and get back to Draven, but would you hurt anyone on the journey? That's the question. I can't free you, or your comrades upstairs, if there's a chance any of you would harm another."

"Can I say something?" Billy bit his bottom lip. "One of the lads is okay, he's like me, but the other, well, he's not so nice and, truth is, I'd rather you didn't let him go. I'm sure he'd do bad things again. He always does, even when we try to stop him. He's knocked me out a few times when I've asked him to stop hurting someone."

Jaxon snarled viciously, his head spinning around when Skar growled. Skar held out a map to Billy. "First, show us where Draven is, second, which one of those two upstairs were you talking about?"

Billy scanned the map, frowning for a moment before nodding toward a spot on the detailed chart. "See that small body of water there?"

In answer, Skar stabbed his finger on the small blue blob.

Billy nodded. "Yes, that's right. His house is off to the left side of there, he uses that lake for water for his property."

Skar held out the map for Jaxon to study. "There's mountains right behind his property and nothing much else around, so it should be fairly easy to get close. I'd say we go in from the mountain and fly right on down to his front door. What do you think?"

"Sounds good." Jaxon turned to Billy again. "So, which one upstairs were you talking about?"

"The big one, he's got dark hair and his eyes are almost black, about as black as his soul, my mom says." Billy shook his head sadly. "He's always been the same and since Draven tricked us all at the same time he's been even worse. He wasn't interested in the food and stuff for the orphans, nope, Draven offered him gold and he leaped right on that. Now that he's enslaved, he's taking it out on anyone and everyone he comes in contact with."

"Bliss," Jaxon raised an eyebrow, "I'm not condemning anyone on the word of a Demon alone, so can you go and check that one out. If it's as Billy here says then we don't have any options regarding his fate. It's sealed, plain and simple."

Bliss nodded, rushing away with a determined look on her face. Skar nodded to her disappearing back. "She's not quite the usual Bliss, is she?"

"No," Jaxon agreed, surprised at the normally quiet and fearful Dragon's behavior. "She's kinda scary right now. I don't think I've ever seen her like this before."

"I agree." Skar smirked. "Who would've guessed our quiet little Bliss had a dark side."

"In this situation I'm willing to use any resources we have, and that includes Bliss."

"Sure, boss, I agree." Skar nodded.

They were both surprised when Bliss rushed back in, her face white with anger, her body trembling. Skar reached out, holding her shoulders. "What's up, little one?"

"That, that . . ." Bliss stopped, taking a deep breath before continuing. "That *thing* upstairs is, is, fuck it all to hell, I have no word for what he is, Jaxon. He's wicked, evil, and deadly. He can't be allowed back out into the world to carry on the atrocities he's been committing. He's disgusting and needs to be dealt with as soon as possible."

Jaxon looked to Billy who cocked an eyebrow. "I told you he was bad."

"Bad doesn't even come close." Bliss shivered. "I feel as if I need a bath after being in his mind for a mere moment. I couldn't stay in there any longer, Jaxon, I'm sorry. I just had to break contact and get out. I thought I was going to throw up."

"That's all right, Bliss." Skar wrapped her in his arms, hugging her briefly. "You did a good job, honey."

"I'm glad I *could* help." Bliss gave them a determined stare. "I'll do whatever I can to help get Sidra back."

Jaxon could feel her guilt pouring from her. "It wasn't your fault. I hope you realize that. We protect innocents at all costs so there really wasn't any other option."

"Doesn't help me to feel any better," Bliss said sadly.

"We'll get her back," Jaxon reiterated. "No matter what it takes."

"I hope so." Bliss shrugged. "I just feel so helpless."

"You've helped us already and if there's anything else I think you can do, then I'll let you know."

"I know I'm not usually part of this side of things, so can I ask what happens to that monster upstairs?" Bliss shuddered again. "And just so you know he's the one with Aric not Amos. The one with Amos looks terrified and I'm certain he's been crying."

Billy exhaled. "That's Snake, he's like a brother to me. He's a little simple up top and his parents weren't very nice to him, they didn't even give him a proper name, just Snake 'cause he's a Snake Demon. My mom took him in when he was really young and she says that I've always got to look out for him. Shit, she's gonna kick my ass for getting him into this crap."

All of them turned, Jaxon's mouth dropping open as he listened. "Billy, when we let you go, I know until we kill Draven that you'll be bound to try and get back to him, but once that's taken care of, I need you to promise me something."

Billy's face split in a huge smile. "You're letting us go? Of course I promise to do anything you say, Sir."

Jaxon just couldn't get his head around Billy, Snake and the whole situation. For all intents and purposes, they appeared like any other family and that was something he was slowly coming to realize. All Demons were not worthy of obliteration.

"I need you to go home to your family and stay there. Don't go looking for quick riches, even if it was to help others, and for goodness sake, boy, if something appears too good to be true, then you can bet your ass, it's a scam of some sort."

"I've learned my lesson." A tear ran down the side of his face. "I can't believe I'm going to see Mom again. I thought, for sure, my time was up."

"You can thank Bliss for that." Jaxon walked over, undoing the ropes that bound the Demon. "I'm trusting you not to try and escape right now. Okay?"

"I'll sit right here and not move a muscle." Billy grinned. "But, Sir, could someone let Snake know he's not going to die. He'll be really scared right now."

Bliss headed out. "I'll do it."

"Bring him down here, Bliss, they can wait together," Jaxon ordered, his heart softening ever so slightly toward Billy and his "brother."

"Thank you," Billy gushed. "We'll stay right here and not move until you say we can."

"Good, because if you try anything then I'm afraid things will get nasty real quick," Skar growled.

"Nope, we'll be good." Billy rubbed his wrists, the skin red from being tied up.

"Skar—" Jaxon motioned with his head to the door. "I think we have someone upstairs that we need to deal with."

"My pleasure." Skar followed Jaxon out of the cellar.

They passed Bliss as she led Snake downstairs. "Thank you," the young Demon hissed as he hugged the wall, giving them as much space as possible to pass.

"If you and Billy behave then you'll be set free soon," Jaxon said as Bliss carried on with Snake.

"What do you want to do with the other fucker?" Skar's voice showing his anger that was obviously boiling under the surface.

"I don't have time for a trial." Jaxon shrugged. "If Bliss was in his head and she saw things he'd done that was so atrocious she almost vomited that's enough evidence for me."

"Me too," Skar sneered. "But you didn't answer my question."

"We end him," Jaxon said matter of factly.

"Yup, I've got that too, Jaxon." Skar held the door open for them to pass through. "I was more interested in the manner we do that."

"Grab a sword," Jaxon said grimly as they passed by Amos who fell in behind.

Aric turned when they walked in, no surprise in his face when Skar appeared, sword in hand. Merely asking. "Sentence to be carried out?"

Jaxon nodded, holding his hand out for the sword. As Master, it fell to him to dole out this kind of sentence. He'd never ask one of his Warriors to do something he could not.

However, Skar shook his head, hatred in his eyes. "No, please, let me."

"If you're sure." Jaxon stepped back, as did Aric.

The Demon shrieked before spouting a mouthful of threats, most of which were the disgusting ways he was going to attack everyone he could, including eviscerating every man, woman, and child in the camp. Jaxon didn't bother responding, none of them did, they merely watched as Skar walked behind him.

Skar tested the weight of the blade in his hand, measuring its length, and adjusting his stance as the Demon continued to spout profanities. Aric shook his head. "Will you just shut up already?"

"He will very soon," Skar mumbled, holding the sword two-handed out to his side. "Like now." Skar's muscles tensed as he swung the blade around and forward, decapitating the Demon easily.

"Told you." Skar stepped back out of the path of the black blood pooling on the floor. "Can you two get rid of the garbage?"

Aric nodded, Amos going forward to help his twin. "We burn it?" Amos asked, screwing his face up at the smell.

"Yes," Jaxon said coldly. "When you're done I need everyone back for a meeting. We have a Wizard to find and destroy."

"I'll let everyone know," Aric said as he and Amos went to work.

"Half an hour. No later," Jaxon stated, turning to leave, his mind focused on doing whatever it took to bring Sidra home.

CHAPTER

TWENTY

Jaxon looked around at his Warriors, noting they were all dressed for battle, except for Bliss who stood off to the side. "You know what's going on. Sidra has been taken and to be honest it's a long story that I don't want to waste time going into. All you need to know is that we have to go to Boulder and take out a Wizard called Draven. Once that's done, I've been assured that Sidra will be returned."

Bliss held up a hand, her face white with worry. "What if this Sarff Demon lied and doesn't bring her back?"

"If that happens then I'll hunt the bitch down and do what it takes to find Sidra." Jaxon shrugged. "Sidra is my Destiny, you all know the importance of that, so I am not ashamed to admit that I'll do anything at all to get her back. If I need to hunt down another Demon to do that, then I'll do it. Nothing will stop me from getting her back. Nothing."

"We're with you, Master, just tell us what you need from us," Kat said firmly.

"All right." Jaxon exhaled, relieved. He'd known they would stand by his side but he'd still been worrying. "Bliss, I'd like you to come, not to take part in any fighting, but after we're finished there might be others there like Billy and Snake who don't deserve to die. I want you to hang back until I call for you. Okay?"

Bliss nodded, biting a fingernail nervously. Jaxon turned his attention to the rest. "We need to keep the camp defended so at least two of you have to stay here." Jaxon held up a hand, stopping the shouts before they started. "This isn't up for discussion so no argument. Allyssa and Zane, I want you to stay here, Brydon's just out on a short recon job, he'll be back soon to help you keep the camp safe. The rest of you are coming with me and we leave as soon as we're ready so get your asses moving and gear up."

"Will we take packs with us?" Terigan asked, already moving toward the door.

"Not everyone." Jaxon shook his head. "Amos and Aric, I want you two to bring a pack each filled with water and food only. We're going straight there, it should take us around three hours if we hustle. We'll scout things out and then we go in, take care of business, and then we're heading straight back here. If Sidra is not returned by the time we get here then we rest up and figure out how to hunt this Sarff woman down. Is that clear?"

"Yes." Echoed around the room as everyone moved quickly, disappearing from the hall, leaving only Bliss and Jaxon.

"I'm not sure how to 'gear up,'" she said sheepishly.

"As you won't be taking part in any fighting you don't need any weapons." Jaxon walked over, giving her a comforting smile. "I'd say to dress as if you were going for a hike, thick, warm clothes and boots. You don't need all the stuff we use, Bliss, I'm just going to use you to ensure nobody is dealt with unfairly. Okay?"

"Sure." Bliss nodded. "I'll go and change. I won't be long, do I come back here?"

"No, go to the field." Jaxon ushered her out the door. "I need to just double check Billy and Snake will stay where they are until we return."

"They might need a drink or some food," Bliss offered. "I'll hurry and drop some off for them if that's all right?"

"That's very thoughtful of you and yes, that's fine. I'll see you in the field when you're ready."

Bliss barely nodded before rushing away.

Jaxon's legs suddenly shook, his heart rate increasing dramatically, now he had a few moments to think. *Sidra, baby, can you hear me?*

I'm going to get you back. I promise you that. I will get you home. Can you hear me?"

He didn't really expect a reply but when he received none, his heart ached with longing to have her in his arms.

"You okay?" Terigan's soft question caused Jaxon to jerk around.

"Not really," he confessed to his closest friend.

Terigan's eyes were full of compassion as he walked over, his large hand landing on Jaxon's shoulder and squeezing gently. "We'll get her back, Jax. I promise we will."

"The only consolation is that I know she's still alive." Jaxon's hand covered his heart. "I'd know if she wasn't."

"I know, that's what I've heard about Destinies." Terigan gave him a shake. "Go get ready and I'll meet you at the field."

"I won't be long." Jaxon paused. "Wait, can you hold on here for a little bit. Bliss is bringing food and water for Billy and his friend. I'd rather she wasn't alone and please reiterate that if they leave that room their freedom and lives are forfeit."

"Will do." Terigan nodded firmly.

"Thanks." Jaxon left, anxious for them to be on their way.

He bumped into Em on the way, her old eyes scanning him intently. "I won't ask and I won't hold you back. I just wanted to say again to be careful around this Wizard. I don't want any of you being injured because he may look like a human male, but he most definitely won't be. He could be very powerful, Jaxon. I just want you to be aware and keep vigilant on this mission. I'm too old to be worrying about you lot."

"I'll keep it in mind," Jaxon replied, barely stopping. "I need to go, Em. We'll be back by morning."

"I hope so," Em said grimly, before walking away.

Jaxon hurried to his cabin, got what he wanted, then jogged to the field. Everyone was there, including Bliss and Terigan. "Okay, guys, we know where we're going and what we have to do. Any questions before we leave because I have to tell you, I'm not in the mood to chat on the way."

Skar silently turned away, jogging forward to morph, his huge black beast taking to the sky with speed. Amos and Aric followed, the remaining Warriors taking Terigan's lead, and mere moments later Jaxon was alone. He nodded grimly to himself before joining his Guard.

"I'll have you home soon," he said to Sidra, knowing she probably didn't hear him. He

hoped that was the case and not that she was *unable* to hear him. If she were unconscious that would explain the silence, but no, he wasn't going there. If he did, he knew it would screw with his mind and right now, he needed to focus on the one thing he knew he could do: destroy Draven.

His beast sped upwards, joining his Warriors, Terigan leading the way towards Boulder. Jaxon was pleased that Terigan's beast kept up a fast pace. This wasn't a time for going slow, they needed to reach their destination quickly. Assess the threat then take it out. Simple. Or that's what he hoped and prayed for. His mind going again and again to his Destiny.

Jaxon worried she was okay, wherever she was, and hoped that she hadn't been mistreated. He wasn't sure how he'd react if she had been. Not well, that's for damn sure.

Terigan interrupted his thoughts, surprising him. *"Jax, we're almost there. You all right? I can sense you, my friend, and I'm worried about you."*

"Are we? Damn it, my mind has been on Sidra and I didn't realize. Sorry, I'm back in the game now."

"Okay, so I think we send in one of us to check this place out first, then we all go in."

Jaxon agreed, that was his thought too. *"I'll send Skar in. He's got the best set of eyes of any of us."*

"True," Terigan conceded reluctantly.

Jaxon opened the link to include everyone. *"All right, so we're almost there. Skar, can you go ahead and do a fly over, check it out and let us know your thoughts."*

"Will do." Skar sped up, leaving them behind as his beast rushed over the mountain below.

"For now we wait," Jaxon told everyone as he slowed to hover at the peak of the range.

It was a few minutes before Skar rejoined them. *"There's a few Demon guards set around the perimeter, but that's a fair distance from the house itself. I'm sure there'll be others inside but I got really close to the ones visible and I'd bet they're lower Demons, similar to Billy, so we should be able to deal with them without too much trouble."*

"Good to know." Jaxon's heart sped up at the thought of coming face to face with Draven. *"Bliss, you stay up here. Do not engage and keep well away from the compound. We'll call for you if we need you."*

"Understood," Bliss replied rather shakily.

"Just stay up here and you'll be fine." Jaxon tried to stem her anxiety, after all, it was the first time she'd gone on an active mission. Her nerves were to be expected.

Swinging his head around, Jaxon locked eyes with each one of the Dragons present. *"Amos and Aric, you two are our aerial support, keep your eyes* peeled and take out anything that tries to come in after us. However, if anyone tries to escape and are not in combat mode, then just keep them contained until we can check and see who they are. There might be others that are there only under duress and I don't want them harmed until Bliss can check them out. Got it?"

"Sure thing, boss," Amos replied immediately.

Aric barely responded, a quick, "Yes," being the only thing he said.

"The rest of us will go down and we'll have to go in and find this Draven guy. From what Billy's told us, he seems to spend all his time underground and the entrance is through a door beneath the staircase in the house. I'll go in first and the rest of you follow. I want Sapphire at the front door to stand guard. Skar, can you check the house first and then come find us?"

"Will do," Skar replied.

Jaxon looked over at Sapphire. "You need to watch our backs, Sapphy, I don't want any surprises sneaking up on us."

"No problem."

"Good, Terigan, you're with me, so let's get to it and find this Wizard before he does any more damage. Then, hopefully, Sidra will be released and we can organize a damn good shindig to celebrate."

"Sounds like a plan," Terigan said coldly. "Let's go find this Witch with grandiose delusions."

"Remember what Em said," Jaxon reminded everyone. *"This Draven guy could be powerful and dangerous. Let's do our best to get everyone home in one piece. So, are we ready Warriors?"*

"Hell yeah." Amos swooped away, staying hidden and flying high to keep watch on things below, Aric following quickly.

Jaxon swooped over the edge of the mountain and plunged down, his wings tucked in at his sides and only unfurling to slow his descent when he was barely twenty feet from the ground. He landed fast and heavy in front of the house, transforming immediately and rushing up the whitewashed stairs. He didn't slow down, or try the handle, rushing the door and shattering the frame around it, slamming it open.

He felt and heard his Dragons behind him so he didn't break stride, even when he saw a bemused Demon standing open-mouthed on the left. Jaxon knew Skar would take care of him so he continued on to the third door beneath the staircase. Counting off one, two, three, he tugged the handle fiercely, almost pulling the door from its hinges.

Jaxon looked inside, seeing the dark steps that led downward. Terigan was right beside him as they started to descend, their enhanced sight helping them in the utter darkness. There very well might be lights but neither of them wanted to announce their arrival, so down they went, sure of foot and hard of heart, toward the man who'd caused so much heartache.

Terigan's hand landed on Jaxon's shoulder. *"We'll get her back, my friend."*

"Thanks," Jaxon answered, knowing his Warriors would do whatever it took to get his Destiny back to him.

The descent seemed to go on and on, but finally they could see a sliver of light below. They sped up, both anxious to find and deal with Draven. As they reached the bottom of the stairs, a large door appeared to the right, the light slipping beneath the bottom where there was a gap. Jaxon grabbed the handle, going slowly and as quietly as possible as he opened the door.

As soon as it was open wide enough for him to make sure there was nobody in the immediate vicinity, Jaxon opened it fully and rushed through. His favorite battle sword was in his hands, with plenty more blades secreted around his body. Terigan had two swords, shorter fighting blades, which he had used with lethal force many times already.

"Which way?" Terigan whispered as they entered the massive cavern, their eyes spinning around to take everything in.

There was a raised area directly in front, with a large table that was covered in books and paper. Off to the side was a raised podium that had a very old looking book on it, open and obviously of importance. Jaxon nodded toward it. "I think after this is done we should take that back to Em."

"She'll have a hissy fit getting her hands on something like that," Terigan whispered back.

"Yes, but more importantly, it might help us in the future." Jaxon pointed with his sword. "Over there, that looks like it leads to the other rooms Billy told us about."

"I don't hear any screaming so guess he's not doling out any abuse right now." Terigan followed behind Jaxon, both of them keeping their wits about them and their eyes constantly scanning for threats.

The area was large, with many parts in shadow, so they kept their senses heightened, on alert and scanning the area vigilantly. A surprise attack was not something either of them wanted, or would allow. "I can't sense anything," Jaxon murmured, not even able to discern a breath being drawn.

"Me neither." Terigan's eyes spun toward a door to their left, footsteps growing louder. "Sounds like we're going to have a visitor."

"Yeah." Jaxon pointed with his sword and they took up positions either side of the rough-hewn wood.

The sound of someone approaching grew louder but it was difficult for them to decide how many approached as the footsteps seemed to echo all around. Jaxon raised an eyebrow, Terigan shrugging as he mouthed. "Not sure. One? Two?"

Jaxon shook his head. He couldn't decide so they lay in wait to see who, or what, opened the door. Steeling himself as the door creaked before being opened wide, a young male walking through, his head bowed so that he didn't even see Jaxon or Terigan as he walked forward. Jaxon held up a finger, staying Terigan to see if another person exited.

At that moment, another man followed the first, his body quivering with obvious fear. The first spoke quietly. "Hurry, go now before he decides he wants to keep you there for more of his sick games."

The second man sped up, although his legs looked as if they were about to give out any moment, heading toward the door Jaxon and Terigan had come through moments before. The first man raised his head, noticing the door was ajar, spinning around to check the cavern. The second man was through the door, closing it firmly behind him, as the first's eyes landed on Jaxon.

Jaxon stepped forward, holding his sword before him in his preferred two-handed grip. "Where is Draven?"

Terigan strode toward the man whose face was a mask of disbelief. "Tell us, now."

"Who are you? What are you doing here? He'll kill you, hurry, leave before he finds you."

Jaxon shook his head. "Not gonna happen so tell us where we can find him."

The man, who looked no older than a teenager, and was one hundred percent human, shook his head. "Please, go, please."

"Boy—" Terigan prodded him with the tip of one of his blades. "You need to speak up now before things get nasty."

A loud, commanding voice boomed around the cavern. "Things are already nasty. Who the hell do you think you are coming here, into my fucking *home*?"

The boy raced away, his legs pumping fast as he tore open the door and fled. Jaxon turned, his face a mask of stone as Draven appeared. He looked the Wizard up and down, noting his small stature, non-descript features, and mousey hair. "You're not what I expected but hell, what do I know about Witches?"

Draven stalked forward, his hands clenching into fists at his sides as he roared, "I am *not* a damn Witch! I'm a Wizard."

Terigan slid off to the side, opening up the space between him and Jaxon. Sneering at the man to divert his attention. "Witch, Wizard, it's all the same to me. I think you're just a guy who's got some delusion of grandeur. Ain't ya?"

Draven's hair seemed to come alive, starting to stick out as electricity sizzled around him, his hands now moving before him as he muttered under his breath. Both Jaxon and Terigan were well warned he was about to let loose some kind of spell but when he threw his hands out to the side, neither of them expected two balls of power to come flying toward them.

Terigan jumped, rolling off to the side, as Jaxon threw himself behind a stone outcrop on the side of the wall. The stone exploded, embedding shards into Jaxon's back, his bellow one of anger and pain.

His friend didn't fare any better as the spell exploded a table and chairs, wood splinters covering him and embedding anywhere they could. Blood started to drip down Terigan's face as he bowled over the debris, springing to his feet.

Draven laughed as he walked further into the cavern. "You are imbeciles. Coming here to my cave and thinking you could hurt me. I'm going to have such fun with you two. Such strong men, it'll take me days to finally finish you off. By then, you fucking morons will be begging for death to take you."

Terigan snorted. "You like to hear yourself talk, don't ya?"

Draven's head spun to spear Terigan with a cold stare. "You really are a fool."

Jaxon lowered his body, centering his strength in his thighs before springing forward. His immense power and speed had him hurtling toward Draven who glared at Terigan. His friend shrugged. "Hey, that hurts. You know what my old gran used to say? 'If you can't say something nice, then don't say anything at all.' So why don't you just shut the fuck up."

Laughter erupted from Draven as he shook his head, a hand reaching out to the side and sending Jaxon flying back with such force that he crashed into the rock, winded. "You'll have to do better than that." Draven smirked as Jaxon hauled his body up from the floor.

"You okay, Jax?" Terigan asked worriedly.

"Fine," Jaxon answered curtly. *"This fucker is beginning to annoy me."*

"Yup, me too." Terigan took a step toward Draven, and ended up on his ass when another

shot of power belted him smack bang in the chest.

Draven chuckled as he slowly walked around aimlessly. "I'm having *fun!* Thanks so much for coming to visit."

Terigan cursed, pulling himself upright via an old stuffed armchair. "That kinda hurt."

Jaxon's temper rose, his friend had barely recovered from being mortally wounded in battle, and only being saved by their Goddess. "Enough of this," he ground out, his eyes taking in the high ceiling and size of the space they were in. "Terigan." Jaxon dropped, raised an eyebrow, and with no other word spoken, Jaxon morphed quickly.

His great beast filled the space, its head almost hitting the ceiling, its wings unable to open, but he didn't need to fly. All he had to do was kill this Witch. Terigan darted off to the side, staying well clear of the Dragon as it stomped a huge foot forward, smashing a table to smithereens. Jaxon heard his friend chuckling as Draven ran towards the raised area with the ancient book on the podium.

Draven started to quickly flick through pages of the book, mumbling as he did. "I know it's in here! Where is it? There's a spell for you scaly bastards and I'll show you how powerful I am. I'll destroy both of you."

Jaxon's Dragon inhaled sharply, sending a quick warning to Terigan. *"Better find cover, Terigan."* Terigan rushed out, dashing around the edge of the cavern and back to the door they'd entered by. As soon as he was clear, Jaxon focused on Draven.

He was still flipping pages over quickly. "It's here, I *know* it's here!"

"Too late," Jaxon thought as his beast rained fire down onto the man, engulfing him in his magical dragon flames. The entire area in front blew up in a fiery conflagration, the smell of burning flesh intermingled with the noise of the firestorm he'd unleashed.

Jaxon huffed out one last burst of flame, making absolutely certain all that was left of Draven was nothing more than a pile of ashes. His Dragon fire so powerful it disintegrated even the man's bones. Satisfied the Witch was destroyed, Jaxon allowed his flames to flicker down and finally stop.

Terigan pushed open the door, sticking his head inside. "He gone?"

Jaxon transformed, nodding as he strode toward his friend. "Yes, and so is the book. Let's not tell Em about it or she'll be giving me an earache for weeks about destroying it."

"No worries." Terigan held the door open for him.

"Let's go and see what's going on upstairs." Jaxon jogged upstairs and into a scene from a bloody horror movie.

Sapphire and Skar had dealt with more than a few Demons, their disgusting black blood soaking the floor for as far as Jaxon could see. Around a dozen or so bodies lay around the area, making it difficult to traverse from the staircase to the front door.

"You two have been busy," Jaxon said wryly. "I was wondering what was keeping you, Skar."

Skar harrumphed loudly. "Sorry, boss, been helping our Sapphy out."

Sapphire grinned. "We make a good team, big guy. Look at all the lovely work we've done."

Terigan looked around, tapping his chin. "Oh, I think we'll need the decorators in."

"Shut up." Sapphire grinned as she spun around. "Everyone is taken care of, except for a few that I don't think needs this sort of *care*."

"Is one of them a young human that came up from below?" Jaxon asked, looking out the front door to see a small group huddling close together, obviously terrified.

"Yes," Sapphire answered over her shoulder. "There's a few humans, and a couple are Demons but they seem harmless and I don't get any bad vibe from them. Might be better to get Bliss to check them all out though, just in case."

"Will do." Jaxon looked up and saw Amos and Aric still circling high above. *"Amos, Aric, everything looking okay from up there?"*

"Yes, Jaxon, everything's fine and nothing's escaped. In fact, none of the perimeter guards even tried to escape, they're in that group in front of the house."

"Good. Okay just keep your eyes peeled." Jaxon looked for Bliss' beast but couldn't see her. *"Bliss, you can come down now. We are in need of your talents."*

"On my way," Bliss replied instantly, her sleek Dragon sliding over the top of the mountain and down towards them.

"Sapphire, Skar, can you and Bliss deal with them?" Jaxon waved a hand toward the assembled group. "I want to get going. I need to get home in case Sidra is released."

"Sure," Skar agreed.

Sapphire's eyes locked with Jaxon's. "Boss, what will you do if you get home and she's not there?"

"If that happens I'll be getting to work to figure out how to track, and find, this Sarff woman. Then I'll be going after her."

"You should wait until we all return." Sapphire frowned. "We can all help you."

"By the time I get back, Brydon, Amber and Opal will be home. If needs be I'll get them to help."

Terigan stepped forward. "I'm going with you."

Jaxon turned, patting Terigan's arm. "That's something I was already certain of, my friend. So, shall we?"

Terigan nodded, striding over the bodies littering the floor. "The sooner we get home the better."

"My thoughts exactly." Jaxon followed his friend, certain Terigan would be at his side for whatever happened.

CHAPTER

TWENTY-ONE

Sidra sighed as she finished her first book, a smile tugging at her lips, even in the hell she found herself in. "Wow, Ms. Elsworth, I wish I could meet you and thank you for your story." Sidra muttered as she clicked the screen back to the home page and searched for book two in the Real World series.

Once she'd found it and opened it, Sidra reached for her bottled water, sipping it slowly and nibbling on a bar. She had no idea how long she was going to be imprisoned, so she was rationing her provisions. At first, she'd kept trying to use her link to reach Jaxon, and each time there was no reply. She'd been driving herself nuts so she'd turned on the e-reader and started the next book.

Sidra had been so engrossed she'd read it from start to finish, with barely a break to sip on some water. "Thank you." She wished she could thank the author in person for helping her in such a horrendous situation. She was sure if she hadn't held the e-reader in her hand when she'd been taken, she would be climbing the walls by now.

For now though, she was relatively comfortable, with supplies, and about to start another book, praying that she wouldn't have time to read the entire series before being rescued. "I think that would definitely have me going batty." She laughed, her eyes settling on the words on the page before her.

She paused, her thoughts drifting to Jaxon, her Destiny.

Sidra no longer doubted what they were to each other. She embraced it with every fiber of her being. Her heart speeding up as she thought on the magnificent man that she'd spend the rest of her life with. His hair that was longer than most and she liked to run her fingers through it, grabbing tightly as he made love to her.

The muscles on his body, so many that she was amazed every time she caught sight of them. Her fingers trailing over his rock hard chest, abs, and down to his rather impressive package. A chuckle escaped her lips as her face blushed with the thoughts running through her head.

"I'm yours, my Dragon, and when I'm out of this shitty hole in the ground, I'm taking you to bed and we're staying there for days." Sidra's voice echoed around her and she shivered, fear lapping her insides at the thought of being imprisoned in this small space until she'd run out of supplies.

"Damn it!" She refocused on her precious story, hoping it would chase away her worst nightmare: never seeing Jaxon's beautiful face ever again.

Jaxon sped back homeward. His only intention was to return as quickly as possible. He'd held up his part of the deal so Sarff better hold up hers. If she didn't, then she'd regret the day she ever thought to blackmail him. He'd hunt her down and make her pay for taking his Destiny from him.

On and on he flew, Terigan at his side, and with every mile that passed, Jaxon thought up a new way to torture Sarff if she didn't keep up her end of the deal. At times, his terror overtook him and a bellow would tear from his throat in anger.

Terigan remained silent, never once interrupting his musings and plans to wreak havoc on Sarff. Not a word passed between them as their great beasts swept across the sky, massive wings beating furiously to speed them homeward.

Only when the mountains that enclosed their valley came into view did his friend speak. *"We're nearly home, Jax."*

"I can see that," Jaxon snapped, immediately regretting his tone. *"Sorry, I'm just worried."*

"Understandable," Terigan replied as they sped across the range, diving down toward the field for landing.

Jaxon waited until the last moment, almost at the edge of the field, before transforming, landing on his feet, and rushing toward the camp, racing across the ground as the sun barely started to show itself, dawn slowly arriving. His heart thudded in his chest as he saw a woman standing in the middle of the camp, rushing toward her with all his speed.

"Sidra?" he asked as he drew nearer, although every one of his senses told him it was not.

Sarff turned toward him, a smile on her face. "Thank you, I felt Draven's demise some time ago."

Jaxon stopped a few feet in front of her, snarling as she smiled. "I did what you asked, now return Sidra to me or . . ."

Sarff held up her hand. "Shush, no need for threats, Dragon. You've released me from that monster's bind and I'm grateful. I'll hold up my end of the bargain. Wait here."

Jaxon dashed forward, his fingers grasping thin air as Sarff disappeared. "Fuck!" he roared, his hands bunched at his sides.

Terigan's hand landed on his shoulder. "Just wait and see. She could be telling you the truth."

"I'll die if I don't get her back, Terigan." Jaxon's heart ached at the loss of his Destiny.

"I know, my friend, I know." Terigan stayed beside him, waiting.

Sidra jumped with fright when Sarff spoke, so enthralled by the story she was reading. "Shit." Sidra dropped the reader onto her lap.

Sarff smirked down at her. "Nope, I'm glad to see that you didn't need to use the temporary bathroom facilities."

Sidra stood, grasping hold of the reader in her hand, squaring her shoulders to glare at the woman. "When the hell am I getting out of here?"

"No need to get snippy, Unicorn." Sarff cocked her head to the side. "Now, I could get paid a fortune if I handed you over to some people, but . . ."

Stepping forward, Sidra glared at the Demon. "If you do that Jaxon and his Warriors will hunt you down. Trust me, Demon, you don't want to make an enemy of the Guild."

Sarff smirked again. "I am well aware of that." She held out her hand. "And since he held up his end of the deal, I'll return you to him."

Sidra hesitated, having no trust whatsoever in any Demon, especially one that had kidnapped and imprisoned her. "How do I know you're telling the truth?"

"You don't." Sarff wiggled her hand. "But I'm your only way out of here, so I guess you'll have to trust me."

"Never," Sidra spat out at the same time she reached for Sarff's hand. "However, I need to get out of this fucking hole so just get on with it."

Sarff held her hand and again Sidra felt as if her body was folding in on itself, her skin feeling as if it were being ripped inside out as Sarff whisked them out of the room of rock. When her feet touched hard ground again, Sidra bent over, barely managing to keep from retching the bar she'd eaten earlier.

"Sidra!" Jaxon's voice entered her consciousness a moment before his arms hauled her up against him. "My Destiny, darling, are you all right?"

Sidra's breathing slowed, her free hand grabbing hold of his clothes as tears ran down her face. "Jaxon?"

"Yes, my love, it's me. Are you okay?"

Terigan spoke in the background, their eyes turning to glance at him. "Good to have you home, Sidra. Jax, I'll let everyone know."

"Thanks," Jaxon answered, turning her face up to look down at her. "Answer me, baby, are you all right. Did she hurt you?"

Sarff sounded insulted as she broke in. "No, I didn't hurt her. My end of the bargain has been carried out. I wish you goodbye, Dragon."

"I don't want to see your face again, Demon," Jaxon growled. "If I do, I won't be held responsible for my actions."

"Yeah, yeah," Sarff scoffed. "Heard it all before."

The Demon disappeared, leaving no trace of ever having been there as Sidra started to laugh. Jaxon stared at her as if she'd lost her marbles, which made her laugh even harder. "Sidra? What's so funny?"

She took several minutes to regain control of herself, hiccupping as she clung to him. "I thought, for a moment, that I wasn't going to see you again. I'm just overcome with emotion right now. I laugh when I'm nervous, Jax, it's one of my little quirks."

"I see." Jaxon grinned down at her. "I thought that Demon had done something to your mind and you'd gone a little loopy."

"I am a little loopy, but that's just me." Sidra reached up, tugging his head down to kiss him so passionately that both of them were left out of breath.

Zeeandra's voice surprised him as she opened a link. *"I see that you've managed to get Sidra home safe and sound. I'm glad, Jaxon."*

Jaxon let Sidra know he was otherwise occupied. "Zeeandra's talking to me, honey, hold on a second.

"Oh, okay." Sidra snuggled closer against him as he replied to his Goddess.

"Yes, I'm glad too. I'd rather not go through that again."

"That is yet to be seen," Zeeandra said cryptically. *"However, that is not my reason for contacting you. I want to warn you that I may be in need of Terigan soon. There is something that only he is suitable for, so be prepared for me to send him far away for a time."*

"I see." Jaxon frowned. *"Anything you request will be carried out but I'll be sad to see him leave so soon after returning home."*

"I know, Jaxon, he is your best friend and you missed him, but this is something only he can do. I'll keep you informed but for now, go and enjoy your time with your Destiny."

"Thank you, I will." Their link broken quickly as he turned his attention back to Sidra, leaning down to kiss her softly.

"I want to go home," she gasped, smiling up at him.

Jaxon reached down, picking her up and cradling her against him tightly. "Then that's what we'll do. Do you need anything? Food, water? Anything?"

"Oh yes, there is definitely something I need but it's not food or water." Sidra nibbled on his neck. "I need *you*, my Destiny."

"Oh." Jaxon inhaled sharply. "Then me you shall have, Twink."

"Good. I'm still not sold on that nickname though."

"I like it, but I'll try and keep its use for when we're alone."

"Hmm, that's okay I guess." Sidra winked at him cheekily. "Just don't call me it in front of everyone or I'll be most unhappy."

"I'll remember that."

Sidra licked her lips, raising an eyebrow. "I hope you don't have any pressing Guild business in the next couple of days, because I'm telling you right now, we are not leaving the bedroom for quite some time."

"Sounds good to me." Jaxon laughed as he pushed open the door, kicking it shut as dawn broke over the camp. "I want nothing more than to take you to bed and check every inch of your body, my love."

"Honestly, I'm fine, but I think you should kiss me all over, just in case."

"Another good plan." Jaxon placed her down on their bed. "One I'm happy to carry out. Right this minute."

"Oh, and you can organize the linking party thingie for next weekend. I don't want us to be disturbed until then, but after that, I want everyone to know how happy I am, Jaxon."

"Boy, you just keep coming up with good plans, dontcha, lass?"

"Yup." Sidra smiled, holding up her precious e-reader. "Put this somewhere safe. Ms. Elsworth and her stories kept me sane while I was gone. Wish she was around so I could go thank her."

"You never know, honey, she might be." Jaxon started to undress, causing her mouth to water.

"If she is I'd love to find her."

"Then I'll get the word out." Jaxon pointed to her mouth. "Stop biting your lip like that, it drives me insane."

Grinning up at him, she shook her head. "In that case I'm going to do it all the time."

"Naughty, lassie." Jaxon's leather pants dropped to the floor, exposing his ardor.

Sidra whimpered softly. "Jaxon, Master of the Guild of Dragon Warriors, I'm totally besotted with you. I love you, my Dragon, now get that delectable ass over here."

"With pleasure." Jaxon stalked toward her. "I love you too, my Cinneamhain, and tonight I'm going to show you just how much."

"Sounds like a plan." Sidra chuckled as his hands undressed her quickly.

"Yes, you're not the only one that can come up with a good plan."

"Indeed." Sidra's mind floated away in utter bliss as her Destiny got to work on her body, taking her higher than she'd ever flown before, and sending her body into a sea of pleasure she hoped she'd never leave.

AUTHOR'S  NOTE

I sincerely hope you enjoyed book one in the Guild of Dragon Warriors and I'd like to thank you for taking the time to read it. If you could possibly spare a moment to leave a review then I'd really appreciate it, as your review could help another reader decide if it is for them.

If you'd like to continue the Guild's stories, then go check out Terigan's Trials. You can find details of it on my website, akmichaels.com or on any of the platforms that sell my books.

I'd like to say a great big thank you to several peeps. My editor, Missy Borucki - thank you very much for helping me make my stories the best they can be. I love that you "get" me and never try to stifle my voice. You're a gem of an editor and I appreciate you very much.

To the Sassy Queens of Design, aka Rebecca and Angel, for giving me another wonderful cover. Also Stracey, the third Sassy Queen, for all the beautiful swag you create for me. You surprise me time and again with the wonderful things you come up with.

I'd like to say a huge thanks also to the girls on

my Street Team, who work very hard for me and whom I adore! Go Ava's Bite Club! I'm very grateful for everything you do for me girls.

Also to my Reader's Group, Ava's Minxes, thank you for your support, girls, and taking time to read my stories. Sue and Nicola, I really appreciate you running the Minxes for me.

Tammy Payne, you are fabulous, and your eagle eyes find things that've been missed, thank you, honey.

My fabulous Beta readers, you are astounding and I appreciate you all for reading for me and helping me improve my stories.

The very talented Casey, from Fancypants Formatting - thank you very much for giving me exactly what I wanted.

Remember guys 'n gals, Live, Love, Read!

Ava

CONTACT AVA

Sign up for my Sassy Lassie's VIP Clan today and you'll get details of my freebies in your welcome email *and* another free book. You can find details of the Clan on my website, akmichaels.com and details of all my other books. Remember to pop over on Facebook and let me know what you thought of Jaxon and his Warriors.

OTHER WORK ❦ BY AVA

This is always changing, and only a small selection of my work, so please check out my website for the most up-to-date information.

A WOLF'S HUNGER SERIES

RAFE: A K MICHAELS
KADE: A K MICHAELS
ZOHAR: A K MICHAELS

A Vampire's Thirst: Victor

A Vampire's Thirst: Dark, Dangerous, and Undeniable!

Victor Strong, ancient Vampire and hard-as-nails businessman, has enjoyed centuries in the human world by following one simple rule: Keep a steely control over your dark side. Then it comes, like a thief in the night, overtaking him mind, body, and soul... a strange, unexplainable 'Thirst' that not even he could deny.

With the craving for blood, and other darker, more enticing desires, rapidly growing out of

311

control, Victor suddenly fears not only for his sanity, but his very life.

Holding on by a thin, unraveling thread, Victor is pulled from the brink of madness by a sweet, tantalizing aroma. So hypnotized by the scent, he is forced to find its owner, compelled to find the most elusive of all things; a mere myth among his kind. The Vampire's Bloods-Mate.

Can he reach her in time? Can she save him from himself? Or will Victor be lost to his dark side forever?

The hunt is on. The battle fierce. Only the strongest survive A Vampire's Thirst!

Book 1 in A K Michaels' brand new series A Vampire's Thirst full of hot as hades alpha males in this smoking paranormal romance story.

Her Highlander's Desire

Have a moping, lovesick friend? No clue how to help her? Why contact Geri Wilder from the Paranormal Dating Agency, of course! Just remember to keep the details hush-hush because not everyone is onboard with the whole supernatural matchmaking thing. As for convincing her mate to let Alinka go halfway around the world...that's all on Tasha's shoulders. Tasha has her hands full, but never underestimate the power of an Alpha female.

The PDA promised results and that is EXACTLY what they delivered.

Fiery, white hot attraction, like fireworks exploding in the night sky, consume both Alinka and Dara. Unable to control their passion, the couple immediately succumbs to the pull of their Soulmate. Shock and fear over the intensity of their feelings forces both to make rash decisions with devastating effects.

Will Fate and Destiny seal their union? Or will one wolf run leaving the other to lick his wounds and pick up the pieces of a broken heart?

A Wolf's Hunger Cannot Be Stopped...Or Can It?

Grab this hot paranormal shifter story from New York Times Bestselling Author, A K Michaels.

Not only is it part of Milly Taiden's Paranormal Dating Agency Kindle World but it's also linked to A K's A Wolf's Hunger series and filled enough hot shifter romance to keep you turning the pages into the wee small hours of the night.

From Scotland, With Sass

Belle is just too sassy for her own good. It's gotten her into hot water one time too many and she knows she's treading a thin line with her Alpha. So what does she do when she's forced to pick up a sexy-as-sin Scotsman and return him to the Pack? Heck, as soon as the Alpha's mate goes near him, she growls at her! She's lucky to make it out of there in one piece, and she's sure it's the hot Highlander who saved her.

What was supposed to be a pick him up, drop him off, and make her getaway kinda day, turns into a scorching hot encounter that takes her breath away, at the same time as her sanity. Mr. Sex-on-Legs Scotsman has her heart racing every time he glances her way, her Wolf acting like a love-sick pup, his beast calling to hers as only a soul-mate can.

With rogue Wolves in the area, willing to take what they want, and what they want is Belle, can the lovers find each other and seal their bond before it's too late?

Her Purr-Fect Surprise

What's Connie to do when she knows her friend Cyndi needs love? There's only one solution: Gerri Wilder at the Paranormal Dating Agency!

Her only problem is how to pay for her services. So she offers everything she has: including herself as a slave. Connie has a nerve-wracking wait to find out if the world-renowned dating guru will help her friend, and at what cost!

When Mitch Mackay arrives at the Silver Streak Pack, he's not happy. He should be at his Alpha's side hunting rogues, not on some obviously made up visit to the Pack Healer. That is until he scents her...his one, his only: his soul-mate. The only trouble is...she's as skittish as a wild horse and as innocent as a new-born lamb, and the first thing she does is ups and faints on him. Shoot. Can he convince her that he's the Cougar for her Wolf? Or will her fear take over and make her run from their one chance at happiness?

And that's if they survive when rogues attack the camp at the worst possible moment: when the Alpha and his men are away hunting to clear the land of the very scourge that threatens their future and their lives.

Book 1 in A K Michaels' Silver Streak Pack full of excitement, paranormal romance, and Shifter hotness! Another addition to the steamy hot Paranormal Dating Agency. Grab your copy now and curl up with Mitch Mackay, a scorching hot Cougar who's sure to set your kindle aflame.

The Black Rose Chronicles

The Black Rose is a highly trained assassin. She is different, exceptional, and one of a kind. An anomaly, she knows she's the only Witch/Wolf hybrid left alive. Only two people know the truth about her: her father and her mentor; her savior, Seth. If anyone even suspected her secret, she would be hunted down, for her unique DNA is beyond value.

She is strong, fearless and powerful. Rose kills with impunity if the target deserves such a sentence. Unfortunately, far too many do in this lawless land filled with Shifters, Vampires, Demons and more. Her latest assignment has the most powerful Vampire in existence in her crosshairs, and don't forget the Demon with a hidden agenda. Can Rose decipher all of the deceit and lies and make the right decision? One that will literally save the world and all of its inhabitants. Human and Paranormal alike.

Book 1 in New York Times Bestselling Author, A K Michaels' award winning series filled with paranormal beings in abundance. Shifters, Vampires, Witches, and more are all in this contemporary fantasy story filled with thrills, excitement and Paranormal Romance.

Reviewers are calling it, "Captivating," "Beautifully written," and "A simply brilliant start to an incredible series."

Highland Wolf Clan Series

Read the book that reviewers are calling "gripping," "suspenseful", with "lots of love and action" and a series "I couldn't put down"!

A man born to be Alpha that walks away from his birthright and Pack. Cameron Sinclair wants nothing to do with either.

When summoned he reluctantly goes to the aid of his Uncle's Pack. What he finds is danger, intrigue, heartache, and the chance of a different life.

His instinct screams at him to walk away but his heart has other ideas. Come and join the Highland Wolf Clan and find out what's in store for Cameron and his Highlanders.

The Witch, The Wolf and The Vampire Series

A witch on the run, hunted by her father...and

pursued by two men who desperately want to make her theirs. You know what they say...what happens in Vegas, stays in Vegas.

Peri is haunted by memories of her father's dark, magical cult, who tortured and imprisoned her throughout her childhood. Even six years after her escape, Peri is still a wanted woman, and is only able to stay alive by tracking criminals as a bounty hunter, constantly on the move and always alone.

Her travels lead her to Las Vegas, where a job turns bad. Wounded, she collapses at the feet of a stunning, ancient vampire named Josef, and gorgeous wolf shifter Gabe. Josef and Gabe tend to Peri's injuries, both of them falling in love with her. Claimed by both the vampire and the werewolf, Peri is caught in the middle.

As the romance unravels, Peri discovers her magic is far more powerful than she realized. Yet her father is searching for her, and Peri doesn't know if she's strong enough to stop him from taking her back. Trapped in a complex love triangle, who will Peri choose? Josef? Gabe? Or perhaps...both?

A thrilling urban fantasy full of adventure and suspense, *The Witch, The Wolf and the Vampire* is an erotic paranormal romance with a throuple taking center stage. This magical dark fantasy will have readers swooning for the next book in

A.K. Michaels' supernatural science fiction series.

The Witch, The Wolf and The Vampire: Next Generation, A Son's Fate

A gripping addition to The Witch, The Wolf and The Vampire series by New York Times Bestselling Author, A K Michaels.

Follow Joey's journey as he says goodbye to his life of luxury, with doting parents, and a sister he loves in 'Sin City'. With each passing day he is more unsettled as his Wolf strives to live as its DNA is programmed: within a Pack. After all, it's not just any Pack he wants. He is determined to join the very Pack that almost killed his father. He has no idea of the hardships ahead, but he faces everything with a deep resolve to gain his dream: Alpha status. Nothing less will suffice, even if he dies trying. Joey will give up everything to win his rightful place and seal his fate.

Joey is certain he won't settle for that alone. No. He craves to be Alpha and he'll do whatever it takes to achieve his goal. Including deceiving his parents as he uses underground fighting clubs to toughen up.

After all, it's not just any Pack he wants. He is determined to join the very Pack that almost killed his father.

Supernatural Enforcement Bureau Series

As Director of the Supernatural Enforcement Bureau, powerful Vampire Ronan, thought he had seen it all...until he discovers that Dragons actually exist. Can he help the Dragon being hunted on his patch? He certainly has the means at his disposal...if they can find it first...before the dark magic-wielding Witches and their Vampire cohorts.

After seeing the magnificent beast with his own eyes he can't turn from the task, even if he wanted to. Especially as his Sire, Josef, gives him a direct command to find the Dragon and keep it safe. No matter the cost.

With rogue Vampires and Witches on its trail, it's only a matter of time before they capture it. That's not something Ronan will allow...not on his watch! He will do whatever it takes to find and save the Dragon, using every powerful being at his disposal, including the dark and dangerous Creed.

Sabrina's Vampire Series

Sabrina's life was a mess, suspended from her

police job, she ran to Vegas for a break, to escape the torment and embarrassment. She followed this up by getting blind drunk and down an alleyway with two thugs who wanted more than a goodnight kiss.

Kyle, a Vampire, hears her scream and against his better judgement enters the alley and saves her. As she collapses into his arms he had a deep need to take her home? He never takes anyone to his home. Soon Sabrina is ingrained in him - he can't get enough - can't let her go and just why are his bites not healing on her neck? When he finds out he is shocked - he must keep her - make her stay.

Will she? Will this woman stay in the arms of a Vampire?

Defender's Blood Series

Alex has no idea her life is about to change beyond her wildest imaginings. She is the last in a long line of very special females born for a dangerous task, and she isn't sure she is up to it. Zach, her vampire protector, is just as sure she is.

Demon attacks, angels and even the ultimate, divine intervention, shake Alex to her very core. Can she do this? Can Zach keep her safe? The alternative is unthinkable: demons once more ruling the earth.

Zach has to ensure that Alex puts a stop to this - and quickly.

Read Defender's Blood, Alex's Destiny – Book 1 in the Defender's series.

Lori's Wolf Pack

Lori's lost in the forest, regretting her idea to go for a hike. Hurt and getting more terrified by the minute, especially when she hears the howls of a large animal nearby. In her haste to get away she falls and knocks herself out.

The animal finds her, having heard her screams.

The Wolf changes and the Alpha looks down at the female. As soon as he picks her up, his body reacts and he, at first, has no idea why. All he knows is his Wolf wants out, wants to mark this human as his.

Lori is oblivious to what's in store over the next few days as the powerful Alpha carries her to his cabin.

Adult content in this novella, no cliffhanger, and a happy ever after.